Gray! For the she couldn't b

Though she couldn't see his face, for it was hidden beneath the brim of a shabby hat, she knew that hard, muscled body. The long legs. The lean hips.

He turned and nodded, while Darcy stared at him in stunned silence. His face seemed strangely distorted. His eyelids were drooped, giving him a sleep-drenched, sensual appearance. It was impossible to tell the color of his eyes. But the shape of them seemed all wrong.

"Captain." His voice was a strange rasp, as though the single word had caused him great effort.

When he turned away, Darcy's heart was drumming painfully inside her chest. Her breathing was none too steady. But as she watched this stranger, she realized he couldn't be Gray. He'd looked right at her.... And there had not been the slightest hint of recognition.

* * *

The Sea Sprite
Harlequin Historical #565—June 2001

RUTH LANGAN

THE SEA SPRITE

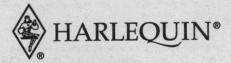

HARLEQUIN®

TORONTO • NEW YORK • LONDON
AMSTERDAM • PARIS • SYDNEY • HAMBURG
STOCKHOLM • ATHENS • TOKYO • MILAN • MADRID
PRAGUE • WARSAW • BUDAPEST • AUCKLAND

ISBN 0-373-29165-5

THE SEA SPRITE

Copyright © 2001 by Ruth Ryan Langan

All rights reserved. Except for use in any review, the reproduction or utilization of this work in whole or in part in any form by any electronic, mechanical or other means, now known or hereafter invented, including xerography, photocopying and recording, or in any information storage or retrieval system, is forbidden without the written permission of the publisher, Harlequin Enterprises Limited, 225 Duncan Mill Road, Don Mills, Ontario, Canada M3B 3K9.

All characters in this book have no existence outside the imagination of the author and have no relation whatsoever to anyone bearing the same name or names. They are not even distantly inspired by any individual known or unknown to the author, and all incidents are pure invention.

This edition published by arrangement with Harlequin Books S.A.

® and TM are trademarks of the publisher. Trademarks indicated with ® are registered in the United States Patent and Trademark Office, the Canadian Trade Marks Office and in other countries.

Visit us at www.eHarlequin.com

Printed in U.S.A.

Please address questions and book requests to:
Harlequin Reader Service
U.S.: 3010 Walden Ave., P.O. Box 1325, Buffalo, NY 14269
Canadian: P.O. Box 609, Fort Erie, Ont. L2A 5X3

For my family, so wonderfully diverse,
who make me so proud. And of course for Tom,
founder and chairman of the board.

Prologue

Cornwall, 1655

"There's a storm moving in, children." Miss Winifred Mellon, nursemaid to the four motherless Lambert children, strode briskly along the rocky shore, cupping her hands and shouting into the wind. The beach near their home, MaryCastle, was strewn with boulders. Some were as big as a small shed, offering the perfect perch for a child to climb and watch the clouds rolling in across the Atlantic.

Young James, at ten and two the oldest of the Lambert children, looked up, then began trailing his best friend, Gray Barton, who was almost ten and three. Gray's father was a sea captain who had already allowed his son to sail with him. In the eyes of the Lambert children, that made Gray someone to be admired, since it was the goal that all of them secretly shared. Now Gray, his cap of black hair ruffling in the wind, scrambled across a series of slippery, egg-shaped rocks, as surefooted as the tumbler they'd once seen in a London park. James did his best to keep up.

"Where are your sisters?" Miss Mellon demanded.

James shrugged. "Last I saw, Ambrosia was pestering Newt to teach her how to spit."

Miss Mellon wrinkled her prim-and-proper nose, while the two boys laughed. Newton Findlay had been a sailor aboard the family ship, the *Undaunted,* until he'd lost a leg to a shark. Now he worked for the Lambert family, and tolerated with good nature the million questions four small children asked on a daily basis.

Despite Winifred Mellon's determined efforts, the three Lambert girls refused to behave like females. They disdained music, handwork, art, in favor of fighting with wooden swords, climbing the mast of their father's ship and swimming in the ocean. Swimming with all manner of vermin for companions. The very thought made the poor woman weak.

"And the other two? Bethany and Darcy?"

James pointed. "Bethany is up on the hill, hoping for a good view of the storm."

The nursemaid turned in time to see the little redhead standing with her arms lifted to the heavens. "What is she doing, James?"

"Waiting to see if lightning will strike."

While the two boys grinned at one another, the nursemaid let out a shriek and lifted her skirts to race as fast as her legs could take her. Minutes later, breathless and bedraggled, she descended the hill, dragging six-year-old Bethany behind her.

When she finally managed to find her voice she thought to ask, "Where's Darcy?"

"Out there." Bethany pointed to dark, churning waves crashing against the shore.

"What do you mean, out there? In the ocean?"

"Aye."

The nursemaid's heart nearly stopped. "Who's with her?"

"Nobody, Winnie."

The poor woman's eyes widened. "Your little sister is alone? In the ocean? With a storm rolling in?"

When the girl nodded, the nursemaid turned as pale as her petticoats and began racing toward the house. "Sweet heaven," she shouted. "Newt! Newton Findlay! You must come at once! Our sweet little Darcy is out in that storm!"

Hearing her cries the old sailor stepped from the shed, where he'd been mending some sails. "Now what's this about our Darcy?"

The nursemaid could hardly get the words out over the panic that was threatening to choke her. "Our baby's taken the skiff, Newton. Look!" She pointed, and the two of them stared at the boiling sea. Barely visible was a tiny boat being tossed about like a piece of bark.

The old sailor took off at a crazy gait, running as fast as his wooden peg would allow. But long before he reached the edge of the water, Gray Barton had already whipped off his shirt and plunged into the frigid Atlantic.

"Oh, sweet heaven." Miss Mellon stood in the foaming surf, her skirts drenched, her high kid boots quickly filling. She was gripping the old sailor's arm so hard she nearly drew blood.

They watched helplessly as wave after wave rolled

over the figure of the lad. Each time he disappeared, they thought surely he'd drowned. But then, just as their hearts stopped, they would catch sight of him again, gamely struggling against waves that were now as high as a ship's rail.

"Oh, Newton." Miss Mellon's tears spilled down her cheeks, blinding her.

"This is all my fault. I've allowed our baby to drown. And now that brave young boy, as well."

"Here, now." The old sailor patted her hand while he continued to watch the feeble progress of the boy. "It's nobody's fault. The lass just purely loves the sea. And she's too young to know the danger."

"Aye. Absolutely fearless." The poor woman's lips quivered, and she began weeping harder. "As is that lad. How will I ever tell Captain Lambert? First his wife. And now his baby. And she was entrusted to my care."

"Hush, now," Newton cautioned. "There's a chance the lad will reach her in time." But the old man's voice lacked conviction. He knew of few men, even seasoned sailors, who could fight such waves. And if the lad did manage to reach the skiff, how could he bring it safely back to shore in such rough seas?

The sky grew darker, and the children huddled around their nursemaid, unusually silent as they realized the seriousness of the situation.

"Is Darcy going to die, Winnie?" Ambrosia demanded.

For the first time in her life, Miss Mellon couldn't find the words to deny the question.

"Is she, Newt?" James tugged on the old man's sleeve.

Unable to speak, Newton drew his arm around the boy and continued staring into the distance, even though it had grown so dark, they could no longer see the skiff or the boy in the water.

Overcome with emotion, Miss Mellon dropped to her knees in the water and held Ambrosia and Bethany against her chest while she sobbed her heart out.

Suddenly James pointed. "Look, Newt!"

The old sailor took a moment, then said, "Well, I'll be."

"What?" Their nursemaid got to her feet and tried to see. But all she could make out was the black boiling ocean.

"There." As lightning streaked across the sky and seemed to dance on the waves, they could see the outline of the little boat.

With each flash of lightning the boat seemed to be moving closer.

"Praise be," Newton muttered as he started into the foaming surf.

Minutes later he was hauling the little skiff onto the beach. Gray climbed out, carrying little Darcy in his arms.

When Miss Mellon tried to take the child from him, Darcy locked her chubby arms around his neck and buried her face in his throat.

"Nay. I want to stay with Gray. Wasn't he brave? He swam all that way just to ride back with me. And what an exciting, bumpy ride it was. I started to worry, but Gray said he'd never let anything bad happen to me. Not ever."

Instead of ordering her down, so he could catch his breath, the boy merely beamed. "It's all right, Miss Mellon. Newt. She's not heavy. She's just a wee bit of a thing. Hardly weighs anything at all." He stared down into her eyes and found her looking up at him adoringly. "No need to fret now. Darcy wasn't even afraid. Just paddling furiously and a little annoyed that she couldn't get back to shore."

He looked up at the others. "Isn't she something?"

"Aye, lad. Something. And so are ye. It's a brave thing ye did."

"I gave her father my solemn promise that I'd always look out for her when he was at sea."

"Did ye now?"

"Aye, sir. And I'd never break a promise."

"So I see." Newton draped an arm around the boy's shoulders and herded him toward their house in the distance.

And though Gray must have been beyond exhaustion, he carried his little burden all the way, finally depositing her on a rug in front of the fire. Then he lay down beside her, draped in a warm, dry blanket.

When the housekeeper came bustling in minutes later with mugs of warm milk, the boy was sound asleep. Curled up beside him was little Darcy, her hand tucked in his.

As the adults gathered around, speculating on the enormity of the boy's heroics, they realized something else, as well. Despite the nearly eight years that separated Gray from Darcy, these two enjoyed a special bond. Both shared a love for and a fascination with the sea. Both were absolutely fearless. And their faith in each other was unshakable.

Newt watched the two asleep. Even their chests rose and fell in silent rhythm. "A more perfect match I've never known." He shook his head before going off to his bed, while muttering, "I hope I'm around to see them grown."

Some people, he realized, were simply born for one another.

Chapter One

"It's hard to imagine that both Ambrosia and Bethany are married now, isn't it, Grandpapa?" Darcy Lambert, youngest of the three Lambert sisters, stood beside her grandfather on the widow's walk, the wide porch that ran the length of the upper floor of their home, MaryCastle. While she talked, Darcy kept her gaze fixed on the horizon, hoping for a glimpse of the tall masts of the *Carrington,* the ship on which Gray Barton served as first mate.

"I've no doubt you'll soon follow them into that sea of matrimony, lass." Geoffrey Lambert touched a hand to her cheek and she closed a hand over his.

"Aye. Gray said this will be his last time at sea under the command of another. Next time, he'll be captain of his own ship. Think of it, Grandpapa. A ship's captain. It's what he's wanted for so long. And he promised that when next he sets sail, I'll be going with him, as his wife and first mate."

The old man sighed. "It's hard for me to think that I'll lose all three of my lasses in the space of a single year."

"You'll not be losing us, Grandpapa." She pointed

to the workmen swarming around the skeleton of a house rising beside theirs. "Ambrosia and Riordan will be living right next door. Bethany and Kane are just a carriage ride away at Penhollow Abbey. As for Gray, I think he'll agree to live here at MaryCastle when we aren't aboard ship. Oh, Grandpapa." She wrapped her arms around his waist and pressed her cheek to his. "Just think of all the lovely babies we can give you."

"Aye." He chuckled. "Another generation to pester old Newt, and drive poor old Winnie to distraction."

Darcy joined in the laughter. "It will invigorate them, Grandpapa. Invigorate all of us."

"Indeed it will." As the wind picked up the old man shivered. "Winter will be upon us before we know it. Come on, lass. Let's get in out of the cold."

"You go, Grandpapa." Darcy drew her shawl firmly around her shoulders. "I'll just stay here a while longer. I have a feeling Gray's ship will be coming home today. I want to be the first one down to the shore to greet him."

"Aye, lass." He touched a hand to her shoulder, before turning away. "But don't stay out here too long. You wouldn't want Gray to find you frozen to this porch."

"Don't worry." She gripped the rail and turned to the sea. "He'll find my heart as warm as when he left. And a fire burning in my soul for only him."

"Our dinner will soon be cold." Mistress Coffey, housekeeper for the Lambert family, glanced around with annoyance. "Where is Darcy?"

Ambrosia, recently returned from next door, where

she and her new husband, Riordan Spencer, were building their home, continued lighting the tapers in the center of the table. "I haven't seen her all afternoon."

"If I had to hazard a guess," her grandfather said, "I'd say she's probably still up on the widow's walk, watching for Gray's ship."

"Then perhaps you ought to speak to her, Geoffrey." Their old nursemaid, Winifred Mellon, clucked her tongue as she slipped into her usual place at the table. "This is the fifth time in as many days that she's missed her dinner."

"You can't blame her for getting nervous, Winnie." Ambrosia kissed her husband's cheek, then linked her arm with his when he entered the dining room. "Gray's ship should have been here more than a month ago."

Riordan brushed a kiss over his wife's lips. "And you, more than anyone my darling, should be aware that ships never reach their destination on time. There are so many things that can create havoc with schedules, not the least of which is the weather." He glanced around as the others took their seats. "I've been hearing from sailors about some terrible storms off the coast of Wales. Wasn't that where Gray's ship was headed?"

"Aye." Geoffrey Lambert suddenly turned away from the table.

"Where are you headed?" the housekeeper demanded.

"I'll go fetch the lass. I don't blame her for keeping her vigil. But she needs to keep up her strength."

The others waited, then gave a sigh of relief when the old man returned with Darcy beside him. Her blond hair was wind-tossed, her cheeks as bright as apples from the chill breeze blowing in off the Atlantic. And though her eyes bore the smudges of sleepless nights, she managed a wide smile at her family.

"Grandpapa persuaded me to come inside and try your fine roast goose, Mistress Coffey."

"You won't be sorry." The housekeeper passed around a platter. "I made your favorite sweet honey glaze and sour cream biscuits."

The old woman began circling the table, filling teacups. They heard the front door open, and the sound of Newton stomping mud from his boots. He seemed to take a particularly long time before walking to the dining room.

"About time." Mistress Coffey shot him a dark look. "Another minute and I'd have had Libby remove your plate from the table." She sniffed as she passed him. "Do I smell spirits?" Sparks nearly flew from her eyes. "Newton Findlay, have you been in the village, drinking at the tavern?"

"Aye." The old sailor paused in the doorway, but made no move to sit at the table. And instead of his usual lively argument with the old woman, which the entire family had come to expect and even enjoy, he was unusually silent.

When he continued to stand, the others paused to look up at him.

"What is it, Newt?" Ambrosia arched a brow. "You look like you've just lost your best friend."

"Not I, lass." He cleared his throat and stared down at the toe of his boot.

For the space of several seconds he struggled to find the words. Then, looking up, he glanced at Darcy. "I heard talk in the village, lass."

"Talk?" She set down her cup with a clatter. Her eyes went wide as a smile curved her mouth. "Gray. Oh, Newt. You've heard from Gray."

"Not exactly, lass. But I've heard about his ship."

"Aye?" Without realizing it, she touched a hand to her heart. "What've you heard, Newt? When will he be home?"

"I heard from a man whose brother sailed aboard the *Carrington* with Gray. They were off the coast of Wales when they found themselves in a gale. Some say it was a hurricane, but they thought they could ride it out. Then there was a terrible fire aboard ship. They're not sure how it started. Maybe a brazier tipped during the storm. At any rate, all hands were forced to abandon ship."

Darcy shoved back her chair and stood, gripping the edge of the table. Her eyes looked suddenly too big for her face. "What about Gray, Newt? Tell me...tell me he made it to shore."

The old sailor shook his head. "His cap'n was wounded in the fire. Gray saw to it that he was loaded into a skiff with the rest of the crew. But Gray himself refused to abandon ship until he was certain all the others were safely away. They saw him, enveloped in flame as the *Carrington* went down."

"They?" Her eyes narrowed. "Who are these who carry such wicked tales?"

"Gray's shipmates, lass. Only three men made it. The rest were lost at sea, including the cap'n and those with him in the skiff."

"Nay." The word was torn from her lips. "Gray is a strong swimmer." She looked around at the others, daring them to argue. "Nothing would stop Gray from making it to shore. Nothing. Not even fire."

"Lass…"

"Nay, Newt." She pushed away from the table. "I would know it, here in my heart." She stared hard at her grandfather, then at her older sister, begging them to understand. "I would have felt the pain if he'd drowned. My own breath would have ceased."

"Darcy…" Ambrosia started to stand but her sister shook her head fiercely.

"He's not dead. He's not. I won't accept that. I can't." Her eyes went wild, like an animal caught in a trap. "Gray survived. I know he did. He had to."

"But lass…"

She held up a hand to stop Newton's words. "I don't care what others have told you. How can I still be alive if Gray isn't? Don't you see? It isn't possible for me to live without him. We're…one. We've always been one. We share the same heart. The same soul. The same spirit."

"Ye may think that, lass. But in fact, ye're two separate lives. And no matter how painful it might be, it's possible to live without Gray."

"Nay. Stop, Newt. It isn't possible. Gray's alive, I tell you."

While the others watched helplessly, she fled the room.

There were no tears. Nor would there be. Darcy refused to allow them. For if she permitted herself to weep, to grieve, she would be admitting that her beloved Gray was dead. And that she would never do.

Instead she returned to the widow's walk, to pace, to stare out to sea. To wait. He would return. She could see it in her mind's eye, the tall masts, the gleaming white sails, the skiff returning the crew to shore. And Gray, striding across the beach, that wonderful smile lighting his handsome, rugged face as he scooped her into those strong arms and swung her around and around.

She closed her eyes and smiled at the image.

She loved him. Had always loved him. And had always known, with some sixth sense, that they would spend their lives together. She'd been born for him alone. And if he had ceased to exist, she would somehow know. She would have felt his spirit touch hers as he passed.

As darkness blanketed the water, the wind picked up. It was then that she heard it. A low moaning sound that caused the hair at the nape of her neck to bristle.

Newton had always told her the sea was a woman. A woman who called out to sailors, causing many to risk their lives for her. But this was a man's voice, low, tormented and filled with suffering.

She covered her ears and dropped to her knees with a sob. "Oh, Gray. Please, Gray. Nay. I can't bear it. You must stop, before you break my poor heart."

But the moaning went on and on, tearing at her heart, searing her mind and soul. Shattered, she slumped to the porch and drifted into unconsciousness.

It was Newton who found her and carried her down the stairs and into the parlor.

"Oh, sweet heaven." Miss Mellon took one look at that still, pale figure and indicated the chaise. "Set her here, Newt."

"Aye." The old man lay down his burden with the

greatest of care, fearful that she might shatter like fragile crystal.

"Geoffrey," the old woman called. "I think some whiskey is called for."

"I quite agree." Captain Lambert poured a generous tumbler and held it to his granddaughter's lips.

As the fiery liquid slipped down her throat, she coughed and choked, then opened her eyes.

"What were you thinking? Your hands are cold as ice." Ambrosia began rubbing her sister's hands between her own.

"I heard…" Darcy swallowed. "I heard Gray calling out to me. He's in terrible pain."

Ambrosia glanced at the others, who were peering down at Darcy with matching looks of concern. "You only thought you heard him, Dar."

"Nay." Darcy shook her head vehemently. "I heard him. As plainly as I'm hearing you now." She turned to Newton. "I heard him, Newt."

"Lass." He closed a gnarled old hand over hers. "Ye know the tricks the sea can play on our minds. She can sigh and moan and even talk, when she's a mind to. But it's the sea talking. Not Gray."

"It was Gray." One big wet tear squeezed from the corner of her eye and began trickling down her cheek. "He's in pain. He needs me. And I don't know how to help him."

"Here now." Geoffrey Lambert pressed the tumbler of whiskey into her hand. "I want to see you drink this. All of it. It'll warm you and help you sleep, lass."

"I don't want to sleep, Grandpapa."

"Then drink it for me." He sat beside her on the chaise and closed a hand over hers, forcing the tumbler to her lips.

She drank, feeling the whiskey burn a path of fire down her throat. Within minutes the tremors that had rocked her began to ease. She became aware of the uneasy looks that passed from one to the other as her family remained around her.

"I'm...fine now. You can all go up to bed."

"Not until you're ready." Ambrosia glanced toward her husband, who nodded his agreement.

"I...suppose I could sleep." Darcy handed the empty tumbler to their housekeeper, then got unsteadily to her feet.

At once Ambrosia put an arm around her sister and began to walk with her toward the stairs. As they climbed to the second story, Ambrosia pressed her cheek to her sister's. "You've had a terrible shock, Dar. It's no wonder your mind is playing tricks on you."

Darcy swallowed back the protest that sprang to her lips. There was no point in upsetting the others.

"If you'd like—" Ambrosia paused outside her sister's room "—I could come inside for a while and we could talk. Or maybe you'd like me to stay with you through the night. We'll sleep together the way we did when we were little, and one or the other of us was feeling fearful."

"Nay." Darcy glanced beyond her to where Riordan Spencer stood. "You have your husband now."

"Riordan doesn't mind..."

Darcy shook her head. "I'm weary now. I'll sleep."

"You're sure?"

"Aye." She brushed her lips over Ambrosia's cheek. "But I thank you for your offer. Good night."

She stepped into her room and closed the door, then leaned against it and listened to the footsteps receding along the hallway. When the house grew empty she walked to the big window overlooking the sea and knelt down, resting her arms along the wide sill.

Sleep, she knew, would be impossible this night. She needed to remain alert and awake, in case Gray called to her again.

She rested her chin on her hands and peered into the darkness, hoping to catch a glimpse of white sail.

Was she slipping into madness? Was she simply denying what she knew to be the truth? Was this the way other people dealt with the loss of a soul mate?

"Oh, Gray." She felt the tears threatening and blinked hard and fast, then was forced to swallow the lump in her throat. She mustn't allow them to start. If she gave in to the weakness, it would shatter her last thread of control. She bit back the sob that tore at her throat. "Gray, how can I live without you? I can't bear it. Oh, I can't bear to think of my future without you."

She pressed a hand to her stomach and fought the rush of sickness that left her lying weakly on the hard wooden floor, her body damp with cold sweat. With a throat raw from unshed tears, and a head throbbing from the effort to stem them, she lapsed into a deep sleep. A sleep filled with visions of a flaming ship sinking slowly beneath the churning black waves of the Atlantic.

"Darcy?" Old Miss Mellon crept into the room, dismayed at the sight of sweet Darcy crumpled beneath the window.

"Aye?" She lifted her head and ran a hand through the hair that hung in tangles around her face. A face pale and tormented.

Sunlight streamed through the window. Already the sun was high in the sky.

"We didn't wake you for Sunday services. We thought it best to let you sleep."

"Thank you, Winnie. I..." Darcy glanced around and realized she'd spent the night on the floor. "That was kind of you."

"Vicar Thatcher Goodwin broke the news to the congregation. He's planning a memorial service this evening for all the lads of the village who served aboard the *Carrington* and were lost at sea."

When Darcy said nothing the old woman took a deep breath. "You must attend, child."

Darcy was already shaking her head. "To do so would be an admission that I believe Gray is..."

"I understand. But the others in the village of Land's End won't understand. They've long known that you and Gray—" she chose her words carefully "—planned a life together. If you should avoid this service, they'll think you don't care enough to come."

Darcy sighed. "I don't care what others think, Winnie. I never have."

The old nursemaid straightened her shoulders. Over the years she'd learned when to yield, and when to fight these obstinate young women. She had come prepared to do righteous battle.

"You may not care what the villagers think. But you owe it to Gray's memory to be there."

"But I—"

Miss Mellon held up a hand. "You listen to me, Darcy. You'll put aside your own feelings this evening. You'll endure the Bible readings and the hymns, even if your heart is broken beyond repair. You'll do it because it's the right thing to do. You'll do it because your family and your friends expect it of you. And most of all you'll do it to honor the memory of the fine young man you've always loved."

Darcy swallowed back the many protests that sprang to her lips and merely nodded.

"Fine." Miss Mellon patted her shoulder. "That's fine, child. You pull yourself together now, and prepare for the service."

She turned away and let herself out of the bedroom. At the bottom of the stairs the rest of the family stood waiting. She gave a terse nod of her head and watched as they sighed their approval.

Without a word she kept on walking and managed to hold her tears in check until she was safely in her own room. Only then did she allow herself to weep for the child who had given her so many frightened moments all those years ago. To grieve for the graceful young woman she'd become. To ache for the heartbroken lass who now would bury the man who had pledged to make her his bride.

Every pew of the little village church was filled. From all over Land's End the people came to pay tribute to the sailors who had been lost aboard the *Carrington.* The women were somber in their dark gowns and bonnets, the children unusually quiet. Men, old and young, nodded with each word spoken by the old vicar, Thatcher Goodwin. Every man, woman and child in Cornwall understood the perils that all sailors faced each time they challenged the Atlantic. She was a demanding mistress. A fickle, often fiery mistress, who stole a man's heart, and often his life, on a whim, leaving widows and orphans to grieve and mourn their losses.

Darcy sat, surrounded by her family, struggling for composure. Throughout the endless prayers and readings, and the hymns that pulled at her heart, she stared straight ahead, refusing to glance at those around her who were weeping. For to do so would be to open herself to pity. And that would only lead to sorrow, which in turn would unleash a floodgate of tears.

She would not join this maudlin crowd in their mourning. Could not. And so she sat, hands tightly fisted in her lap, eyes dry and staring, without really focusing on anything.

She had turned inward. There was her strength. There was her salvation from this mass hysteria. She imagined herself alone, on a cliff, staring down at the foaming sea. It could not touch her. It could not hurt her. And soon, when it realized her strength, it would deliver up the man it had tried to take from her.

When at last the tedious service was ended, she breathed a sigh of relief and followed her sisters down the aisle.

She was startled when her hand was grasped, and a high-pitched voice, like the sound of seabirds fighting over a morsel of fish, broke through her wall of reserve.

"Oh, Darcy. I couldn't believe my ears when I heard that Gray was one of those who'd lost his life aboard the *Carrington*." Edwina Cannon physically restrained her, and drew her arms around her even when she tried to pull away. "I know just how you feel."

The young woman noted with satisfaction that several people had paused to glance her way. Since she liked nothing better than finding herself the center of attention, Edwina continued in an even louder, higher tone. "It was the same for me when my beloved Silas was lost to me. He was far too young. And so was your Gray. I was devastated. Simply devastated." She gave an exaggerated sigh. "But I managed to pull myself together in time. And so shall you."

Darcy pushed herself free of Edwina's arms, and felt her face flame as she realized how many people were staring at them. "Thank you, Edwina. Now I really must go."

"Nay." Edwina's fingernails bit into Darcy's flesh as she clamped a hand around her wrist. "These good people have come to offer their sympathy." She turned and gave a dimpled smile to those who were watching and listening. She was clearly relishing her role as chief mourner. "It is simply good manners to linger and accept the condolences of all who knew and loved Gray."

Darcy's eyes grew stormy, a sure sign that she was about to explode. Seeing it, her sisters stepped between her and the other young woman.

Bethany's teeth were so tightly clamped, she could hardly speak. But she managed a thin smile. "Thank you for your concern, Edwina. But we really must leave now."

"But I—"

The shrill voice was silenced as Bethany closed her arm around Edwina's shoulder and dragged her into a pew. At the same instant, Ambrosia caught Darcy's hand and pulled her toward the entrance of the church, where the congregation was now milling about.

"This way, lass." Geoffrey, seeing their dilemma, motioned toward a side door.

Within minutes they'd slipped unseen through the door. Waiting just beyond the steps was Newton, with their carriage. As soon as everyone had climbed aboard, he cracked the whip and the team started off at a trot.

Ambrosia and Bethany turned to see Edwina Cannon and her mother just stepping outside, surrounded by hoards of villagers.

"Look at her," Bethany muttered. "If I know Edwina, she'll continue to hold the crowd enthralled for an hour or more on the pain of her own loss."

"Aye." Ambrosia lifted her voice in a perfect imitation of Edwina's shrill tones. "Poor me. Nobody has ever suffered as I have."

As the others tittered at her sarcasm, she glanced at Darcy, who had retreated into her own dark silence.

Chapter Two

"That was a fine meal, Mistress Coffey." Riordan Spencer could always make the old housekeeper blush with a simple compliment. "I think you'll regret the fact that we're building our home so close. Ambrosia and I will probably be over every night to sample your fine cooking."

"I should hope so." Mistress Coffey circled the table pouring tea. "I only wish we could persuade Bethany and Kane to come more often."

"We would, if it didn't make Mistress Dove so nervous." Bethany sipped her tea and smiled at her new husband. "Every time we come here, we have to spend two days reassuring her that we still appreciate her."

"Well, it does my heart good to see my three lasses together again." The old woman glanced at Darcy, so pale and quiet. She hadn't spoken a single word throughout the meal.

For the past several weeks she'd been like a ghost. At first they'd seen her spend hours on the widow's walk, staring into the distance. But now, with the first biting slap of winter, she'd begun slipping off to her room instead, to stare out the window for hours.

Bethany's husband, the earl of Alsmeeth, glanced across the table. "How's the house coming, Riordan?"

"The workmen are doing a fine job. In fact, Ambrosia and I are hoping to move in before spring." Riordan sipped his ale. "I should be glad. But it means I'll have to pass up a lucrative offer to run supplies between Scotland and Wales."

"Ah, well." Geoffrey Lambert smiled. "With winter winds howling, you'll be happier sitting by the fire with your wife. And I'm sure Ambrosia will be happier knowing you'll be home with her."

"True enough." Riordan smiled at his wife. "That's why I told the harbormaster to find another ship's captain."

At that Darcy's head came up. "Has he found someone yet?"

Riordan shrugged. "I doubt it. I just sent word today."

"I'd like to take the commission."

The others merely looked at her.

Geoffrey Lambert cleared his throat. "This isn't to some exotic island, lass, where the sun shines year-round. We're talking about navigating the waters around Scotland and Wales in the dead of winter. There are fierce storms and—"

"I know, Grandpapa. But I'd like to do it."

"Perhaps. But where would you find a crew willing to come aboard?"

"There are sailors in the village just begging for work."

"I suppose you could find enough to man the *Undaunted*. But what about a first mate?"

Darcy turned. "Would you sail with me, Newt, as first mate?"

The old man thought about the winters of his youth, when he'd battled waves taller than mountains, and had watched shipmates lose all feeling in their hands and feet, before tumbling into the black waters from sheer exhaustion. And then he thought about the comfort of MaryCastle in winter, with its snug rooms warmed by log fires, filled with the wonderful fragrance of bread baking and soup simmering. After a pint of ale at the tavern, he liked nothing better than to return to the warmth of his bed, knowing there would be no demands made of him on the morrow except an occasional hitch of the team to a sleigh.

And then he looked into those hopeful blue eyes. And he could no more refuse than he could stop breathing.

"Aye, lass. If ye want me aboard, ye know I'll be there."

She placed a hand over his. "Thank you." She looked at the others. "I really want to do this. I need to do it. Do you understand?"

One after another they nodded, before looking away. The pain was still sharply etched on her face. A pain that had all their hearts rubbed raw.

"It's settled then. I'll go to the village at first light and tell the harbormaster I'll take the commission. And Newt and I will hire a crew." She shoved away from the table, and slowly circled it, brushing kisses across the cheeks of her family, before climbing the stairs to her bedroom.

She had found a way to get closer to Gray. Even if it meant merely passing over his eternal resting place. For, though she hadn't yet accepted his death, the truth was, hope had begun to fade. If he were alive, she reasoned, he would have found a way to get word to her. And so this was all she could do for him now. But at least it was better than sitting home mourning her loss.

For the first time in weeks she slept soundly.

The air was sharp as needles, burning the lungs of those sailors unlucky enough to be above deck. To add to their misery, it began to sleet. Icy fangs that bit into the flesh and made them yearn for home and hearth.

From high above the rigging came the shout, "Ship with no flag. Moving fast on port."

"There's time to outrun her," one of the sailors called.

"The *Undaunted* doesn't run." Darcy held the wheel steady and gave a call to lower the sails. "She fights."

"But cap'n—"

She cut off the sailor's protest with a quelling look. "Take up your positions and prepare for battle."

"Aye, cap'n." Amid grumbling and complaining, the cannons were uncovered and loaded with gunpowder.

A sailor began passing among the crew, handing out an assortment of weapons. Swords, pistols and knives disappeared inside heavy jackets, as did the fingers, numb with cold.

Hearing the call, Newton came above deck and approached Darcy, who was working frantically to turn the ship in order to face the oncoming danger.

"The crew is weary, lass. They've swabbed the deck clean of the blood from the last fight. They're not up to another encounter."

"Our job is to fight pirates, Newt."

"Aye, lass. That it is. But in order to do that, we need to be strong. There's still time to outrun them and reach the safety of a harbor."

"You'd have us turn tail and run like cowards?"

"I'd have us survive, lass." He touched a hand to her arm. "Look at ye, Darcy. Ye're nearly skin and bones. We've been a month at sea, with scores of skirmishes."

"Then we'll make it one more. I'm not weary, Newt."

"Maybe not. But ye can't say the same for the crew. It's time to put into shore now. Let them eat something besides fish. Let them sip ale in a tavern, and sleep in real beds, with a warm female beside them. Otherwise, ye'll soon have to deal with ye'r crew jumping ship the first chance they get."

She sighed. He had a point. She'd noticed the restlessness of the men, but had chosen to ignore it. Besides, they had another task to see to. There was a cargo in the hold which they'd agreed to deliver.

She studied the distant ship struggling to keep up with the *Undaunted*. It would be a simple matter to take shelter in one of the many harbors that dotted the coastline. After a night in port, they could continue their journey and deliver their cargo. And if the pirates were still waiting, her crew would be fresh and ready to fight.

Reluctantly she nodded. "All right, Newt. Give the order to hoist the sails."

The old man sighed with relief. If the crew had been forced into one more fight, he wasn't certain they'd have had the heart for it.

The order was given and the sails were soon billowing in the stiff wind. As she steered toward port, Darcy heard the happy murmur that went up among the crew. Despite the bitter cold, the sailors crowded the rail as they drew close to land. The thought of a warm fire, and an even warmer woman in their beds, had them eager to drop anchor and head to shore.

When Darcy went to the strongbox in her cabin, Newton urged her to be cautious. "I wouldn't give the men all their pay, lass."

"But I owe them."

"Aye. And ye'll pay them when ye return to home port. For now, ye'd be wise to give them only half. Knowing these lads, they'll spend as much as they have in their pockets, be it a quid or a pound."

She considered, then nodded in agreement.

Darcy stood alone on deck and watched as the skiff deposited the last of the crew ashore. Then she went belowdecks to take stock of their supplies, noting that they were down to a single barrel of fresh water.

A short time later she heard footsteps overhead. Newton poked his head around the door of her cabin.

"I brought the skiff back for ye, lass."

"Thanks, Newt. But I won't be going ashore."

"What do ye mean? Ye'd spend the night here in ye'r cabin?"

"And why not? I have an extra blanket. And as long as I have my knife, I'm safe."

"I know ye are, lass. There's not many who could outfight ye. But I thought ye might want to go ashore here, since we've made it to the coast of Wales."

"Wales?"

"It's just a small island offshore. But it's Wales, nonetheless." He saw the way her eyes widened, before they narrowed with the memory. He kept his tone casual. "This is a rare chance to sleep in a feather bed, lass, with a fire to warm ye." Before she could refuse he put a hand beneath her elbow. "Come on, Darcy. I know the tavern owner. His wife's a fine cook. We'll share a bowl of soup and a tumbler of ale. And he'll put ye up in a room by ye'rself, all warm and snug in the attic."

She shrugged, then gave him a slow smile. "You've always known just the thing to bring me around, haven't you, Newt?"

He merely grinned as he led the way to the ship's rail. Darcy followed him down the rope ladder, then sat in the bow of the skiff while he rowed to shore. Once there they walked along the wharf until they reached the tavern.

Inside the air was heavy with the smells of wood fire and meat sizzling in grease. Of bread baking and, as they moved deeper into the public rooms, of sweat and unwashed bodies. Darcy wrinkled her nose, preferring the sting of clean night air carrying the tang of saltwater. Still, there was the promise of a feather bed. And a cozy fire. And it had been so long.

As she trailed behind Newton she was aware that the raucous conversations became more hushed as she passed the tables of sailors. She saw heads come up to stare, and voices lowered to whispers.

"That's 'er then? Ye'r cap'n?"

"Aye."

"She's too pretty to be a sailor. But I wouldn't mind taking her to my bunk."

"She'd as soon slit ye'r throat. She may be beautiful, but this one sleeps alone. She's untouchable. Keeps to 'erself, she does. But in a fight, she's a fierce brawler, she is. Maybe the most fearless fighter I've ever seen."

"Fearless? Or foolish? I've heard the lass has a death wish." An old sailor's lips curled in derision. "I'd not sail with such a captain."

"And why's that?"

"Because she's bound to take her crew down with her."

At that several of the men at the table fell silent, mulling over the seed of suspicion that had been planted. Since they'd signed on with her, they'd been involved in more battles than most would see in a year or more.

Could it be true that Darcy Lambert preferred death over life? Was that why she seemed hell-bent on destruction?

"It's rumored she lost her love to the sea. Maybe she hopes to join 'im."

Although Darcy overheard many of the slanderous remarks, she chose to ignore them. Instead, trailing a lad of perhaps nine or ten, she marched through the public rooms with her head high, looking neither right nor left. When she and Newton were shown to a private room, she accepted a tankard of ale and stood warming herself in front of the fire.

"Don't mind the men out there." Newt accepted a tankard from the lad and paused beside her. "Nothing sailors like better'n a good tale. They'll repeat it in every port until it grows as many tentacles as an octopus."

"I know, Newt." She tipped the tankard and drained it, then stared into the flames.

"But they may have a point, lass." He stood beside her, staring keenly at the flames dancing on a draught of air. "I've been watching ye. There've been plenty of times ye could have avoided a fight. Instead, ye steered the *Undaunted* into the path of danger."

"Have you forgotten what it is we do for our king, Newt?" She turned to him with a frown, then fell silent as she noticed for the first time that the lad was still in the room, listening intently.

When the boy saw her look his way, he took his leave, closing the door firmly behind him.

Alone, Darcy turned to Newton. "We're privateers. Just as Papa and James were. It's our duty to rid the ocean of pirates who would do harm to those who sail for England."

"Ye needn't remind me of duty, lass. I was seeing to it before ye were born." The old man drained his tankard and set it on the scarred wooden table, then turned to her. "But lately ye've begun to take risks with the lives of ye'r men."

"They knew the risks when they signed on. We never lied to them."

"Nor did we tell them we'd seek out every pirate sailing the Atlantic."

They both fell silent as the lad returned with a tray. He took his time depositing two bowls of steaming soup and a loaf of hard-crusted bread on the table.

"Would you like more ale, miss?"

"Aye. Thank you."

"And you, sir?"

"Aye." When his tankard was full Newt narrowed his gaze on the lad until he backed up, then took his leave.

When the door closed behind the lad, Darcy turned on Newton. "What would you have me do, Newt? Avoid any further battles?"

"Nay, lass." Patiently the old sailor held his tongue as he drew out the chair for her in a courtly gesture. When she was seated, he walked around the table and sat across from her. "But ye know in ye'r heart that ye'r pushing ye'rself and ye'r men to the limit with these endless brawls. It may help to take ye'r mind off ye'r pain, but it's a dangerous game ye'r playing. And I've a duty to remind ye when I think ye've overstepped ye'r bounds."

Darcy picked up her spoon and began to eat mechanically. Across from her, Newton broke the bread and handed her a chunk. "Here, lass. It's fresh from the oven." His voice lowered with feeling. "Take a moment to savor it."

She set down her spoon and tasted the bread. Then she sighed from the pure pleasure of it.

His weathered face crinkled into a wide smile. "Ye see? Sometimes it's the little things in life that ye need to enjoy. It makes the big things that much easier to bear."

She reached out and placed her hand over his.

"You're so good to me, Newt. How do you put up with me when I'm in one of my moods?"

"They never last long, lass. And I always know that ye'r sunny nature will win in the end."

The two fell into a companionable silence as they enjoyed their first tasty meal since leaving home. Outside the wind raged and howled. Inside the tavern they were warmed not only by the fire, but by the warmth of their friendship as well.

"This way, miss." Holding a candle aloft, the lad climbed narrow stairs to the very top floor of the tavern, then stood aside, allowing Darcy to enter first.

"Oh, my."

Tucked under the eaves was a small cozy room with a single bed and a scarred wooden night table on which rested a pitcher and bowl.

The lad set the candle on the night table. "To my mind, even though it's small, it's the best room in Timmeron Tavern, miss."

"Aye. It's fine." The room was comfortably warmed by the stone fireplace that soared through the roof. A small, narrow window looked out over the wharf. The curtains and the bedlinens were freshly washed.

"Will you be needing anything, miss?"

"Nay, thank you."

When the lad hesitated, she glanced at him. "What is it?"

He shrugged. "Is it true then? What the sailors are saying below?"

"What have you heard?"

"That you're a ship's captain. That you fight like a man. Is it true?"

"Aye." Darcy couldn't help smiling at the look of astonishment on his face.

"But you're no bigger than me." He seemed to be taking her measure, and realized that his head came nearly to her chin. "How is it that you have your own ship?"

She sank down on the edge of the bed. "The *Undaunted* was my father's. And now she's mine."

The boy looked at her with new respect. "I went to sea once. Aboard my uncle's ship, the *Mary M.*"

"I've not heard of her."

He shrugged. "She was a small ship. But seaworthy. She ran cargo around the coast of Wales." His voice lowered. "But she sank in a storm, and my uncle went down with her."

"I'm sorry. Did he have a wife and children?"

"Nay. Just us. My mum and me."

"Have you no father?"

The boy shook his head, avoiding her eyes. Darcy could feel the lad's shame and was instantly sorry for the question. "You lived with your uncle?"

"Aye. Until he died. Then we were forced to move to the village. My mum took a job here at the tavern."

"How does she fare here?"

He stared at a spot on the toe of his scuffed boot. "She died more'n a year ago."

She should have guessed as much. Judging by the shabby, ill-fitting clothes, the lad was barely getting by. "I'm sorry. Are you on your own now?"

He nodded. "The owner lets me work here sometimes. And I have a place to sleep. In the shed with Gryf.''

''Gryf? Is he a brother?''

''Nay. He's just a friend. He's a bit slow still, as he's recovering from injuries. But left on his own he can do anything.''

''Such as?''

The lad pondered a moment. ''Such as cutting my hair.''

Darcy had to bite back a laugh. The lad had the look of a shaggy dog, with only big dark eyes visible beneath the fringe of hair the color of autumn leaves.

''Do you consider that a fine haircut?''

''Aye. Before Gryf cut it, I had to tie it back with a length of leather. The sailors were always teasing me about looking more like a lass.''

''Then Gryf did a fine job for you. What else can he do?''

He gave it some thought. ''I've seen him mend nets in the village, and trim sails. He's a fine fisherman. He helped cut logs for the fire. He can cook a bit, and—'' he had a sudden inspiration ''—if you'd like, he'll fetch up a tub and buckets of warm water for a bath. And while you sleep, he'll wash your clothes and have them dried and looking like new by morning. For a coin, of course.''

''Of course.'' The little beggar, she thought. He'd have his friend do any amount of drudge work for a price, and he'd probably keep the coins for himself.

Still, visions of a warm bath had her heart soaring. She'd been wearing these filthy rags for weeks, without the time to change them between bloody battles. The thought of a real bath, and clean clothes after a good night's sleep, was almost more than she could resist. ''How much?''

The lad thought quickly. ''Ten and sixpence.''

She narrowed her eyes in challenge. ''You wouldn't be thinking of stealing my clothes, would you?''

''Nay, Captain. Gryf and I have no use for a lady's clothes. Will I have him fetch a tub?''

It was simply too tempting. How could she refuse? ''Aye. And a square of linen and some soap.''

''It'll cost you another pence.''

''I'd thought as much.''

The lad's smile would rival the sun. ''I'll have Gryf here before you can pry off those boots, Captain.'' He turned away.

''Wait.''

He paused, turned.

''What is your name?''

''Whit.''

''All right, Whit. I'm Darcy Lambert.'' She offered her handshake and though he held back at first, the boy finally managed to accept.

''Have your friend Gryf hurry.''

''Aye, Captain Lambert.''

The door slammed and Whit's footsteps could be heard racing down the stairs. True to his word, within a short time there was a knock on the door and he was standing there with a round tub.

''Gryf is heating kettles of water.'' He handed Darcy a square of snowy white linen. ''You'd best stand to one side, Captain, while I set this as close to the chimney as possible. That way you'll be warm while you bathe.''

''Thank you, Whit. That's most thoughtful.'' She watched as he set the tub down.

She turned toward the door as a man entered with a bucket of steaming water in each hand.

Gray! For the space of a heartbeat she couldn't breathe. Couldn't move. Though she couldn't see his face, for it was hidden beneath the brim of a shabby hat, she knew that hard, muscled body. The long legs. The lean hips.

''This is the ship's captain I was telling you about, Gryf.''

He turned and nodded, while Darcy stared at him in stunned silence. What little she could see of his face seemed strangely distorted. His eyelids were drooped and puffy, giving him a sleep-drenched, sensual appearance. It was impossible to tell the color of his eyes. But the shape of them seemed all wrong.

''Captain.'' His voice was a strange rasp, as though the single word had caused him great effort.

When he turned away, Darcy's heart was drumming painfully inside her chest. Her breathing was none too steady. But as she watched this stranger, she realized he couldn't be Gray. That hadn't been his voice. And the face had been all wrong, the lower half covered by a rough, scraggly beard. Furthermore, he'd looked right at her. And there had not been the slightest hint of recognition.

While she watched, he went about his work in a slow, methodical manner, pouring first one bucket, then the other. Like Whit he wore cast-off clothes that were ill-fitting. The breeches, several sizes too big, were tied at his waist with a strand of rope. His tattered shirt strained across the muscles of his back and shoulders.

When the buckets were empty he trudged down the stairs, only to return minutes later with two more buckets.

"Thank—thank you." Now that she'd found her voice, Darcy tried a tentative smile.

He didn't return it. He merely nodded and took his leave.

"Why does your friend speak in that strange whisper?"

"It hurts too much." Whit handed her a blob of yellow soap before walking to the door. "I'll just wait outside. When you're ready, hand out your clothes. I'll see that they're returned to you before morning."

She paused in the doorway. "All right. But I'm warning you, Whit, if this is a scheme, I'll find you and your friend, Gryf, and cut out both your thieving little hearts."

The boy shivered at her tone. At this moment he had no doubt that all the tales he'd heard about this female were true. There was a look of a brawler about her. She looked as though she'd enjoy a good fight.

Minutes later the door opened a crack and a hand slipped through, holding out a pair of faded breeches and a colorful shirt, as well as a delicate chemise.

"I'll expect these outside my door by dawn, Whit."

"Aye, Captain. They'll be here. Looking like new."

Darcy closed the door and listened as his footsteps descended the stairs. Then she eased herself into the tub and closed her eyes. Newt was right, she thought with a smile. It was the little things in life that made the big things easier to endure. She'd endure whatever hell came her way later. Right now, she'd just found heaven.

Draped in the linen square, her hair fragrant after a thorough scrubbing, Darcy crossed to the window to stare out at the darkened sea.

Somewhere there in the distance Gray's ship had gone down. The *Undaunted* may have actually passed over the spot this day.

Why hadn't she felt something special? Why hadn't his soul touched hers? She felt tears sting her eyes and turned away, annoyed at this fresh wave of grief, brought about, no doubt, by the encounter with the stranger, Gryf. For a moment she'd been certain her beloved had returned to her.

It was that hard, muscled body. Those long legs. The big, work-worn hands. But where Gray had always been a bundle of energy, cutting a swift, sure path through life, this man moved like a child who was just learning to walk. And his face, what little she'd seen of it, wasn't Gray's face. Where Gray had been strikingly handsome and smooth-shaven, Gryf's chin was covered with a dark stubble. And the eyes. Those red-rimmed, bloodshot eyes. They were so sad and haunting. Not at all the lively, dancing eyes of her beloved.

She put a hand to her heart. How long would this continue? Was she doomed to feel this terrible sadness for a lifetime?

What she wouldn't give for one full day without a thought to the man she'd loved and lost.

Newt was right, of course. Gray was the reason she'd leapt into so many battles. She'd hoped each new plunge into danger would help to ease her burden. But that had given her only momentary relief. What was worse, she hadn't given a thought to the sailors under her command. She'd selfishly placed them in harm's way to assuage her own grief. A grief that was still there, sometimes as jagged as a knife blade, at other times just a dark bruise around her heart. A bruise which sometimes faded, but returned even more painfully with the light of each new day.

Annoyed with her thoughts she placed her boots beside the bed, and slipped her knife under the pillow. Then she crawled naked between the covers.

She'd feared that sleep would be a long time coming. Instead, it crept up on her quickly, while she was still trying to recall the curve of Gray's lips whenever he smiled.

Chapter Three

Darcy heard the footfall on the stairs and was awake instantly. Not Newton, she knew. His peg leg made a distinctive tap on the steps. And not Whit. His were the hurried, impatient footsteps of a child.

Gryf. Though she knew not why, her heart missed a beat. That tall, silent man touched something in her. He seemed wounded and…lost. Aye. Lost. A ship cut adrift from its moorings. And that made her think of Gray. What if her beloved wasn't dead, only lost? What if, even now, he was struggling to make his way back? If so, she would hope that strangers would be kind enough to lend a hand.

She shook her head, annoyed that once again she'd allowed her thoughts to circle back to Gray, and the hole he'd left in her heart.

A glance at the window told her it was still dark outside, with soft bands of dawn light just beginning to color the sky.

The room had grown cold during the night. The fire on the hearth below stairs must have been allowed to burn to embers once the tavern had emptied of patrons.

She sat up, drawing the blanket around her for warmth. Padding lightly across the floor, she opened the door a crack and peered around. Assured that there was nobody there, she looked down. As promised, her clothes were neatly folded in a pile just outside the door. She snatched them up and stepped back inside, noting that they were still warm from the hot stones that had been carefully moved over them to iron out the wrinkles.

Working quickly she slipped into her chemise, noting how soft and clean it felt against her skin. She breathed in the fragrance of evergreen, and wondered if Gryf had dried her clothes on the branches of nearby trees. It gave her a strange feeling to know that he'd had his hands on her most intimate garment.

She drew on her shirt, then shimmied into her breeches and finally her boots. In front of a tall looking glass she twisted her hair into a coil and left it falling over one breast.

She turned at the sound of a knock on the door.

"Are ye awake, lass?"

"Aye, Newt." With a smile she hurried to the door and threw it open. Seeing the look on his face, her smile faded. "What is it? What's happened?"

"Bad news, lass. Several of the crew deserted us."

"Deserted... Are you sure?"

"Aye. Their beds are empty. They fled in the night."

"How many?"

"Six."

Six able-bodied seamen. Gone. She straightened

her shoulders. "We'll need to hire on new sailors as soon as possible."

"Aye, lass." He paused a beat before saying, "There's more."

She waited, her heart sinking.

"They left without paying. The tavern owner says he'll hold ye responsible for whatever they owe."

She gave a deep sigh. Then nodded. "Aye, I'll pay, Newt. I'm grateful you talked me into withholding half their wages. Maybe if I'd paid them all I owed them, I'd have lost even more of the men. And I'd have had no way to hire on a new crew, without enough money to entice them."

"Aye. There's that, lass." He gave her a sharp look. "Ye're not angry that I persuaded you to drop anchor here in Timmeron?"

She shook her head. "It wouldn't matter where we anchored, Newt. They'd have left anyway. And it isn't your fault. It's mine. I'm the one who drove them to this."

"Don't be so hard on ye'rself, lass."

"Why not? You said yourself that I'd pushed them beyond their limits."

"Hush now, lass." He patted her shoulder. "In all the years I've sailed, I've never known a ship to return to home port with its original crew intact. There are always those who can't finish the task they set for themselves."

Aware that he was trying to calm her fears, she gave him a gentle smile and closed a hand over his. "Thanks for that reassurance, Newt. Now, let's go below stairs and see if there are any sailors desperate enough to hire on in the dead of winter."

Darcy led the way down the stairs, where they were shown to one of the public rooms. As soon as they were seated a wench hurried over and began serving them bowls of gruel and thick slices of bread still warm from the oven, which they washed down with cups of scalding tea.

The room began filling up with men. Sailors, farmers from the nearby village, and even a few travelers.

Glancing around, Newton stood and announced in a loud voice, "We need a few good hands aboard our ship, the *Undaunted,* which sails this day. Ours is a cargo ship, plying the waters between Scotland and Wales. If ye'r of a mind, Cap'n Lambert will be paying a gold coin to every man who signs on."

The men mumbled among themselves, but not a single one came forward.

Darcy glanced at Newton as he took the seat beside her on the wooden bench. "I know it's winter, Newt. But some of these men look like they need work. Should I offer two coins?"

He shook his head. "I've a feeling ye'r crew had more to say before they left than ye'd have liked. Ale has a way of doing that to men. And once they get started, they tend to add a bit more…fancy frills to the tale, leaving the truth forgotten. Even two coins won't be enough to overcome whatever fear they've planted in the hearts of these men."

Darcy could only imagine what had been said. And it wouldn't take too many…fancy frills. She had, in truth, pushed her crew to their limits before seeing the wisdom of Newton's advice and permitting them to come ashore.

She sighed. "Go ahead, Newt. Offer two coins."

"Ye'll not have enough to buy the supplies we need."

"We'll eat more fish and less mutton. Go on, Newt."

He got to his feet and cleared his throat before changing the offer to two gold coins. But still the men remained silent.

Darcy lowered her head and stared at the gruel, congealing in her bowl. She had suddenly lost her appetite. Now she and Newton would have to work around the clock to keep the *Undaunted* afloat without the proper crew.

A youthful voice called, "You can count on me, Captain."

Darcy turned to see young Whit standing in the doorway. His boots were covered with dung, and his hands and face were filthy.

"Whit. Do you never sleep?"

"Not when there's coin to be earned."

As he walked closer she wrinkled her nose. "You smell like a barnyard."

"Aye. A nearby farmer pays Gryf and me to muck the stalls each morning and milk the cows. I drew the short straw this morrow and had to do the mucking."

Darcy couldn't help smiling. "Is there anything you and Gryf won't do for pay?"

"Nothing that I can think of, Captain. Now, if you're looking for able-bodied seamen, Gryf and I are willing to sign on."

"Just a moment." Darcy held up her hand. "I don't think you have the right to speak for your friend in this matter."

"And why not?"

"Because this is something that requires a good deal of thought."

He waited for a moment, then said, "There now. I've thought it over. And I'm willing to sign aboard, as long as you'll take Gryf as well. What are our duties?"

Darcy turned to Newton. "I'll leave it to you to explain to the lad."

The old sailor cleared his throat. "What we do is dangerous, lad. There's more to signing aboard ship than swabbing a deck."

"I'm not afraid of storms. Or of pirates."

The old man narrowed his gaze. "If ye'r not afraid, ye should be."

"Why?" The lad looked from the old man to Darcy. "Because the captain has a death wish?"

Darcy blanched.

So, it was as they'd feared. The crew had grown loose-lipped from ale and had revealed more than they should have about the *Undaunted* and her captain. And probably had embellished their tales a bit more with every tankard they downed.

"If I've a death wish, it's the death of pirates, not my crew."

The boy merely looked at her and shrugged. "I'm not afraid, Captain."

"Listen, lad." Newton put a hand on the boy's shoulder and felt him flinch before he brought his fists up as if to defend himself.

At once the old man took a step back and slanted him a look. There was no hiding the fear he read in the boy's eyes.

He deliberately kept his tone easy. "If I were to

sign ye aboard the *Undaunted,* the first thing I'd require of ye would be that ye never speak such things about the captain again.''

"You mean, about her death wish?"

Newton's tone sharpened. "Do I have ye'r word on it, lad?"

Whit looked over at Darcy before averting his gaze. "Aye, sir."

"Good." Newton nodded toward the door. "Now go and find ye'r friend. If he wants to sign aboard, I'll need to hear it from his own lips."

"Aye, sir." The boy turned and raced from the room.

Newton waited until he was gone before turning to Darcy. "I wasn't going to take him. He's just a mite of a lad. But it might be best if we take him with us. If he brings along his friend, we'll be assured of at least two more hands before we leave port."

"There is that, of course." She studied the old man before saying, "But there's more to it than that, isn't there, Newt?"

He stared hard at the tabletop. "There's usually a good reason why a lad that young doesn't like being touched. I'd be willing to wager he's been beaten a time or two."

Her hand went to her mouth. "Do you think his friend Gryf...?"

He shook his head. "The lad seems to have real affection for his friend. But I'm thinking we'll be doing him a favor if we take him away from the Timmeron. Maybe we'll be doing both of them a favor."

By the time they'd finished their meal, Whit was back, trailed by his friend. Like Whit, Gryf's boots were covered with dung, his clothes smelling of a barnyard.

As he approached their table, Darcy felt that peculiar twinge inside and struggled to make out his eyes hidden beneath the brim of a battered old seaman's cap. In the light of morning they were still bloodshot, but they appeared to be dark. Gray's eyes had been the color of coffee beans. And always laughing.

"Here we are, Captain," Whit called. "Gryf agrees that he's willing to sign aboard your ship."

"I'll hear it from his lips, if you don't mind, Whit." Darcy stared into the face of this man. "What say you, Gryf?"

He nodded. "Aye. I'm willing to sign aboard." His voice was like that of a man who'd been choked nearly to death. Every word was an effort.

"Ye comprehend the risks?" Newton demanded.

Gryf turned to the boy and gave him a smile. "Whit and I feel we have nothing to lose."

"Only ye'r life." Newton peered up at the man. "Can ye write ye'r name?"

"Aye."

The old sailor opened a page of the ship's log, then turned it around and handed the man a quill. "If ye'r certain of ye'r decision, sign here."

Gryf scratched a word, then straightened.

Darcy studied the single name. "What is your family name?"

He shrugged. "I know not."

"What do you mean? Are you a foundling then?"

"Perhaps. I know not." He paused, swallowed, then spoke again in that same painful rasp. "This is the name I was given by the family that nursed me back to health after the fire.''

"Fire?" Darcy's heart leapt to her throat. Her face lost all its color.

Seeing her expression, Newt was quick to interrupt. "A ship's fire, man?"

Gryf shook his head, but it was the boy who answered for him. "It hurts him to speak too much. His throat is still raw from the smoke and flames. 'Twas not a ship's fire, but a tavern fire. Gryf was found lying in the ashes, badly burned.''

Darcy's hopes plummeted. She had to remind herself to breathe in and out as the boy continued.

"A kind family took Gryf in until the worst of his burns were healed. But they were unable to find anyone in Timmeron who recognized him. It could be because his face and body were so badly burned. And Gryf himself hasn't been able to remember anything about his life before the fire.''

"How did they come by the name Gryf?"

"It was their grandfather's name. He'd been much revered in their family. He came originally from Cornwall, and had an accent much like Gryf's.''

Darcy's eyes went wide. "So you may have come from Cornwall?"

The man shrugged, embarrassed at so much attention. "I may have. I know not."

"And your friendship with the lad?" Newt studied the boy who was staring up at this man with such fondness.

"I knew I was a burden to the family who had nursed me back to health, so I walked to the village to find work. That's when Whit and I...met. The lad had no place to sleep, so we agreed to share the shed, and we've been together since.''

"Ye seem willing to work hard," Newt muttered. "But can ye handle the work of a sailor?''

"I'm willing to try.''

"Do ye like the sea?'' Newt asked.

Again that shrug of the shoulders. "I think so. At least I have no fear of it. And I feel drawn to it. More so than to the land.''

Newton glanced at Darcy, who was studying the man with a look of fascination. Feeling his gaze on her she turned to the old man and nodded.

"All right then. Ye and the lad are welcome.'' He turned the ship's log toward Whit. "Sign here, lad, and ye're a member of the crew.''

The boy scratched his name, then grinned at his friend before turning to Newton. "You promised us each two gold coins.''

"I did. But since ye'r not yet a man, and we have no way of knowing how much ye can do aboard ship, I thought I'd pay a single gold coin each.''

The boy shook his head. "Nay. Fair's fair. Two gold coins each, or we have no deal.''

Again Newt turned toward Darcy, who was biting back a grin. It was easy to see why this boy had survived on his own. When he dug in his heels, he was as obstinate as a mule.

"Pay them, Newt. Whit's right. Fair's fair.''

To their delight the old sailor placed two gold coins in each of their outstretched palms.

"All right. If ye have anything ye wish to bring, get it now, then meet me at the skiff. We'll be ferrying supplies out to the *Undaunted*. As soon as I hire the rest of the crew, we'll haul anchor.''

He watched as the man and boy hurried off to pack their belongings. Then he turned to Darcy, who was staring after them with a strange, haunted look on her face.

''I know what ye're thinking, lass.''

''Do you, Newt?'' She turned. ''Do you think he resembles Gray?''

''Not a bit of it.'' He paused. ''Perhaps at first glance. The same size, I suppose. But the face and voice aren't his.''

''He was badly burned, Newt.''

''Aye. But it was a tavern fire, lass. Not a ship's fire.''

''He said he doesn't remember. Not even his name.''

''Don't torment ye'rself this way, lass. He's a poor, unfortunate wretch who was in the wrong place at the wrong time, and now he must pay the price. But don't make him into something he can never be.''

''But I felt something when I first saw him. Did you feel it, too?''

The old man shook his head firmly, determined to nip this before it became a full-blown obsession. ''Get hold of ye'rself, lass. Or ye'll be seeing Gray in every man ye meet.''

''But he's tall enough. And his hands...''

''Enough, lass.'' He got to his feet. ''If ye don't mind going to the village to buy the supplies we need, I'll scour the waterfront and see if I can persuade a few sailors to sign aboard.''

For a moment longer she continued to stare at the

man and boy as they pushed through the doorway of the tavern and disappeared from view.

Then, with a thoughtful look on her face, she sighed and stood up, mentally scolding herself for the thoughts she was entertaining.

"Aye, Newt. I'll see to the supplies."

She strode out of the tavern and made her way to the village, determined to put these fanciful thoughts to rest. It was the knowledge that she was in Wales, where Gray's ship had gone down, that was causing her such confusion. Once they were out to sea, her mind would be clear.

Of that she had no doubt.

Chapter Four

"Here ye are, lass." Newt smiled at Darcy as she arrived at the dock.

"How many seamen were you able to hire, Newt?" She climbed down from the wagon loaded with supplies.

He nodded toward the cluster of men. "Only two more. But they seem able enough. We'll have to make do with a smaller crew until we reach our next port."

He turned to the men. "Let's get these supplies loaded into the skiff, mates."

The men worked quickly, grunting as they hefted sacks of flour to their shoulders and struggled under barrels of fresh water. Darcy noted that, despite Gryf's injuries, he didn't evade the hard work required. He handed the smallest parcels to Whit and saved the heaviest items for himself.

After several runs to the ship anchored in the bay, the supplies were finally loaded and the crew went belowdecks to settle their meager belongings into their quarters. Before Whit and Gryf could follow, Darcy handed them some parcels.

"What's this, Captain?" Whit asked.

"Clothes. Some sturdy breeches and tall boots, as well as warm coats."

She could feel Gryf studying her as he accepted his parcel, though he said not a word.

As the two walked away she caught sight of Newton's arched brow. "I want my crew to look like sailors, not a pack of shabby pirates," she muttered.

"Ah. Is that what ye're up to?" He gave her a long, steady look. "Ye wouldn't be hoping proper seaman's clothing might help Gryff look a bit more like…"

"I wasn't hoping for anything." Knowing her cheeks were flushed, she turned away and busied herself on deck.

The old sailor walked away shaking his head.

As they prepared to haul anchor, Darcy took the wheel, maneuvering the big ship through the channel until they were into open sea. Then, turning the wheel over to Newton, she climbed the rigging and began trimming the sails.

On deck Whit watched with a look of amazement. Beside him Gryf lifted a hand to shield the sun from his eyes as he studied the woman high above. With one hand gripping a rope, Darcy reached out and loosened a knot in the rigging, then climbed even higher, until she'd reached the very top of the mast. From there she peered in every direction, studying the steady, rhythmic roll of the waves, searching for any darkened shape that might be a pirate ship on the horizon. Satisfied that their path was clear, she skimmed down the rigging with all the grace of a dancer.

When she landed on deck Whit couldn't hide the note of admiration in his tone. "How'd you learn to do that, Captain?"

She smiled. "I've been doing it all my life."

"Could you teach me?"

"I can try." She lowered her voice and glanced at the old sailor who was steering the ship. "It was Newton who taught me everything I know about ships, and life at sea. Listen to all he tells you, Whit. There's not a better teacher anywhere."

Just then the old man shouted, "Lad. Quit ye'r gibbering and give Gryf a hand with those ropes. And be quick about it."

"Aye, sir." Whit hurried to Gryf's side and began the tedious task of carefully coiling the ropes that littered the deck and carrying them down to the hold. Under his breath he muttered, "I don't see how this is going to teach me to climb like the captain."

Gryf couldn't help laughing. In that strained voice he said, "I doubt such a thing can be taught, Whit."

"Then how did the captain learn?"

"By doing. From the looks of her, it comes as natural to her as breathing."

"Do you think I'll ever be that good, Gryf?"

"I don't see why not." He deposited the last of the rope coils in a darkened corner of the hold and headed for the ladder, with the boy trailing behind. As he started up he said gently, "As long as you want it badly enough to keep trying."

"I do want it. I've always wanted to be a ship's captain like my uncle. And now that I'm aboard ship again, I want it even more." He paused for breath, before continuing up the ladder. "What do you want, Gryf?"

Gryf stepped up onto the deck and offered his hand to the boy. Together they secured the heavy door that covered the ship's hold. "I'm sure there was a time when, like you, I wanted all sorts of things, Whit. Now I'd settle for just knowing who I am and where I belong."

"That's easy." The boy gave his biggest, brightest smile. "You're my best friend. And no matter what your real name is, you belong right here aboard the *Undaunted*. We both do."

As Whit walked away Gryf couldn't help laughing at the lad's youthful innocence. What he wouldn't give for such complacency. But the worry was constantly there, nagging at the edges of his mind. Someone, somewhere knew him. Someone was bound to recognize him. That was why he'd accepted this chance to leave Timmeron. It was a small, poor fishing village. Everyone knew everyone. Yet nobody knew him. That meant that he'd come to Timmeron from somewhere else. But where? And what had he been doing in that tavern the night it caught fire?

"Ahoy, Gryf." Newton's voice broke through his thoughts. "Find the lad and send him belowdecks to lend a hand to Fielding in the galley."

"Aye, sir." Gryf went in search of Whit and found him following Darcy up the ropes of the rigging.

"Look, Gryf. The captain said I could climb with her, as long as I was careful."

"I see. And that's fine. But now's not the time, Whit. Newton has ordered you below to help in the galley."

"The galley?" The boy's voice took on a note of alarm. "How am I supposed to learn to be a sailor helping the cook?"

Darcy paused and stared down at him. "Remember what I told you, Whit. Do everything Newt tells you."

"But I—"

"Without question."

He caught the sharp edge of her tone and nodded. "Aye, Captain."

Reluctantly he descended to the deck and hurried away.

Darcy looked down at Gryf, and felt her heart lurch at the way he was watching her. Whenever she caught him looking at her like that, she felt that strange curling sensation deep inside. It was simply pity, she reminded herself. The man was wounded, and struggling to recover. She would feel the same for anyone in his situation.

Before she could stop herself she called, "Care to join me?"

He shook his head. "I've a job to do, as well. Newt wanted someone to work belowdecks, hanging the hammocks in the crew's quarters."

That would suit him, she thought. He much preferred the darkness below to the sunshine above. All day he'd made himself invisible while the rest of the crew fought to be in the fresh air.

She nodded. "Then you'd best see to it."

"Aye, Captain."

As he walked slowly away, Darcy remained where she was, staring after him. There it was again. That uneasy feeling in the pit of her stomach at the sight of those wide shoulders and narrow hips. Now that he was dressed in proper seaman's clothing, his resemblance to Gray was even more pronounced.

When she looked up and caught Newton watching her she flushed and returned her attention to the rigging. But all the while she worked she thought about Gryf. And wondered what he'd look like without that hat hiding his eyes and that beard covering the lower half of his face.

She couldn't help herself. Though she knew it was absolutely impossible, she wanted him to look like Gray. To *be* Gray.

As she climbed higher she actually hoped she'd catch sight of a pirate ship. Maybe a good fight would be just the thing to stop this foolishness and bring her crashing back to reality.

Too many days of foul weather had the crew tense and edgy. They'd been buffeted by winds and storm-tossed waves that spilled over the rail, making it impossible to cross from one side of the ship to the other without risking life and limb. Darcy and Newton had taken turns at the wheel, spelling each other for a few hours of needed sleep. Like her crew, Darcy's temper was on a short tether. For days now she'd barked orders and bitten heads off for the simplest infraction.

Now, finally, the storms had subsided. As day slid into evening, the seas gentled. The crew, grateful for this break in the weather, went off to their quarters to gamble or just to rest.

"You've put in too many hours at the wheel. Go to bed, Newt." Darcy came up behind the old man and touched a hand to his shoulder.

"What about ye, lass? Ye're just as weary."

"Nay. I've had my sleep. Or as much as I can manage at one time. It's your turn now. You look like you could use it."

"Aye. I'll not argue with ye. It's been too long a day." He turned away, and as she held the wheel steady, Darcy heard the steady tap of his peg as he descended the stairs to his quarters.

She sighed as the darkness closed in around her. She'd been desperate for some quiet time to restore her soul. She'd been driving the crew to distraction with her own anger and frustration. And now, as the silence settled around her, she had time to reflect and regret her impulsiveness. She had to stop pushing so hard. Hadn't Newt urged her to relax and savor the moment? She was having a difficult time remembering his advice. But for now, she intended to enjoy these few moments of privacy.

It took her a while to realize she wasn't alone. She caught a whiff of smoke on the air. The sweet scent of pipe tobacco.

Annoyed, she turned her head and saw a figure standing at the rail.

Gryf. Her heart gave a sudden lurch before settling back to its natural rhythm.

Gray had smoked a pipe. He'd returned home from months at sea and said he'd learned to enjoy the comfort of a pipe and tobacco, especially late at night when he'd stood alone at the rail and thought about home. About her.

The pain came, so swiftly, so unexpectedly, she nearly doubled over from it. Then she drew in a deep breath to steady herself and slanted a look toward the man at the rail. He seemed so alone. So lost.

As if sensing that she was watching him, Gryf turned, then started toward her.

"I thought I was alone on deck." She wondered if her voice sounded as breathy to him as it did in her own ears.

"Sorry. I came up to smoke. I hope you don't mind."

"Nay. I'm…fond of the smell of tobacco. Do you come up here often late at night to smoke?"

"Aye. And to see the stars. They've been missing for a few nights."

"I noticed."

He pointed with the stem of his pipe. "There's Pegasus."

She looked at him with surprise. "So it is. The winged horse." She took a hand from the wheel to point over his shoulder. "Do you recognize that one?"

He turned, stared. "Aye. Orion, the hunter. And chasing him is Scorpius, the giant scorpion."

"How do you know these things?"

He shrugged. "I know not how. I just do. Why do you ask?"

She tried to swallow, but her throat felt too tight. "A…friend returned from sea with tales of the Greek myths. About Pegasus, and Orion and Scorpius. And about the other stars and constellations."

"Perhaps I heard them from a sailor, as well."

"Or perhaps you were a sailor."

"Perhaps. I know not."

He was standing a little too close. She could feel

the heat of his body. Could breathe in the sweet smell of tobacco. The scent of it stirred so many memories.

"My grandfather loved the stars. He knew them all. Their names. Their myths."

"Is he a sailor?"

"Aye. As was my father and brother."

"Was." He heard the pain in her voice. "They're dead?"

She nodded. "My father and my brother, James, died at sea. When we learned of it, my sisters and I agreed to carry on our family business."

"That's quite an undertaking. Did you find much resistance with the crew?"

"Perhaps at first they resisted. But they soon came around when they realized that we were all seasoned sailors. Now we're accepted for what we can do."

"If you're any indication of the skill your sisters possess, I can see why you're accepted without question."

She felt herself blushing, and was grateful for the darkness.

For long minutes they fell silent, while he smoked and she steadied the wheel.

Darcy took a deep breath. "This is my favorite time of day."

"Why?"

"I suppose because the chores are done. The crew is resting. And I feel...close to those I loved and lost. I can indulge myself with all sorts of memories. Memories of happier times."

As soon as the words were spoken, she realized how cruel they must be to someone who had no such memories.

"Forgive me, Gryf. I'd forgotten…"

"It's all right." He tamped out the tobacco on the rail. When the pipe was cool he set it in his pocket. "Most people have their memories. I just have great empty holes where my memories should be."

Moonglow shimmered across the darkened water, turning it into a sea of gold.

He leaned on the rail to study the beauty of the scene before him. "This is my favorite time, as well. Though not for the same reasons as you, Captain. Without memories, I often feel alone in the company of others. But when the darkness closes in, it gives me comfort."

"I've noticed that you often keep to yourself."

He chuckled. "Not for long, if Whit has anything to say about it."

"The lad seems to have genuine affection for you."

"I return the feeling. He's good for me. He's constantly dragging me out of myself, forcing me to forget about my problems."

"You're good for him, as well. He trusts you. I'm not certain he trusts others yet, though he seems to be willing to accept Newton as a teacher, and to accept the fact that I'm captain of this ship."

He turned to face her. "You're an…interesting captain."

A breeze ruffled her hair and he idly reached up to smooth it. A simple gesture, but far too intimate between a captain and a member of the crew. Yet even while he was cursing himself for acting in haste, he couldn't seem to pull away. Instead, he allowed his fingers to play with the silken strands. And then, to make matters worse, he trailed an index finger from her cheek to her jaw, and found himself wondering what it would feel like to press his lips just there.

At his boldness, both of them stiffened.

Darcy couldn't swallow. Her throat was dry as dust. And though she longed to break the silence, she couldn't think of a thing to say. She knew her reaction was far too strong for a simple touch, but there was no denying the way her heart was pounding.

Instead of stepping back a pace, he startled her by stepping closer to breathe her in. "Your hair smells like the sea."

Her fingers tightened on the wheel and she kept her gaze straight ahead, determined not to make too much of this. "We all smell of the sea."

"Nay. You smell like—" he pressed his face to her hair, sending a series of tremors along her spine "—a cool clear pond on a hot summer day. All fresh and clean and pure. And there's a hint of—" he breathed, paused, sending her pulse rate streaking upward "—the perfume of flowers from some exotic island carried across the sea. That's it. Somehow, you manage to smell both simple and exotic."

She started to step back. "You musn't..."

He lifted a handful of her hair and watched through narrowed eyes as the strands sifted through his fingers. "I knew it would feel like this. As soft and silken as water spilling over a dam. Did you know that when you're climbing the rigging, your hair rivals the sun?"

"Gryf..." She was gripping the wheel with both hands, afraid that if she let go she would surely fall to the deck. Her legs were trembling. Her heart stuttering with each touch of those big work-worn hands.

"I watch you, flitting high among the sails like a little yellow bird. I try not to watch, but it's impossible to look away. You're—" he put his hands on her shoulders and turned her to face him "—absolutely mesmerizing." He lifted a hand to her cheek. "And though I have no right, I must do something I've longed to do from the first time I laid eyes on you."

As he lowered his face to hers her heart stuttered again, then began racing until she could hardly breathe. Sweet heaven, he was going to kiss her. What was worse, she was going to permit it. There was no way she could stop herself.

It occurred to her that she could issue a command in that stern voice she had perfected. A command that would have him backing all the way to the ship's rail. But she spoke not a word as his lips hovered over hers.

His mouth found hers and her mind was wiped clean of every thought save one. She had never in her life been kissed like this. At first it was the merest brush of mouth to mouth. Then, as he gradually deepened the kiss, his tongue found hers, dueled, and sent heat spiraling all the way to her toes.

Somehow her arms found their way around his neck, though she couldn't recall moving. With an animal sound low in his throat he changed the angle of the kiss. All she could do was hold on as his lips moved over hers with a thoroughness that had her trembling.

This was no sweetheart's kiss, all soft and hesitant.

This was a plundering—a taking—by a man filled with a deep, abiding hunger. With lips and teeth and tongue, he took her on a wild ride that left her breathless. He framed her face with his hands and stared down into eyes that were wide with surprise and alarm.

"You taste as sweet, as exotic, as you smell. The way I've always imagined a mermaid would, if she were to lure me to her hidden palace far beneath the sea."

"I'm—" she struggled for control "—no mermaid, Gryf."

"Nay. You're far better. Flesh and blood. And so tempting I have to have one more taste."

He bent to her. And though she knew better, she couldn't seem to stop herself. She stood on tiptoe to offer what he wanted.

Their mouths met, trembled, then came together with all the flash and fury of a thunderstorm.

Gryf knew he'd overstepped his bounds. But he knew just as certainly that he couldn't stop now that he'd started. The taste of her, the feel of her in his arms, had his heart thundering, and his willpower crumbling.

Still, he had to try to do the right thing. One last kiss, he promised himself as he lingered over her lips, thrilling to the way she sighed and clung. One last kiss and he'd walk away. But the lure of those lips was too much for him. He would gladly lose himself in the sweetness of this woman, and never stop until they were both sated.

He knew, by the way she kissed him, that she was

an innocent. He knew, too, that he'd taken her too far, too fast.

Calling on every ounce of strength he could muster, he lifted his head and took a step back, breaking contact.

For the space of several moments they stood very still, their breathing ragged, their heartbeats thundering.

After several deep draughts of air he met her look. "I'm sorry I interrupted your solitude, Captain Lambert. But I'm not sorry for what just happened."

Now that she had her wits about her, she felt a rush of remorse for what she'd just done. How could she be so disloyal to Gray's memory?

Seeing the quick smile that tugged at his lips she felt her temper rising. "Be careful, seaman, or you could find yourself swabbing the deck for the rest of our voyage."

His smile deepened, and she felt a tiny thrill of alarm. It was so like another's smile. "If so, it will be worth whatever punishment you deem necessary. And now, let me give you fair warning, Captain Lambert. If the opportunity presents itself again, I'll do the same."

He turned away. "I'll leave you to your solitude now. Good night, Captain."

Darcy watched as he descended to the crew's quarters. Then she lifted her head and watched the path of a shooting star.

Grandpapa had always said it was the perfect time to make a wish. But she found herself torn. Until this moment, her one, her only wish would have been for the return of Gray. Now she found herself wishing that the mysterious Gryf could somehow become her lost love. For his kisses were far more potent that any she'd ever shared with her childhood hero.

Oh, what was happening to her? Her beloved Gray was hardly gone, and she was already giving her kisses to another. It didn't matter that he reminded her of Gray. He was Gryf. As Newt had said, a poor unfortunate wretch who had been at the wrong place at the wrong time. And here she was, letting him think that he could mean something to her.

She closed her eyes, blotting out the sight of all those stars glittering in the velvet darkness. The sight of them mocked her. As did the moon, all hazy and round and golden.

She couldn't deny that it had felt wonderful to be held in Gryf's arms and kissed until she was breathless. She ought to be blissfully happy.

She'd never felt so miserable in her life.

Chapter Five

At the soft footfall, the little boy sat up in the darkness. "That you, Gryf?"

"Aye, lad."

"What were you doing above deck?"

"Smoking. Watching the stars." Kissing the captain. And wanting more than just her kisses. What he'd wanted, more than anything in this world, was to take her, right there.

The very thought of it mocked him. Whatever had he been thinking?

"Why do you like the night, Gryf?"

"Because nobody can see me. Now go to sleep, Whit."

"Aye. I need no coaxing." The boy rolled to his side and listened to the muffled thud of boots dropping to the floor, and the soft rustling sounds as the man crawled into his hammock.

Suddenly, as the implication of the man's words sank in, he sat up. "You mean you're hiding?"

"Something like that."

"You don't need to hide in the dark, Gryf. Nobody stares at you."

The man gave a grunt of disagreement.

"They don't, Gryf. Truly they don't. They accept that you've been burned, and that you'll some day heal. But they don't stare at you. Well...except maybe the captain. But you look at her a lot, too, when you think nobody's looking."

The boy's words hit a nerve. He hadn't thought anybody else had noticed the way he watched her. But it couldn't be helped. She was a fascinating creature.

"That's enough, Whit." His tone was rougher than he intended. "Go to sleep."

"Aye." The boy lay back down and settled himself comfortably. Within minutes his breathing was slow and deep.

Gryf folded his hands under his head and stared at the tiny path of moonlight filtering through the porthole of the crew's quarters.

He couldn't deny that he'd been caught up short by the sight of Captain Darcy Lambert. What man in his right mind wouldn't be? She was like a perfect porcelain figurine. All soft golden hair and eyes as blue as the sea. As if that weren't enough, she became, aboard ship, a beautiful, brilliant butterfly, flitting high in the rigging. Dancing across the ropes and sails, climbing all the way to the very top of the mast.

He loved watching her. The way she moved, with such fierce energy. The way she held the ship's wheel steady even when the winds threatened to blow her clean away.

She looked tiny and fragile. But beneath the delicate looks there was such strength. It was there in her eyes. In her voice. In the way she took command over a ship filled with men twice her size.

There was a fearlessness in her that touched something deep inside him. What a magnificent mate she would make for any man strong enough to win her heart.

A mate. He had no right to such thoughts. If his scarred face and body weren't enough, there was one other fact, much more important than his disfigurement. For all he knew, he may already have a wife and children waiting for him somewhere. Until he knew who he was and where he'd come from, he had no right to pursue a woman, even one as magnificent as the captain.

Still, the mere thought of the way she'd tasted had the blood roaring in his temples. If she were another kind of woman, he might simply enjoy the moment and take his pleasure before moving on in his search for himself. But she was too sweet, too innocent, to be used in such a manner. And though he had no idea what sort of man he'd once been, he was inclined to think his former self would agree with his current reluctance to take what wasn't his by right.

He didn't believe he'd been a womanizer before his accident. He'd had plenty of chances to indulge himself while he'd recovered from his wounds. The farmer and his wife who'd nursed him back to health had been both kind and trusting. Too trusting. They often left their pretty daughter alone to dress his wounds and feed him. And the girl, on the verge of womanhood, had offered much more. She had made it all too plain that she would be his for the taking. Which was why he'd fled to the village as soon as he was able. Though she was pretty and willing, she'd held no appeal to him.

There had been a wench at the tavern in Timmeron. She'd practically thrown herself at him, until he'd told her that he needed time to recover from his burns. Not exactly the truth, but not a lie, either. He hadn't wanted to hurt her feelings. He knew too well the sting of rejection. There had been plenty of people in the village who had refused to hire him, not because he couldn't do the work, but because they couldn't bear to look upon him. In truth, he'd learned to prefer his own company to that of others.

So why did the captain of the *Undaunted* capture his fancy when others didn't? It might be the fact that she was the prettiest female he'd ever set eyes on. Or the fact that her fearlessness touched something inside him. Or perhaps she reminded him of someone he'd known in that other life.

Catching a glimmer of starlight through the port-hole, he thought about Darcy's reaction when he'd known the names of the stars, and the myths behind them. There had been at first an eagerness about her, and then a sadness. What lay behind that? he wondered. What secret sadness did Captain Darcy Lambert harbor in her heart?

Darcy Lambert. The name was as sweet as the woman who bore it.

He closed his eyes, determined to put her out of his mind. If it took the entire night.

The morning sun seemed to be rising out of the sea in a blazing ball of fire. The sky was painted red with it. There was a fine breeze billowing the sails.

The *Undaunted* made good time, slicing through the water toward a distant harbor. On deck, Gryf and the others checked the lines while Darcy and several of the crew trimmed the sails.

Darcy's voice, from high in the rigging, called out, "Land dead ahead."

"That'd be Brenallyn," Newton shouted. "We've a cargo to pick up there." He began shouting orders to the crew and there was a flurry of activity as they prepared to drop anchor. Gryf stood by the rail and watched as Darcy skimmed down the rigging, hand over hand until she reached the deck. When she caught sight of him staring at her, she colored and turned away, busying herself at the wheel while Newton began barking orders.

"Lower the skiff, mates. Ye there, Gryf. Ye'll accompany me to the docks and see to the cargo."

"Aye, sir."

"What about me, Newt?" Whit looked up with pleading eyes that reminded Newton of a puppy the Lambert children had once had. All big eyes and wiggling body with clumsy feet that were always tracking dirt on Mistress Coffey's spotless floors.

"Aye, lad. But ye'll stay close. If ye wander off, we'll leave port without ye."

"Aye, sir." The lad shot a grin at Gryf, then raced to the port railing to watch as the skiff was lowered into the water. When it splashed down, he was the first one down the rope ladder.

When Newton and Gryf and several other sailors were aboard, the boy glanced up to the railing hopefully. "What about the captain?"

"She isn't coming, lad. She's needed aboard ship. I can deal with the harbormaster myself."

Gryf could read the disappointment in the boy's eyes. It occurred to him that Whit wasn't the only one who'd been hoping Darcy would come along.

She'd avoided him all day. Not that he blamed her. She was a ship's captain, and he was an inept sailor who'd only been hired aboard because she was desperate for a crew.

Last night might have meant something to him, but to her it was probably no more than a moment's distraction.

He smiled to himself. And what a distraction. She'd robbed him of a night's sleep. Still, it had been worth it. If truth be told, he'd do it again, given the chance. What man in his right mind wouldn't? He could spend many a lonely night just thinking about the way she'd responded to his kisses.

Newton's voice brought him up short. "Where's ye'r mind today, Gryf? I said grab that line. And be quick about it."

Reflexively he reached out a hand and caught the rope being tossed by a man on the dock. With one quick twist he had the skiff secured.

Newton studied the perfect knot, then glanced at the man who had formed it without giving it a second thought. "I'd say ye've done that sort of thing before."

Gryf shrugged. "I may have. I don't recall."

"Ye may not remember, but I've no doubt ye'r a man of the sea." Newt stepped ashore. "I'll be no more than an hour. Ye men have time for a walk up the lane, or a tankard in the tavern. I'll expect all of ye here on the docks when I return."

He strode away and the men scattered. Most of them headed toward the tavern.

Whit moved along beside Gryf, eager for adventure. "Where are we going?"

The man shrugged. "I thought I'd drop by the village church. See if the vicar knows me."

For a minute the boy frowned. He'd hoped for something a bit more exciting than a visit to the village church. Then he brightened as he skipped along beside his friend. It looked like a long walk from here to the white building standing at the very top of the hill. Maybe between here and there they'd pass a pastry shop, and he might persuade Gryf to let him fill the hole in his stomach caused by Fielding's miserly cooking aboard ship. After all, he still had the two coins he'd been paid for signing aboard the *Undaunted*. It was an unexpected delight to know he could spend it all on himself if he chose. And all because of the man beside him. If it hadn't been for Gryf, he'd still be locked in a life of misery.

The thought of what he'd left behind had him shivering.

He thought about the man he'd encountered that dark, rainy night. A man whose scarred face had him cringing in terror. And when Gryf had spoken in that strange, raspy voice, he'd tried to get away.

Now he could only thank the fates that had brought this man to him. If it weren't for Gryf, he shuddered to think where he'd be by now.

He reached up and caught that big, work-worn hand in his. "Know what I think, Gryf?"

"What, lad?"

"I think signing aboard the *Undaunted* was just about the smartest thing we've ever done. And when I learn all I can about sailing, I think one day you and I will own a fine big ship just like the *Undaunted*. What do you think of that?"

"I think that's a fine dream, Whit." The man winked at the boy, before turning his attention to the church in the distance. On his face was a look of hope. Somewhere, someone had to know his name.

Beside him, the boy watched the change in his expression and sensed that this was no mere walk along a village lane. He tried, as he had so often, to imagine what it must be like for this man to have no memory of his past.

Odd, the boy thought. Gryf wanted desperately to find someone who knew him, so that he could remember his past. While all the lad wanted was to forget his painful past and find a place where nobody knew his name. Then and only then would he feel safe from the terror he'd left behind. Hopefully for good.

Darcy was seated at the little desk bolted to the floor of the captain's cabin. It gave her such pleasure to sleep in her father's bunk, and work at his desk. Her desk, she mentally corrected. The *Undaunted* and everything in it was hers now. Hers and her sisters'.

She unrolled the map, marked in her father's scrawling hand, and studied the route she planned to take when they left port. There would be many days of open sea before they would anchor again. She hoped Newton was able to entice a few more sailors to hire on while they were anchored here.

She looked up at the sound of men's laughter and recognized Newton's voice, shouting orders. At once she shoved away from the desk and went above deck.

The men were carrying their barrels of cargo up the rope ladder and across the deck, where several more of the crew waited to carry them to the hold.

When she caught sight of Gryf's face, she pulled Whit aside.

"What's wrong with your friend, lad? He looks so sad."

The boy shrugged. "He didn't get the good news he was hoping for."

"Good news?"

"Aye. From the vicar."

"The vicar?" She paused. "He went to church?"

"Aye, Captain. Hoping the vicar might recognize him. It's why he signed on aboard ship. He hoped that someone, in one of our ports of call, might recognize him and help him find those he left behind."

"I see." And she could see. The pain and disappointment were there in the way he moved, a slow, torturous walk like that of a man deeply wounded. In the way his shoulders slumped. In the way his mouth twisted down into a frown of concentration.

His crippling pain touched her own heart deeply. It was something she understood completely. Hadn't the pain of her own loss been nearly overpowering? Hadn't she dragged herself around for weeks, until this voyage had given her renewed vigor?

As she walked away she pondered how she could help Gryf rise above his misery. He needed something more than simple, mundane chores. What he needed was a challenge.

Newton strode across the deck and paused beside her. "I was able to hire on two more crew."

"That's great, Newt. We'll need every hand in the days to come."

"Aye, lass. There's a good bit of ocean between here and our next port." He glanced at the line of sailors hauling cargo belowdecks and frowned when he caught sight of Gryf. "The man may not know it yet, but I'd wager a gold sovereign he was a sailor before his accident."

Darcy's brows shot up. "Why do you say that, Newt?"

"I've been watching him. What he does isn't always thought out. It's instinctive. It takes a man of the sea to react the way he does."

"Then he could be..." The words slipped out before she could stop them. But at Newton's dark look, she tried to cover it by saying, "That would explain how he knew about Pegasus and Orion and Scorpius. He not only recognized them, but knew the Greek myths behind them."

"Most sailors have heard those stories, lass."

"But Gray..."

Newt shook his head. "I'm warning ye, Darcy. This isn't Gray you're dealing with. It's Gryf. Don't make him something he can't be. If ye try, two people will be hurt by it."

Instead of arguing, she squared her shoulders. "Aye. You're right, Newt." She watched as Gryf disappeared into the hold. "I'm thinking that we need another sailor to handle the ship's wheel during storms. If you think Gryf's a capable sailor, why not see how he handles the wheel?"

"Good thinking, lass. I'll talk to him once we're underway." But as Newt walked away, he found himself worried about the lass. How long would it take before she accepted the loss of her childhood love?

The next hours were spent storing the cargo, and preparing the ship to leave port. By the time the skiff was raised and lashed to the deck, and the anchor hauled, Darcy was high in the rigging. Far below she could see Newton standing beside Gryf, who was handling the wheel.

For a moment she closed her eyes and conjured an image of Gray, walking toward her across the beach. Gray laughing as he caught her up in his arms and swung her around and around, then slowly lowered her to the ground and brought his mouth to hers.

Theirs had been a comfortable love. A love that had begun in childhood, and had blossomed slowly. They had always known they were destined for one another. They were kindred spirits. They thought alike, wanted the same things and acted in perfect harmony.

But had there ever been that all-consuming fire? That heat and flare of passion that had sizzled when Gryf had touched her?

She couldn't remember. No matter how hard she tried, Darcy couldn't recall a single time when she'd felt anything even remotely like what she'd felt in Gryf's arms. In that single kiss, time had stopped. Her mind had been wiped clean of every single thought. All she'd known, all she'd wanted was him. And it shamed her to admit that she would have given more. It was Gryf who had ended it. If not, she would have been sorely tempted to give in to the passion of the moment and lie with him there in the moonlight.

She felt a sob tear from her throat at the realization that she had felt more in that one instant with Gryf than she had in all the years she'd known and loved Gray.

Despite their declarations of undying love, they'd been as pure and chaste as children. They'd kissed. Aye, they'd kissed. And touched. But neither of them had taken it further.

Had Gray wanted to? she wondered. After all, he had been a man while she was still a mere lass. Had he simply waited, knowing she was too innocent? Or had he been as lacking in passion as she?

Had they both been fooling themselves, thinking friendship was the same as love? Had they simply gone along all those years because neither of them wanted to hurt the other? She shook her head, overwhelmed by such thoughts. They were too painful to contemplate.

She'd loved Gray. And he'd loved her. Exclusively. Completely. And the fact that there had been so little passion had more to do with her tender age than any lack between them.

Wasn't that so?

Oh, Papa. Her eyes filled, and she lifted her face heavenward. *I feel so lost. So afraid. I fear I'm losing a love I've known for a lifetime. And all because of a man who doesn't even know his own name. Was it love I felt for Gray? And if so, how can I feel such things for another man so soon after losing Gray? Am I being shallow and selfish, wanting something I shouldn't have? Am I being foolish, thinking I can*

find in Gryf's arms what I once found in Gray's? Oh,
Papa. Help me. Please, help me.

Was it her imagination, or had the clouds parted at
that very moment? She looked up to see the beginnings of a golden, glorious sun bursting forth. Darcy
blinked, then swallowed back her fears and glanced
down at the man standing at the ship's wheel.

She was becoming silly and fanciful. He was just
another sailor, she reminded herself. A man hired on
to help in this voyage. She was still captain of this
ship. And captain of her own destiny, as well. Her
future wasn't in the stars or the clouds. And it certainly wasn't in one man's hands. Her future would
be whatever she chose to make of it.

For now she would sort out her thoughts, tread
carefully. And just to be safe, she would remember
to keep some distance between herself and the man
who made her so uncomfortable.

Chapter Six

"I've swabbed the deck, Newt." Whit wiped a shirtsleeve across his sweaty face. "And helped Fielding with the soup in the galley. He says he won't be needing me for an hour or more."

"That's fine, lad."

"Is there anything else you need me to do?"

Newton flicked a glance over the lad, who seemed always to be running from one chore to another. "Nay, lad. Ye might ask the others if they need ye'r help."

"I was wondering..." Whit clasped his hands behind his back, striving for a careless pose. "Could I climb the rigging? The captain said I could, whenever my chores were finished."

Newton glanced up to see Darcy hanging from a rope high above their heads. "Ye'r apt to get dizzy, lad."

"Nay, sir. I've climbed trees, and even climbed on the roof of our old shed, and never once got dizzy."

"This isn't a tree or a shed, lad. It's more like a mountain. With the mountain moving beneath ye. A word of warning. There are grown men who can't climb that high without being sick.''

"I won't get sick, Newt. I give you my word.''

"It's not a matter of making a promise, lad. Some do, some don't, is all.'' The old man considered for a moment. Then, seeing the pleading look in those puppy-dog eyes, he relented. "All right. But just so's ye understand, ye must make the climb slowly, so's ye'r head doesn't spin. And if ye should feel ye'rself growing dizzy, let the cap'n know at once. She can hold on to you until ye get ye're wits about ye.''

"Aye, sir.'' Whit bounded to the rail and climbed it, then grabbed hold of a rope, pulling himself up.

"Ahoy, Cap'n.'' Newt cupped his hand to his mouth to make himself heard. "The lad's coming up to join ye.''

"Aye, Newt.'' Darcy leaned far over the sails, then catching sight of Whit, danced down the rigging and met him halfway.

The two began climbing together, with Darcy staying close beside the boy.

Gryf, standing at the wheel, couldn't help smiling at the sight of the boy, looking a bit awkward, and the young woman just a step behind him, moving with all the grace of an angel.

"Ye think he'll be sick?'' Newt asked.

Gryf shrugged. "There's no way of knowing until he tries. But I'm glad you gave him his chance, Newt. The lad's dazzled by our captain.''

"He's not the only one, I'm thinking.'' Newton turned and pinned him with a fierce look. "I've seen ye watching her a time or two.''

"Aye. Can you blame me?'' Gryf met his look

without flinching. "She's enough to dazzle any man."

"That she is. But for all her fearlessness, she's a sweet, innocent lass. Do ye understand what I'm saying?"

"I understand."

The two men stood a moment, each taking the measure of the other. Finally Newt turned away and busied himself with the crew. But each time he glanced over, he could see Gryf looking upward with a look on his face that was pure male appreciation. The very thought had his blood boiling, and his protective instincts rising to the challenge.

But though it rankled, the old man had to admit to himself that he understood completely. The lass was enough to dazzle even a saint. And from the look in Gryf's eyes, the man's thoughts were far from saintly.

Newt sighed. It was just one more thing he'd have to see to. The lass was a minnow swimming in a pool of sharks, at least where men were concerned.

"Have you ever been this high before, Whit?" Darcy gripped the rope with one hand, leaving the other free to catch the lad if he should show signs of growing dizzy.

"Nay, Captain." He held on for dear life, pausing halfway up the rigging to stare out at the Atlantic spread out before him. "Oh, look how far you can see."

"Aye. Sometimes when I'm up here, I think I can see clear across the ocean to distant lands."

"Look at Newt down there by the rail." The boy grinned. "He looks no bigger than a shadow."

Darcy laughed. "You'd better not let him hear you say that."

"I'll remember. And there's Gryf." Without realizing it the lad's tone softened.

"You care about him, don't you, Whit?"

"Aye, Captain. He's my best friend. Without Gryf, I wouldn't be here."

"You mean here on the *Undaunted*."

"I mean here in this life. Without Gryf, I'd surely be dead by now."

"But why?" She pulled her gaze from the man far below to stare at the lad who clung to the rigging.

"When he found me I was more dead than alive."

Darcy gasped. "Why, lad? What happened to you?"

He looked away, afraid to meet her eyes. "I was…beaten."

"Do you know who did it?"

"Aye."

"Was this person punished?"

"Nay."

"But why? Surely you went to the authorities and told them what had happened."

"Nay." His voice sounded almost breathless, though she couldn't tell if it was from the effort of climbing, or because the breeze had caught it and carried it away.

"Can you tell me what happened, Whit?"

"Nay, Captain. I'll not talk about it. To you or to anyone."

Darcy could see, by the hard tight set of his mouth, that the boy had no intention of saying more. She thought about the hurt she carried in her own heart.

It would be impossible to speak of it without breaking down, and that she would never do. Perhaps it was the same for the lad. Perhaps the feelings he'd locked inside himself were simply too painful to share.

She said simply, "I'm glad it was Gryf who found you."

"Aye." Whit looked away, then pulled himself a little higher in the rigging. "After my mother died, nobody wanted me. Nobody except Gryf."

"And what of the one who beat you?"

"I lived in fear that I'd be found and beaten again. But Gryf said not to worry. He gave me his word that as long as he was around, nobody would ever lay a hand on me again."

"And he's kept his promise?" Darcy looked far below on the deck, where the man stood holding the wheel steady with those big, competent hands. The same hands that had touched her and held her and made her yearn for more.

"Aye. Gryf's a man of his word." The boy smiled, determined to put the past behind him. "Come on, Captain. I'll race you to the top."

Darcy couldn't help laughing as Whit scrambled hand over hand until he was at the very top of the rigging. And though his movements were clumsy, it was clear that he was one of those rare sailors who had no fear of heights. In no time, she was certain, this lad would be climbing as easily as she.

Coming up behind him she pointed. "Land. That would be Scotland, our next port of call."

"Scotland." Whit shook his head. "Who would ever believe I'd sail to such a land?" He turned in a wide arc, studying the dark-blue Atlantic glistening around them. From here it was possible to see for miles in any direction.

Suddenly he pointed. "What's that, Captain?"

Darcy gave a gasp of surprise. "Sweet heaven. I was listening to your tale instead of doing what I came up here to do." She leaned down and shouted, "Ship with no flag. Coming up on the port side with full sail. Prepare for attack."

From far below came Newton's command. "All hands on deck. Uncover the cannons, mates."

Darcy turned to Whit. "We must get below at once. I'll lead the way. You do exactly what I do. Understand?"

"Aye, Captain."

She moved deliberately, seeing to it that the lad remained just one step above her. If he should make a single misstep, she was prepared to catch him and spare him crashing to the deck below.

When they had finally descended the rigging, Darcy leapt to the deck and waited until Whit joined her.

She caught him by the shoulder. "You'll go below at once, Whit. You're to close yourself in my cabin and stay there, no matter what."

In a rare display of defiance, he put his hands on his hips and faced her. "And miss the battle?"

"Aye. That's the plan. Now go."

"But, Captain—"

"That's an order, Whit. Go below now."

He glanced at Gryf and saw the man nod firmly. And though the protest sprang to his lips, he swallowed it down and did as he was told.

Darcy turned to Gryf. "Which do you prefer? Sword, pistol or knife?"

"I'll take a sword."

"Aye." She fumbled among the weapons which a sailor had just deposited on deck and tossed Gryf a sword. Then she tucked a knife in her waist and kept another in her hand.

Behind her there was a flurry of activity as the cannons were uncovered and moved closer to the ship's rail. Several members of the crew loaded them with gunpowder and stood at attention, awaiting the orders to fire.

The pirate ship loomed ever closer, until the men aboard could be seen, crowding the rail. They were a ragged bunch, young and old standing shoulder to shoulder, prepared to toss their ropes.

There was the acrid smell of gunpowder as the first volley was fired. The *Undaunted* shuddered as it took a hit to the bow. The crew retaliated with a series of deafening volleys, and the pirate ship took a hit as well. Still it kept coming, until the two ships were close enough to hear the shouts and curses as the pirates began tossing their ropes across the bow and climbing, hand over hand until they landed on the deck of the *Undaunted.*

The captain of the pirates remained safely aboard his own ship, holding the wheel, where he shouted orders to his men.

As the screaming cutthroats streamed aboard, Gryf took up a position beside Darcy. "You should go below now and join Whit in your cabin, Captain."

"You think I'd run and hide, leaving my men to fight alone?"

"You're a female."

"I'm captain of this ship." She caught sight of a pirate racing toward them, sword aloft. In one clean movement she tossed her knife, striking the man in the chest.

He let out a screech of pain and fell to the deck, clutching his chest. As a second pirate took up his sword, Darcy pulled another knife from her waist and dropped him beside his mate.

While Gryf watched in disbelief she calmly bent down to retrieve her knives, then leapt into battle with several more of the attackers. Shaking his head, Gryf had no choice but to admire her, even as he cursed the fact that she was leaving herself open to danger.

"Watch your back," he shouted as he came up behind Darcy and ran his blade through a pirate about to strike.

Darcy spun around, then seeing what he'd done, shot him a look of gratitude before resuming the fight.

"Here, lass." Newton tossed her a sword and she battled a pirate all the way to the rail before managing to drop him.

When she turned, she caught sight of Gryf engaged in a swordfight with three cursing men. While she watched he dispatched first one, then another. And though the third pirate managed to slice Gryf's arm, this man soon joined his comrades in a bloody pool.

Seeing Gryf join Newt in yet another battle, Darcy took in a long, deep breath and realized that she'd been afraid for him. Afraid that he might not know how to handle a weapon while engaged in combat.

She knew that such fear was a dangerous thing. She couldn't afford such distractions, but there it was.

And though she tried to tell herself it was merely because she felt responsible for all her crew, she knew that to be a lie. Gryf had become a definite distraction.

"Behind ye, lass." Newt's warning had her whirling. Too late, she found herself face-to-face with the tip of a pirate's blade.

Before she could toss her knife she saw the man's eyes widen moments before he slumped to the deck. Gryf stood over him, removing his sword from the dead man's back.

"I'm grateful."

"As am I." He gave her a heart-stopping smile as he turned away.

Just then, out of the corner of her eye, Darcy spotted a blur of movement and turned to see young Whit ducking and dodging a pirate's sword.

"Go back at once, Whit," she shouted.

"Nay, Captain."

Just then a voice from the pirate ship called, "See the lad, mates? I want him dead. A gold sovereign to the one who does the deed."

At that, Whit was momentarily distracted. That was all the pirate needed. As he moved in for the kill, Gryf closed the distance between them and shouted for Whit to take cover. Instead, the boy picked up a sword from a fallen pirate and swung it like a club, catching the pirate on the side of the head. Enraged, the man turned on him. But Whit managed to evade the blade that sliced cleanly through the air. As the man lunged toward him, Whit ducked again, and the man, screaming obscenities, went sprawling over the ship's rail and tumbled into the foaming waters below.

"Are you hurt, lad?" Gryf lowered his sword and touched a hand to the boy's arm.

"He never touched me, Gryf." The boy's smile froze as he caught sight of a pirate, sword lifted, suddenly looming behind his friend.

"Nay!" The word was torn from Whit's lips as the pirate brought the sword down with all his might.

But before it could strike Gryf's head, the pirate suddenly stiffened, then dropped to the deck. The sword fell harmlessly at his side. As he fell, face-down, the hilt of Darcy's knife was clearly visible in his back.

The man and boy watched in stunned silence as she turned away and leapt into yet another battle with two pirates who were bearing down on Newton. There were a series of cries as the two men joined the others in the swirling waters beyond the ship's railing.

"Retreat, mates," came a cry from the captain of the pirate ship. "They've beaten us this time."

Those still able to walk stumbled toward the rail, reaching out for the ropes that would haul them back to their own ship. Mates helped mates until all those still alive had taken their leave. The ropes holding the two ships together were chopped in two, and the pirate ship began drifting away.

As it did, the captain of the pirate ship shouted, "You haven't seen the last of us. We'll meet again. And when we do, we'll not stop until every last one of you lies in a watery grave."

On the *Undaunted,* there was an eerie silence as the survivors stared around at the carnage. The bodies of several pirates littered the deck. A deck that ran red with blood.

"Did any among our crew die at the hands of those cutthroats?" Darcy demanded in a loud voice.

Newton looked around, mentally tallying the crew. Satisfied that all were standing, he shook his head. "I see a few wounds, but no fallen mates, lass."

"Good." She idly wiped the bloody blade of her knife on her breeches, then tucked it at her waist.

When she turned, she fixed Whit with a look of fury. "You disobeyed my order, boy."

"Aye, Captain."

"I'll set your punishment later. And be warned, it will be severe, so that you'll understand just how important it is that every man aboard this ship follows my command." She saw the boy cringe, and knew she'd just struck fear into his heart. "Now, Whit, tell me why you defied me."

The lad hung his head.

She walked closer, her eyes as cold as her voice. "You could have lost your life, and caused the death of your friend, as well. Is that what you wanted, boy?"

"Nay, Captain."

"And still you chose to disobey me and come above deck. What have you to say for yourself, Whit?"

"I...know I shouldn't have disobeyed your order, captain. But I...thought I recognized a voice. I needed to see for myself."

She flicked a glance at Gryf, who was standing beside the lad. She could see that he was as puzzled as she. "And whose voice did you hear?"

The boy refused to speak.

"You'll tell me, Whit. As captain I demand to know."

The boy's lips trembled, but to his credit he held back the tears that threatened. "It was the captain of the pirate ship."

"Aye. The one who ordered you killed. You recognized him? Who is he? And why was he offering a reward to his men to kill you?"

His voice was little more than a whisper. "He's the one who beat me senseless."

"Why? How does he know you, lad?"

"He's my—" He had to suck in a breath before he could manage to whisper "—he's my uncle."

Chapter Seven

Darcy couldn't speak over the pain in her heart. Pain for a lad who had been beaten by his own kin. Pain at the knowledge that the boy had overheard that hideous order to kill him.

Seeing her dismay, Newton was quick to take charge. With a few staccato commands, he set the crew cleaning the deck and returning the weapons to the hold. Soon enough, order was restored from the chaos.

While the work went on around them, he suggested that Darcy meet with Whit and Gryf below deck in her cabin. Numbly she nodded, then led the way.

She took her seat at the desk, leaving the man and boy to stand just inside the door. Then she folded her hands atop the desk and struggled to compose herself.

Gryf glanced around, noting the tidy bunk, the carefully rolled maps in pigeonholes above the desk and chair, which, like the bunk, were bolted to the floor so they wouldn't roll in rough seas. He found himself appreciating the simplicity of this seaworthy vessel. It suited the woman who commanded it.

"Now, Whit." Darcy leaned back and pinned the boy with a look that could make seasoned sailors shiver in their boots. "You'll tell me everything."

He shook his head. "I...can't."

"Can't? Or won't?"

Gryf started to speak and she shot him a quelling look. Then she turned back to the boy. "You'll tell me what happened between your uncle and you, lad. And you'll tell me the truth."

The boy stared hard at the toe of his boot, struggling for the courage to speak over his pain. "Aye, Captain."

Darcy fixed him with a look. "Is this the uncle who was supposed to have drowned aboard the *Mary M*?"

"Nay, Captain." He took a deep breath. "When my mother died, I was visited by a woman claiming to be my mother's younger sister. Though I'd never met her, I believed she was speaking the truth, for she looked like my mother. The same hair, the color of flame. The same green eyes. She took me to her home, outside the village of Timmeron, where I was introduced to her husband, who said he was a fisherman. The next morning, without warning, he apprenticed me to a cruel seaman. I didn't mind the work, though it meant getting up before dawn so that I could get the fishing boat ready for the day's catch. But I worked all day without food, and every night, when I finished all my chores, the old man would beat me."

Darcy bit back her anger, afraid to glance at Gryf. "Did he beat you because he didn't like the way you worked?"

"I think not. He seemed to beat me for no reason

except that it...pleased him. He used to laugh as he wielded his stick. So one night, after he fell asleep, I ran away and returned to my uncle's house. He was gone, and I asked my aunt to hide me. But she refused."

"She refused?" Darcy could hardly hide her surprise. "What sort of woman refuses to help her own kin?"

"She said she wasn't really my mother's sister. She said that it had been my uncle who had ordered her to say those things, though she knew not why. And so I ran away and hid, seeking shelter in sheds and barns with the animals. But when my uncle returned from the sea he came searching for me. When he found me hiding in the meadow outside the village of Timmeron, he beat me. He—" the lad glanced at Gryf, then away "—said I'd shamed him by running away, and he beat me until I thought I'd die. I believe he thought I was already dead, or else he'd have never left without finishing what he'd started. When I finally awoke sometime the next morning, I couldn't stand, and so I began crawling. I must have crawled out into a dirt lane, for that's when Gryf came upon me."

Darcy looked at Gryf now, whose eyes had gone as hard as flint. She knew, from the look of him, that he was suffering for the lad as much as she.

"I...was afraid of Gryf at first, because of his scars and all, and tried to fight him." The lad avoided Gryf's eyes as he spoke. "At first, when I caught sight of his face, I thought he was a monster and I tried to get away from him. If I hadn't been so weak, I'd have made good my escape. But since I couldn't run, or even walk, I couldn't stop Gryf from carrying me to town. Once there he begged a room at the tavern. The tavern owner wouldn't let either of us inside." The boy gave a weak laugh. "Not that I blame him. The sight of the two of us would have frightened away all his patrons. Me with my bloody wounds, and Gryf with his scars. But for a fee, the owner gave us the use of the shed. Gryf made a bed of straw and dressed my wounds, then brought me food, and tended me until I was strong enough to leave my pallet. We've been together ever since."

Darcy had to swallow twice to dislodge the lump that was threatening to choke her. Finally she said, "I don't claim to understand such cruelty, Whit. Nor will I ever, I suppose. But this I know. The desire for vengeance, even though it's a natural enough feeling, can destroy even the best of men. So, no matter how you feel about your uncle, you need to accept this fact, lad. The crew of the *Undaunted* is pledged to fight those who would attack helpless vessels. If your uncle's ship crosses our path again, we'll have to fight him. And, as before, I'll expect you to obey my command to take shelter below. Though you feel you have a compelling reason to exact revenge against the man who left you for dead, aboard this ship you will remain in my cabin."

"But I—"

"Not a word, Whit. That's what being a seaman aboard the *Undaunted* is all about. When the captain gives an order, it's given for the good of all. One man's vengeance can never take precedence over the good of the entire crew. Do you understand?"

The boy swallowed, then nodded.

"I want the name of your uncle, and the name of his ship."

"His name is York. Wylie York. And his ship is the *Sinner.*"

Darcy didn't have to worry about committing the name to her memory. It was seared into her brain. As was the face of the man who'd ordered a child to be killed. "You may go above deck now, and offer to assist Newt and the others."

"Aye, Captain."

She waited until the door of the cabin closed behind him. Then she looked up to find Gryf staring at her with a look of fury.

"You have something to say?"

He nodded. "Aye. If there's justice in this world, Whit's uncle will find his at the end of a sword."

She surprised him by slamming a hand against the desktop with such force it sent a curled map flying. "Aye. I agree."

"But you just said—"

"I said Whit must obey orders. I'd rather not have his uncle's blood on the hands of one so young. But if that cruel pirate is ever in my sights, he'll surely taste the blade of my knife in his evil black heart."

"So." He felt a wave of relief. "Our heartless captain isn't so heartless after all. But I'll give you this, Captain Lambert. You managed to fool the lad. And even fool me until now."

For the first time Gryf managed to laugh. It was a rare sound that brought a smile to Darcy's lips. But her smile suddenly faded when he turned to leave and she caught sight of his bloodstained sleeve.

"You're wounded."

"It's just a cut."

"Aye. A cut that's dripping on my floor." She was on her feet and pointing to the chair she'd just vacated. "Take off your shirt and sit. I'll fetch some hot water from the galley."

"Nay. You don't want to see—"

Before he could give voice to his protest she was gone. Minutes later she returned carrying a basin of water and a clean linen towel.

As she'd ordered, he had removed his shirt. His first inclination had been to simply stalk out of her cabin and head for the deck. He'd be damned if he'd allow her to see his scars. Captain or no, she was a woman first. And no woman would be able to look at what the fire had done to his flesh without being sickened.

But then he'd had a second thought. One he'd resigned himself to. Let her see and turn away. Then he'd be able to do the same. And that kiss they'd shared would be just a pleasant memory. Both of them would be able to move on with their lives.

For a moment, as she stood behind him, all Darcy could do was stare helplessly at the puckered scars that crisscrossed Gryf's back and neck. The thought of how he must have suffered had her closing her eyes against a wave of pain.

He cast a glance over his shoulder. "You're awfully quiet. I hope you aren't one of those timid females who gets sick at the sight of anything unpleasant."

"N-nay." She would have heard the challenge in his tone if she hadn't been so moved. She set down the basin, wringing out a cloth before touching it to his wound.

Gryf clenched his teeth. It was going to take all his willpower to get through this without flinching. He'd expected her to simply look at him and run. But now that she was staying, he was forced to do the same.

But oh, the touch of her fingers against his flesh as she washed his wound was causing a series of tremors that were threatening to be his undoing. How he'd longed for those hands on him. Moving over him. Arousing him.

He took several deep, unsteady breaths to pull himself together. She wasn't a lover, touching him with desire. She was the captain of a ship, seeing to the needs of one of her crew.

He closed his eyes and tried to think of something, anything, that would keep him from being moved by her touch.

Darcy could see that the cut wasn't deep. But it was bleeding profusely, forcing her to stem the flow with a tourniquet, before she could dress it with linen.

All the while she worked, she couldn't stop looking at the patchwork of scars that covered Gryf's back. How he must have suffered. And was suffering still.

No wonder he'd moved so slowly when she'd first seen him. After such burns, each bend of an arm or leg would have caused excruciating pain. It would be like an infant learning each movement.

She glanced at his lowered head. No wonder he wore that hat, with the brim pulled down to hide his face. No wonder he grew that dark scraggly beard to hide the scars that must surely mar his face as well.

Her first thought had been that the sight of those

scars would wipe away any romantic feeling she might have for him. Instead, they seemed to have sharpened all her senses. She was achingly aware of the way his muscles bunched and tensed with each touch of her fingers. And though she should have been repulsed by his scars, she was, if anything, even more drawn to this courageous man.

"This will sting a bit," she muttered as she smeared ointment from a vial and smoothed it over his wound.

"A bit?" He sucked in a breath. "It burns like the fire of hell."

"You'd know about that, wouldn't you?"

The moment the words were out of her mouth she regretted them. But it was too late. They hung between them for the space of several seconds. Finally he stood and caught her hands between his, stilling her movements.

"I tried to warn you, Captain."

"I know you did."

"And now you're sickened by the sight of me."

"Is that what you think? That somehow the scars would repulse me? You're so wrong. I never dreamed…" She closed her eyes and tried again. "Oh, Gryf. I can't bear to think of how much pain you've been made to suffer."

"There's that gentle heart again." He smiled. "Which you try to keep so carefully hidden. Don't grieve for me, Darcy. I don't remember much of it. Just bits and pieces of the pain. I was in and out of consciousness for so long, the family who took me in and nursed me back to health were also preparing a shroud, thinking that I wouldn't survive."

"But you did."

"Aye. I've always thought there must have been a compelling reason why I fought my way back. Perhaps there was someone, somewhere, waiting for me. Someone more important than my own life." He gave a wry smile. "How the gods must be laughing at the fact that now that I'm here, I can't remember who or what it was that brought me to this."

"Oh, Gryf."

"Shhh." He saw the glitter of a single tear in her eye and wiped it with his thumb. "Don't weep for me, Darcy. I may be luckier than we know."

"How can you say such a thing?"

He smiled down into her eyes. "Perhaps I'm carrying some terrible secret in my heart, which, if I recall it, will cause me grave pain. Or perhaps send me to prison."

"I don't believe that of you, Gryf. I've watched you with young Whit. You're so gentle with him. So good and kind and noble."

"Don't make me into something I can never be." He ran a finger over her lower lip, all the while staring into her eyes. "The things I'm thinking right now are neither good nor kind nor noble."

At her arched brow his smile faded. "Unless you order otherwise, Captain, I'm going to have to kiss you again this very moment."

Taking her silence for acceptance, he lowered his mouth to hers and watched as the shock registered in her eyes.

As before, there was nothing sweet or gentle about his kiss. And as she gasped, he took it even deeper, sending a shaft of desire straight to her core.

His mouth moved over hers, taking, demanding. In reply she reached up to encircle his neck with her arms. Her hands encountered the warmth of bare flesh, and she felt a tingling that began in her fingertips and swept through her in waves that threatened to swamp her.

"I've been desperate to taste your lips again." He spoke the words inside her mouth as he took her fully into the kiss.

"Wait, Gryf." She started to push away but he held her firmly against him, running those big clever hands along her spine, lighting fires wherever he touched.

He'd meant it to be nothing more than a simple kiss. But he should have known better. The moment his lips touched hers, he felt the tug of passion, as compelling as any riptide. He was assaulted by wave after wave of need that swamped him, pulling him down, down, until he was drowning in her. Her taste, as sweet as a summer breeze. Her touch, as gentle as the kiss of a snowflake. Her scent, of ocean and woman and faintly, of some exotic island flower.

"Gryf, we musn't…" Pushing against his chest she started to back up, but his hands were already at her shoulders, holding her roughly against him when she would have turned away.

And then, without any warning, her arms were around his waist and she was clinging to him, offering more.

With a muffled oath his arms came around her in a fierce embrace. She was dragged against him, breasts flattened to his chest, thighs pressed to his.

He heard her sigh as he took the kiss deeper. And then he was lost. Lost in a kiss that was both sweet and bold. He could taste her hunger. A hunger that matched his own.

With a need born of desperation he plunged his hands into her hair and pressed kisses across her eyelids, her cheek, her jaw, before returning to claim her lips. They were the sweetest lips he'd ever tasted. He wanted, more than anything, to fill himself with her. To take everything, and then to take more.

"Oh, Darcy. You feel so good here in my arms. So right. As though made for me alone."

His words had her choking back a sob. How could he possibly know what it meant to her to hear such things, when they'd already been spoken by another?

She clung to him, feeling so many conflicting emotions. On the one hand she felt more alive than she could ever remember. At this moment, all her senses seemed heightened by the nearness of this man who was slowly capturing her heart and soul. On the other hand, she knew she had no right to lead him on this way. Yet, she was helpless to stop the growing tide of desire. She could no more resist this man than she could stop the rain that had begun pelting the deck above them. With a sigh, she gave herself up to the pleasure of the moment.

Gryf could taste the loneliness in her. It spoke to the loneliness in his own heart. And though he knew he had no right to such liberties, the need for her was too great. He wanted one more heart-stopping kiss. One more moment to hold her just so, her heartbeat keeping time to his own.

If that kiss should lead to something more, so be it. He had already slipped over the edge, and was taking her with him. The thought had the breath backing up in his throat as he feasted on her.

She could feel her last thread of reason slipping away. Suddenly, all the sane and sensible things in her well-ordered life didn't seem to matter at all. The only thing that mattered was here. Now. This man. The taste of him, dark and mysterious. The feel of that hard, muscled flesh against her fingertips. And the all-compelling tug of desire that curled deep inside her.

She wanted him. Wanted this. More than anything she could remember, she wanted him to go on holding her, kissing her, until her head was spinning, and her body quivering with need for him. Only him.

Take me. Though she didn't say the words aloud, she thought them, and sensed somehow that he had heard, or sensed, exactly what she wanted. His hands moved over her, taking her higher, then higher still, until all she could see, all she could taste, was him.

"Darcy, lass." There was a quick rap on the cabin door.

At the sound of Newton's voice, followed by the opening of the door, Darcy and Gryf lifted their heads, then nervously stepped apart.

The old man peered at the two of them, noting the flush on Darcy's cheeks as Gryf reached for his shirt.

"I was…dressing Gryf's wound."

"Aye. I see." The old man stayed where he was as Gryf buttoned his shirt and tucked it into his breeches. He could see that the man's hands were none too steady. And that his breath was coming in quick bursts, as though his lungs were starved for air.

What's more, Darcy looked no calmer. Her chest

rose and fell with each labored breath. She locked her hands together to keep them from trembling. And her gaze was fastened on Gryf, following every movement he made.

Newton's eyes narrowed.

"If ye'r finished here, the crew needs ye'r help above decks, Gryf. It's raining harder now, and I want that blood swabbed before night falls."

"I'll see to it." Gryf turned to Darcy, wishing with all his might that he could touch her one last time. "Thank you for seeing to my wound." He reached down and picked up the basin of water and the bloody cloth. "I'll take these to the galley on my way out."

When he was gone Newton turned to the lass, who looked exactly the way she always had when she was a little girl, and her old nurse, Miss Mellon, had caught her snatching cookies from a platter before supper.

"We're still two or three days away from land. I'm thinking that after we deliver our cargo, we ought to stay put for a day or so, while the crew repairs the hole in the bow."

She nodded. "Alright. If you think so, Newt."

"I do." He lowered his voice. "I'm also thinking that ye're playing with fire, lass. And I'd not like to see ye burned."

"I'll...be fine, Newt."

He touched a hand to her shoulder. "It's too soon, Darcy. Ye haven't given ye'r poor heart time to heal."

"Maybe this is what my heart needs. I...care about Gryf and the lad."

"I'm not denying he's a fine man. And the lad's

lucky to have him for a friend. But it's ye I'm worried about. Ye're making him into something he can't be. No man can take the place of Gray in ye'r heart, lass.''

"I'm not asking him to."

He looked at her a long time before patting her shoulder. "I hope not, lass. I hope not. For both ye'r sakes."

He turned away and let himself out.

When he was gone, Darcy folded her arms across her chest and stood, head bowed, eyes closed. Sometimes, when Gryf was kissing her, she found herself comparing his mouth to Gray's. Comparing his halting, raspy voice to the smooth deep tones she'd known since childhood. Even comparing his touch, his taste.

She pressed her hands to her temples, to blot out the thoughts that kept creeping into her mind. Thoughts of another man, another time.

Newton was right. It was all too much, too soon. But she just didn't seem able to stop herself. She wanted Gray back. But she wanted Gryf, as well. Oh, what was happening to her? How was she ever going to be able to resolve this?

Newt was right about something else. If she and Gryf continued down this path, both of them might be wounded again. And this time the wounds could prove to be more than their already shattered hearts could endure.

Chapter Eight

Darcy threw herself into a flurry of work. Work had always been her refuge. And her salvation. She found that if she worked hard enough, and long enough, she would fall into bed, too exhausted to think.

The only problem was, even in sleep she found no relief. Her dreams were filled with visions of Gray and Gryf. Visions that had her waking in the dark, heart pounding, lungs straining.

The combination of work-filled days and sleep-deprived nights was beginning to take its toll. She was, as always, driving the crew to distraction with her demands. The deck was never clean enough. The sails never mended properly. The knots in the rigging never unfastened to her complete satisfaction.

"Land dead ahead, Captain." The sailor's voice filtered down from the rigging.

Darcy glanced over as Newton approached.

As usual, the old man wasted no time with formalities. "I know ye'd like to make up for the time we lost in that battle, but I still think it best if we take a few days in port, to give the crew time to repair that hole in the port side.''

''Aye. It has me worried, too, Newt. Though we've taken on no water, I'd hate to see what might happen if we encountered storms.''

''And well we might, lass. It's a wonder we've been this long without winter showing us her nastier side.'' He glanced at the crew, preparing to dock. ''Besides, it'll give us all a rest. We've earned it.''

Darcy said nothing.

He lowered his voice so the crew wouldn't overhear. ''Especially ye, lass. Ye're driving ye'rself too hard these days. And the crew along with ye.''

''I'm fine, Newt.'' She saw him studying her a little too closely and felt the beginnings of a blush on her cheeks. ''You know I thrive on hard work.''

''Aye. That ye do.'' He turned away. ''I think ye should go ashore with me.''

When she didn't argue, he took it as a clear sign that she was distracted. Ordinarily, she much preferred to stay aboard ship and leave the business of delivering the cargo to him.

Following the direction of her gaze, he saw Gryf swinging down from the rigging, with Whit following eagerly behind him. Aye. That was the distraction. And it had the old man more worried than he cared to admit. He stormed off, bellowing orders to the sailors who swarmed about the deck.

''Lower the anchor,'' he shouted.

As the crew scrambled to anchor the ship and lower the skiff to the water, Newton turned to see Darcy avidly watching every movement Gryf made. It only strengthened his determination to put some distance between these two. For their own good.

"I've changed my mind, lass." He retrieved his coat, since the wind had whipped the waves into froth. "Ye can stay aboard and set the crew to work on repairing the damage while I take a few men ashore with the cargo."

"All right, Newt. That sounds fine to me."

He turned away and began calling out to those who would accompany him in the skiff. "Ye there, Will. And Gryf. And Fielding, ye'll want to replenish our supplies. The rest of ye will stay with the cap'n and get to work on that hull."

"What about me, Newt?" Whit turned pleading eyes to him, and the old sailor had to look away in order to resist.

"Nay, lad. Ye'll stay here with the cap'n. That's an order."

He turned away with a sense of satisfaction. He'd pulled that off smoothly. The lass didn't have a hint of what he had in mind. For that matter, he wasn't sure about it himself. He only knew he wanted some time alone with the man who was giving Darcy such nerves.

"Easy there, lads."

Newton stood on the wharf and directed the dock workers who were retrieving the cargo from the skiff. When it was unloaded he watched as the items were checked for damage. Then he entered the small waterfront office where he accepted the money due them. He and the company representative shook hands before he took his leave.

Outside, his three crew members waited in the rain. The old man took some bills from his pocket and handed them to the cook.

"Here, Fielding. Take Will with ye and see to some fresh meat for the crew. When ye return with it, Gryf and I will be waiting to take ye back to the ship."

"Aye, sir."

When the two men walked away, Newt turned to the man beside him. "Since we have some time, I thought we'd warm ourselves at the tavern."

The two darted through the rain, grateful when they reached the comfort of a warm room. They stood a moment in front of a roaring fire on the hearth, allowing the heat to chase the chill from their bones.

Newton pointed to a table drawn up in front of the fireplace. When they were seated a wench approached with tankards.

Before she even walked away Newton had drained his tankard and set it on the scarred wooden table. Gryf did the same, then stretched out his long legs toward the warmth of the fire.

Newton cleared his throat. He knew he was a plain-spoken man, but right now, he wished he'd been blessed with the skill of an oracle. He took a deep breath and plunged in. "Ye have eyes for the cap'n."

Gryf smiled. "What man in his right mind wouldn't?"

"But ye've done more than look."

Gryf held his silence, wondering where this was headed.

The silence disturbed the old man more than words would have. Perhaps he'd hoped Gryf would offer a denial. Or at least a few words of apology. He wasn't certain just what he'd expected. But not this tense, unexpected silence.

He sighed. "I think ye should know. The lass suffered a heartache recently."

He saw Gryf's head come up sharply.

"I'd sensed as much. Can you tell me about it, Newt?"

"I can. The lad she's loved since she was just a wee lass was lost at sea." Until this moment, he'd had no intention of talking about something so intimate. But now he realized this was his chance to watch Gryf's reaction. Darcy wasn't the only one who wondered about the mysterious man's true identity. After all, he was the same height as Gray. Had the same look about him sometimes. The way he squared his shoulders and stared out to sea. The way he planted his feet on the deck and faced into the wind. Like a man born to the sea. Like Gray.

The old man waited the space of a heartbeat before saying, "His name was Graham Barton."

There was no flicker of recognition in Gryf's eyes at the mention of that name. In fact, no reaction of any kind. Newton wasn't sure if he was relieved or disappointed. Had he, like Darcy, wanted him to be Gray? Or had he only hoped to clear up the mystery once and for all? If so, he'd been mistaken. Now there were only more questions.

"And she loved this man?"

"That she did. We…her family…feared she might never recover. But this voyage seemed like the right thing to take her out of her grief and get back to the business of living."

That would explain this ship and crew braving the

winter in this part of the Atlantic. Gryf nodded. "Darcy's a strong woman, Newt. You can sense it in her. She's a survivor."

"Aye. That she is. But I'm not sure she's ready to open her heart to another yet. It's too soon. The wound is still raw."

Gryf idly rubbed his shoulder. "I'd know a bit about wounds and how long they can take to heal."

The serving wench returned with bowls of hot soup and a plate of crusty bread. When she walked away the old man reached for the bread and broke off a hunk. "Then ye understand why I worry about the lass. Her poor heart was broken. Shattered, if truth be told. She's not ready for any more pain."

Gryf's voice was low with anger. "What makes you think I'd cause her pain?"

"Because—" the old man tasted his soup, then crumbled the bread over the surface and decided to be as bluntly honest as possible "—I think she's getting ye all mixed up in her mind with the lad she lost."

He saw the flash of pain or perhaps anger in Gryf's eyes as he digested that bit of news. It wasn't something a man wanted to hear. Not if he cared about the woman involved.

"Ye'r like him, ye see. In many ways." It had to be done, the old man consoled himself. For Darcy's sake. Though he'd never believed in meddling, this was different. She thought of herself as so tough. But underneath that hard shell she'd built around herself, she was still that little girl who'd once wrapped her chubby arms around his neck and wept against his throat when her kitten was crushed under the wheels of an errant carriage. She'd cried as though her heart would never mend. And in that moment, his own had shattered as well.

She was as much his daughter as if he'd given her life. He'd die for her. Aye. And meddle, if that's what it took to keep her safe.

Gryf studied the old man, and could see what it had cost him to reveal Darcy's secret. "I'm...grateful to you for telling me this, Newt."

The old sailor nodded and bent to his soup. And noticed that the man across the table had suddenly lost his appetite.

"Nay, Whit. Like this. Smooth, even strokes." Darcy took the tool from the lad's hand and began planing the length of wood until it was smooth to the touch.

"I see. Like this." He ran a finger over the velvet finish. "Let me try, Captain."

She handed it back to him and the lad followed her example. She was grateful now that she'd remained aboard ship with the boy. They hadn't had a chance to talk since she'd forced him to reveal his awful secret. She hoped this time together might ease any lingering tension between them.

"You've a quick mind, Whit."

His smile was bright and open. "That's what Gryf tells me. He said I can do anything I set my mind to."

"And what is it you hope to do?"

"Be a ship's captain like you."

She couldn't help chuckling, even though she

found herself flattered. "There are easier ways to make your way in this world."

"Aye. But none as satisfying."

"It is that." She took up a plane and began smoothing the other end of the wood. The two worked in companionable silence, while the crew sawed and hammered nearby, repairing the damage to the bow of the ship.

"Gryf told me that sailing gets in a man's blood. The longer he stays at sea, the more he needs of it."

"Does Gryf think he was a sailor before his accident?"

The lad shrugged. "He can't recall. But I'm sure of it. I've seen him do things even some of the other crew members can't."

"Such as?"

"The first time he climbed the rigging with me, he never had to look at where to put his feet. Just walked up the ropes like he was walking up a ladder. It's the same with the ropes. Newt said Gryf can tie a knot better than anybody he's ever seen."

"Newt said that?" When the boy nodded, she arched a brow. "That's quite a tribute to Gryf. Old Newt rarely pays a compliment."

"Gryf paid you a compliment, too."

Darcy's interest sharpened. "What did he say?"

"Gryf said that you're just about the prettiest ship's captain he's ever laid eyes on."

She couldn't help blushing, even as she tried to pretend the words were meaningless. "I'm probably the first female captain he's ever seen."

"Why are you captain of this ship instead of Newt?"

"Because the *Undaunted* belongs to my family. Newt was first mate aboard the *Undaunted* when my grandfather was captain. He'd thought that part of his life was over. But now that my father and brother are gone, my sisters and I decided to carry on the family business, and we've asked Newt to join us."

"It must be nice to have family."

She paused in her work. "Is there no one except your uncle?"

He shook his head.

"But now you have Gryf."

"Aye." His face lit with a happy smile. "And he's better than anyone in the world."

"Ahoy, the *Undaunted*." At Newton's shout, Darcy and Whit hurried to the rail to watch as the old sailor and the others climbed the rope ladder to the deck.

Fielding happily hauled his supplies across the deck, heading toward the galley.

When Gryf hauled himself over the rail, Darcy stood back as the boy rushed to his side. In that instant she found herself wishing that she could be as free to rush to him as the lad was.

The boy's eyes were bright with curiosity. "Did you bring me anything, Gryf?"

"I might have." The man kept his features carefully masked.

"What is it? What'd you bring?" Now the lad was fairly quivering with excitement.

Gryf reached into his pocket and removed a handful of cookies.

The boy's eyes widened. "Where'd you get these, Gryf?"

"From the cook at the tavern. I told her I knew of a lad who had a yearning for anything sweet."

The boy looked up at him adoringly as he bit into the first confection. Then, remembering his manners, he held out his hand to Darcy. "Have one, Captain."

She shook her head in refusal. "You keep them, Whit. And save one for a special treat later tonight."

"I will. Thanks, Gryf." The boy carried his treasure off to the crew's quarters.

Darcy watched him leave, then turned to Gryf with a smile. "That was sweet of you. I doubt Whit has had many gifts in his young life."

"Aye. It occurred to me." There was no answering smile. In fact, he seemed almost eager to flee her side as he abruptly turned away.

Puzzled, she watched as he crossed the deck and picked up a hammer. Minutes later he joined the rest of the crew in their work, effectively shutting her out.

She returned to her own work, wondering what had brought this about. Perhaps Gryf and the others had had words while they were ashore. Or perhaps she was merely imagining a slight when none had been intended.

Darcy finished writing in the ship's log and set aside her book and quill. She'd been closed in her cabin for hours, attending to business. Now she wanted to take a turn around the deck before going to sleep. She picked up her heavy winter coat and blew out the candle before heading for the steps.

An icy wind caught her hair, whipping it across her cheeks as she stepped on deck. She paused to give her eyes a chance to adjust to the darkness. Then she looked around. Everyone, it seemed, had retired for the night. She felt a vague sense of dismay, which she quickly shrugged aside; then she caught the sharp bite of tobacco on the night air and turned to see a shadowy figure all alone at the rail.

Gryf. Her heart missed a beat before starting to race. Though she wouldn't admit it to herself, she'd been hoping he would be here.

"Aren't you freezing?"

He didn't turn. He'd heard the light footfall on the deck, and knew instinctively it was Darcy. "I hadn't noticed the cold."

"Hadn't noticed?" She laughed. "You must be made of stone."

"If only that were true." He took a last puff on his pipe, then tapped it on the rail, watching the burning ashes drop into the dark water below.

"You sound so...somber. You must have some serious thoughts on your mind."

"Aye." He closed his hand around the bowl of the pipe. Finding it cool to the touch, he returned it to his pocket and turned up the collar of his seaman's coat. "I seem better able to sort through my thoughts out here, where I can see the moon and stars."

"I love looking at them, too." She lifted her face to the wind and watched the path of moonlight shimmer across the waves. "Do you mind if we watch them together?"

"How can I object? You're the captain."

She turned to him, feeling the thread of anger beneath the words. Without thinking she put a hand over his. And felt him flinch.

Flinch? Her heart did a quick little flutter in her chest.

"What's wrong, Gryf? Have I said or done something to upset you?"

"It isn't you, Darcy." He turned then, and looked at her for the first time. He felt a razor's edge of pain around his heart at the way she was watching him. God in heaven, how was he supposed to ignore the invitation in that trusting smile? "It's me. I need time by myself."

"Oh. Aye. Of course."

He watched her smile fade from joyful to puzzled, her eyes go from happy to sad.

"I'll—I'll leave you alone, then." She started to turn away and he caught her by the arm to stop her.

"Wait." He'd meant only to soothe. To offer an apology for his disturbing behavior. "Darcy..."

The look she turned on him was so hopeful, he instantly hated himself. Still, he couldn't help reaching out to brush a strand of her hair from her cheek.

For a moment she stiffened, then moved against his hand like a kitten.

What happened next was completely without rhyme or reason. Giving not a single thought to the consequences, he swore, low and deep in his throat, and dragged her against him, savaging her mouth.

Darcy's first thought was to push free of the arms imprisoning her and slap his arrogant face. Was she supposed to ignore the fact that he'd just tried to snub her? Now did he think it would all be forgotten by a kiss?

In truth, it could. In the space of a single instant, everything that had happened before this moment was wiped from her mind as his mouth moved over hers and took.

This was no tender coaxing. No sweet caressing. This was a savage mating of mouth to mouth. A quick, greedy assault. And though it frightened her, it was also deeply, distressingly arousing. For it uncovered a raw, primitive hunger in her that demanded satisfaction.

He tangled a fist in her hair and pulled her head back, plundering her lips. She was instantly caught up in a quick flare of desire. Without a thought to where this would lead, she moaned and clung and gave what he demanded.

And what he demanded was more. All. His hands moved over her, igniting fires wherever they touched. He couldn't get enough of her. He wanted to touch her everywhere. And did.

At her moan of pleasure, he suddenly froze. As quickly as it began, it ended. He lifted his head and held her a little away, staring down into her eyes already glazed with passion. His own were dark and troubled and as turbulent as a storm-tossed sea.

It infuriated him that even when he kissed her in anger, she responded with such generosity.

What he wanted, more than anything in the world, was to accept the invitation in those eyes and crush her against him. To take what she was so obviously offering, and to hell with the man she'd loved and lost. It was no concern of his.

But it was. It was. Now that he knew about her loss, it wasn't something he could forget or ignore. It ate at him. Tore at his soul. And mocked him. He'd be damned if he'd try to fill the role of a dead man.

"Good night, Captain." He lowered his hand to his side and turned away, leaving her standing alone at the ship's rail, while he stalked off to the crew's quarters to brood.

Chapter Nine

Darcy stood alone at the rail, listening to Gryf's footsteps fade.

What had just happened here? She wasn't quite certain. There had been such raw passion. And then a fierce, barely controlled anger in those dark eyes and in his tone of voice. An anger that she felt was directed at her. But what had she said or done to cause it?

She searched her mind, wondering what had set him off. One minute he was touching her, kissing her, drawing her into his web of passion. The next he was distant, aloof. And doing everything possible to push her away.

She'd sensed an almost barely controlled violence in his kiss. As though he'd wanted to devour her. She shivered. It excited her. And that worried her. It was true that she lived in a man's world, a world of villains and pirates and bloody battles. But she'd always managed to hold herself apart from the other passions which the rest of her shipmates indulged.

The thought came unbidden. Maybe he simply

needed a woman. Any woman. Perhaps, on his trip to the village, he'd seen the others take their pleasure with one of the tavern wenches. There were always village wenches lurking about the taverns, hoping to snag the interest of a sailor with coin in his pocket.

She knew so little about Gryf. He was a solitary figure, keeping to the shadows to hide his scars. Perhaps a tavern wench had been unwilling to overlook his disfigurement.

Disfigurement. The very word offended her. Despite the puckered scars on his neck and back, he was easy on the eye. And though he continued to hide from the world under that beard and the brim of a hat, what she'd seen so far was dangerously attractive. Aye. Attractive enough to catch the eye of any woman.

The thought brought a shaft of pain directly to her heart. She couldn't bear to think about him in the arms of another. Still, what right did she have to such thoughts? He was little more than a stranger. A sailor who'd been hired to fill in for missing crew members. And when this voyage was over, he'd no doubt sign onto another ship and sail away to some far-flung country, never to be seen again.

Well, let him go. And good riddance.

Men, she thought with a sudden rush of fury. She'd never understand them. And wasn't inclined to even try.

If Gryf thought he could play her for a fool, he was mistaken. He'd find in her a worthy opponent. She could avoid him, no matter how confining the space between them. She'd show him.

She swallowed the hard lump that had settled in

her throat like a stone. Not disappointment, she told herself. Anger. And she'd always known just how to deal with anger.

Newt stood in the shadows, wondering how long Darcy would remain topside in the bitter wind.

He'd overheard the words exchanged between the lass and Gryf. And though he was suffering a twinge of guilt for his part in all this, he couldn't help rejoicing that one of them had had the good sense to put a stop to this thing that had begun to develop between them.

An innocent like Darcy needed protection from her foolish heart. And he'd given his word to her grandfather and the others that he'd watch out for her. Even if it meant causing her momentary pain.

Still, the guilt gnawed at him. He'd always believed that, in matters of the heart, some things seemed to have no rhyme or reason. He could see why Darcy was attracted to the lonely sailor. He looked so much like Gray, he even had Newt wondering. But that didn't explain Gryf's intense interest in a lass he barely knew. Unless she somehow stirred memories in him. Memories that, though buried beneath layers of pain, were struggling to break through. If that was the case, the memories would continue creeping up to the surface, until his past would merge with his present. In the meantime, it was Darcy's heart that needed tending. And Newt intended to do what he had to, to keep her safe.

The old man shivered in the cold and tucked his hands in his pockets before crossing the deck to stand beside her.

"Ye're up late, lass."

"Aye."

"Was that Gryf I saw leaving?"

"It was."

He heard something in her voice, though whether it was pain or anger he couldn't be certain. He glanced over. She was looking up at the sky.

"What are ye thinking, lass?"

"About the time Gray returned from his first voyage aboard his father's ship, and told me about the great hunter, Orion. No matter how hard Orion tried, he couldn't defeat the scorpion. When he tried to escape, the scorpion stung him to death with its poisonous tail. And ever since, the scorpion is always chasing after Orion in the night sky."

She pointed. "There they are, Newt. The hunter. The scorpion."

"Gray was a fine storyteller, lass. No one could tell a tale better."

"Aye." She was silent for a full minute before she whispered, "Gryf tells a fine tale, as well."

He glanced over and saw a hint of moisture glittering on her lashes. He didn't think he could bear it if she started to weep on his shoulder. "We'd best get in out of this cold."

"Cold?" She looked around. "I hadn't noticed."

"Then ye'r blood is hotter than mine, lass. Come."

Newton led the way below deck.

At the door to her cabin she paused. "Good night, Newt."

"'Night, lass."

The old man waited until he heard the latch set before he continued along to the quarters he shared with the crew. Inside, he made his way among the hammocks until he came to his. Wrapping the blanket around himself he rolled into bed. Shrugging aside the guilt that stabbed at his conscience, he was soon asleep.

Across the room Gryf lay in his hammock, brooding. He'd heard the old man come in. Listened as the men around him sighed, and the fat cook, Fielding, snored. But the sleep he longed for eluded him. All he could think about was Darcy Lambert.

What was it about this woman that kept nagging at the edges of his mind? Was she like someone he'd known and loved? Could he actually be this man for whom she was grieving? It didn't seem likely. The name had meant nothing to him. Besides, her man had gone down in a ship. And his wounds had been caused by a tavern fire.

Still, he'd been instantly attracted. That first night, when he saw her in the tavern room, he'd thought her different from any other woman. Dressed like a seaman, in breeches and boots, instead of the usual demure gowns the women in the village wore. And that golden hair, all free and flowing, instead of hidden beneath a bonnet. No wonder he'd noticed her. Every man in that tavern had taken note of her. But for his part, it had been attraction, not recognition.

He rolled to his side, trying to get comfortable. He couldn't fault Newton for trying to warn him off. The old man loved her. He had a right to look out for her, especially since she'd been thrust into a man's world.

Odd, that one who looked like that, with that cloud of golden hair and eyes bluer than any sky, should choose such a profession. If she were dressed in an elegant gown, and thrust into the proper setting, she could pass for royalty. But even the rough garb of a sailor couldn't mask her beauty, a beauty laced with a toughness that helped her survive in this life she'd chosen.

Still, for all her skill as a sailor, she was an innocent when it came to men. She may have loved a lad, but she hadn't loved a man. Not the way a woman loved a man, at any rate. It was obvious in the way she kissed. As though her lips had never before touched a man's. And in the way she responded, with the sort of open trust that was at once endearing and worrisome.

Still, she wasn't exactly a helpless female. He'd seen the way she fought. There wasn't a man among them who could toss a knife with as much accuracy as Darcy. She'd handled a sword with equal skill. In fact, when it came to a battle with hardened cutthroats, he'd rather have Darcy Lambert at his side than most of the sailors aboard this ship.

She was, quite simply, a most amazing woman. No wonder he was attracted to her. His eyes opened, and he watched a flicker of moonlight dance across the ceiling. Aye. He was still attracted to her. Even knowing that she'd loved and lost another. And now, having been warned that she might be confused at times about his true identity, what was the harm of it? He'd let her know that he was Gryf. A simple sailor. And that he was attracted to Darcy Lambert, a not-so-simple sea captain.

He smiled in the darkness. There now, this conflict hadn't been so difficult after all. Perhaps one of the best things about having no memory of the past was the fact that he couldn't tell if he'd lived by the rules of other men, or had lived by his own.

For now, he would be content to make up the rules as he went along. One day at a time. Especially where Darcy Lambert was concerned.

Relieved in his mind, he slept.

"We'll stay here in port today and finish the necessary repairs, mates." Newton stood in the center of a cluster of sailors. "Until I'm satisfied that the *Undaunted* is seaworthy."

Gryf, standing on the fringe of the circle, watched as Darcy made her way topside. As always she wore men's breeches tucked into tall boots and a colorful shirt with billowing sleeves. Her wind-tossed hair was a mass of long yellow tangles that framed a face kissed by the sun.

When she caught sight of him she turned away and busied herself filling a dipper from a bucket of water.

He ambled over and assumed a careless pose. "Good morrow, Captain."

She drank. Swallowed. And struggled to keep her emotions banked. "Good morrow."

In the uncomfortable silence between them they heard young Whit shout a question.

"If there's time, will we be allowed to go ashore and visit the village?"

Much to the delight of the others Newton nodded. "Ye will. After ye'r chores are done. But I'll expect ye to return to the ship before dark." He and Darcy had discussed it, and agreed that, though a night on shore would be a lovely break with routine, they couldn't afford to have any more of their crew taking off, and leaving them shorthanded. The best way to see to it was to demand that they return at night to the *Undaunted.*

Darcy and Gryf strolled over to join the rest of the crew, careful to keep their distance from each other as they did.

Whit was practically dancing with eagerness at the thought of setting foot in a new country. "Do the Scots speak our language, Newt?"

The old man grinned. "In a manner of speaking."

"What does that mean?" the boy asked.

Newton winked at those sailors who had some knowledge of the country and were already laughing among themselves. "I guess ye'll just have to see for ye'rself, lad."

The boy couldn't keep the enthusiasm from his voice. "When can we start our chores?"

Newton chuckled. "If the cap'n and I had known that all it took to make ye so eager to work was a simple trek to the village, we'd have started putting into port more often. Now mates, let's see to those repairs. The sooner they're done, the sooner ye can be off to ye'r pleasures."

The men fell to their chores with renewed enthusiasm. Though they wouldn't admit it, they were as excited about spending the afternoon in a Scottish village as Whit was. The thought of hot tavern food, and equally hot wenches, had them hoping to make the hours fly as quickly as possible.

The air sang with the sound of hammers and saws as they repaired the holes and replaced boards burned by cannon fire. The cook used this time to take stock of his supplies, while others were put to work repairing damage to the sails and rigging.

By noon they gathered on deck for a cold meal before lowering the skiff that would take the first of the crew to the docks.

When it left, bound for shore, young Whit looked around for Darcy. Seeing her working high in the rigging he shouted, "Come on, Captain. We're heading to the village."

She gave him a smile as she started her descent. "You go ahead, Whit. I'm going to stay aboard and get some work done."

The lad turned to Gryf. "Tell her she has to come, Gryf."

The man placed a hand on the boy's shoulder. "She's a grown woman, lad. She knows what she wants to do."

The boy's eyes were wide and pleading. "But if you ask her to come, she'll do it."

Gryf considered for less than a minute. After all, this was the perfect opportunity to declare a truce. Besides, the idea of spending an afternoon in the company of both Darcy and Whit was far more appealing than the thought of attempting to entertain the lad alone.

He paused below the rigging and waited until she leapt onto the deck. "Whit's not the only one who wishes you'd come along."

He saw her eyes widen a fraction before she hid her surprise behind a negligent shrug. "I'm not much for drinking ale in taverns with my crew."

"Neither am I. And with Whit by my side, I'm thinking I'll have to find something more interesting than a tavern to explore. The lad needs to see some of the lands he's never seen before.'' His tone lowered. ''Come on, Darcy. Even the ship's captain needs a break from routine.''

She couldn't help the shy smile that tugged at the corners of her mouth. Or the little shiver along her spine at the urgency in his tone.

''All right.'' Seeing Newton rowing the skiff toward them, she called, ''Give me a minute.''

She fled down the steps and into her cabin. Minutes later she returned wearing a simple gown of pale bleached wool, with a high, modest neckline and long tapered sleeves. Over it she wore a shawl in the same shade. She'd run a brush through her tangles and swept her hair from her face with mother-of-pearl combs.

Gryf couldn't help staring as she climbed down the rope ladder and settled herself in the skiff. But though he kept his thoughts to himself, Whit wasn't nearly as reserved.

''Captain, you look like a…lady.''

''Thank you, Whit.'' She felt the color rise to her cheeks when she caught the way Gryf was watching her. She was suddenly grateful that she'd taken the time to change.

''But why'd you dress like that?''

''So the good people of this village aren't scandalized. I doubt they've seen a woman in men's breeches before.''

The lad giggled. ''Neither have I. You're the first.''

''Am I?'' She chuckled. ''Then you ought to see my sisters.''

''You have sisters? What are their names?''

Gryf was grateful for the lad's questions, for they were things he was eager to know, as well. It was obvious that Darcy was much more comfortable talking about herself when she thought only the lad was listening.

"My sisters are Ambrosia and Bethany." At the mention of their names her tone softened, and she realized how much she missed them. "Ambrosia is the oldest. She's married to a sea captain, Riorden Spencer. Bethany is the middle sister, and she's wed to Kane Preston, the earl of Alsmeeth."

"An earl?" The lad seemed suitably impressed. "Does she live in a big house filled with servants?"

"Aye. But that isn't why she wed him. Theirs is a love match."

Gryf head the yearning in her tone and was surprised by the way it touched him.

"Do your sisters captain a ship as well?" the boy asked.

"Aye. We take turns as captain of the *Undaunted*."

"Can they fight as fiercely as you?"

She laughed. "They're as fierce as any pirate. Ambrosia is tall enough to handle a sword with ease. Bethany's skilled with a dueling pistol." She touched a hand to the knife at her waist. "This is my weapon. By the time I was your age, Whit, I could take a single leaf from a tree with my blade."

The lad turned to Newton. "Could she truly? Or does she jest?"

The old man nodded. "It's the truth, lad. No one in our little village wanted to fight with the Lambert sisters. They enjoyed nothing better than a good brawl. They sent many a bold lad home to his papa in a fright.''

Gryf found himself smiling at the image of a dainty, blue-eyed, blond-haired demon sending lads running home in tears. If he hadn't seen her skill and fearlessness with his own eyes, he probably would have expressed doubts of his own.

As the skiff pulled to the dock, a seaman tossed a rope and Gryf secured the vessel. Before he could reach for Darcy's hand she hiked her skirts and leapt out.

She turned as Whit climbed out behind her. ''Welcome to Scotland, lad.''

''Scotland. Who would have believed this? Just weeks ago I thought I'd never even live to see another morning. And now I'm in Scotland.''

The boy surprised her by catching her hand. She looked down at their linked fingers. There was something so sweet in his gesture, so trusting, she felt her heart contract, before swelling with affection. It couldn't be easy for this lad to trust, a fact that made it all the sweeter.

''Do you think we can see all of the village before dark, Captain?''

She squeezed his hand. ''I doubt it. Not that there's all that much to see. One fishing village is pretty much like another. But let's just relax and see as much of it as we can.''

''Aye.'' He turned and called to the man who walked a few paces behind them, ''Hurry, Gryf. Half the day is already gone. Before we know it, it'll be time to head back to the ship.''

Darcy turned to Newton. "Are you coming with us?"

The old sailor shook his head. "Nay, lass. I'll join my mates for a pint in the tavern." He stared pointedly at Gryf. "The skiff will be leaving promptly at sundown. I'll expect ye to be on time."

"We'll be here." Gryf walked beside Whit, deliberately keeping the lad between himself and Darcy. He could feel the old man watching him, and worrying about the hours that the lass would be out of his sight.

"Where will we go first, Gryf?" the boy asked.

"Let's just walk up to the village before we decide." He was determined to keep this day light and innocent. Not just for the sake of the worried old man, but because he wasn't ready to completely let go of all that Newton had told him. Despite what he'd decided last night, he was still feeling a little tender about being confused with a dead man.

But for now he intended to put it behind him and simply enjoy what was left of the day. For, from the looks of that leaden sky with its dark-edged clouds billowing in from the north, winter was planning to pay a nasty visit.

This may be the last pleasant day left to them.

Chapter Ten

"Does this place have a name?" Whit strolled along beside Darcy on the way to the village.

"This string of islands is called the Outer Isles. This one is called Orkney." Darcy swung his hand in hers as they walked along the rutted road.

"Not a very pretty name."

"Aye. And it deserves a pretty name, for it's really a pretty place, don't you think?"

In many ways it looked like any other fishing village, with taverns lining the wharf, and a row of small shops. Farther along were the cottages, and up on the hill, a church. Yet, though it wasn't a prosperous village, everything seemed so neat and tidy. And the people, for the most part, happy and smiling.

Trailing slightly behind them, Gryf noted the way several of the young men in the village stood a little taller, and squared their shoulders, as Darcy passed. Probably hoping she'd notice them. To her credit, she never even looked their way. She was too intent upon the lad beside her.

It was another reason why she did such strange

things to his heart, he realized. Though she was truly beautiful, she never gave it a thought. Nor did she use her beauty, as some women might. She seemed truly unconcerned with her looks.

Darcy pointed to the chapel on the hill. "Here in Scotland a church is called a kirk."

Whit looked at her. "Why?"

"It just is."

He turned to Gryf. "Will you visit the...kirk here to see if the vicar recognizes you?"

Gryf shook his head. "I know without asking that I didn't come from Scotland."

"And how would you know that?"

Gryf gave the lad a gentle smile. "Because of my accent."

"Oh. Aye." Satisfied, the boy turned back to Darcy. "If I call it a church, will the people know what I mean?"

She couldn't help laughing. "Aye. Some of them might. But others might have a difficult time understanding you. When you're in a new land, with new people, it's wise to learn as many of their words as possible."

She nodded toward a boy and girl hauling a small wooden cart. "Would you like to stop and talk with them?"

"I would." He let go of her hand and raced up the lane to the children.

It pleased Darcy to note that, though they were from different lands, they accepted each other in the way of children everywhere.

"What are you hauling?" Whit asked.

"Kippers." The girl's voice was high-pitched. Beside her, her little brother stared at the stranger.

Whit peered down into the bucket. "It looks like fish."

"Aye. 'Tis. And these—" the girl unwrapped a square of linen to reveal freshly baked confections "—are scones."

"Scones. They look like biscuits. Where are you taking them?"

"Hame." The lad smiled. "Our mum just had a wee bairn, and we've been stayin' wi' our aunt in a hut by the loch. Now it's time te gae' hame." He caught his sister's hand, the two began hauling the little cart over the bumps in the road.

When the children were gone, Whit started back toward Darcy and Gryf. On his face was a look of astonishment.

"What is it, lad?" Darcy asked with concern.

He shrugged. "I thought Newt said they spoke English. But I didn't understand anything they said."

Darcy began laughing.

Gryf joined in. "He said his mother just had a new baby, and he and his sister had been staying with their aunt in a hut by the lake. Now they were going home. Presumably with a fine dinner of fish and biscuits for the whole family."

Whit stared at the man with a look of admiration. "How'd you understand all that, Gryff?"

"It takes a bit of concentration." He was still laughing. "But I'm willing to bet by the time we leave here tonight, you'll be able to understand a few words as well."

Whit stood still a moment, considering. "Do you think you could have heard such words before?"

Darcy caught the look of surprise on Gryf's face. Then the slow nod of agreement. "It could be, lad. Maybe that's why it was so easy for me to figure out what they were saying."

As they walked, Darcy couldn't help remembering that Gray had often journeyed to Scotland. The very thought had her heart racing. Still, she cautioned, most sailors in this part of the world sailed to Scotland. She'd be a fool to pin her hopes on such a weak premise. But she couldn't help herself. Even the smallest link with Gray had her hopes soaring, even though she was mentally calling herself every sort of fool.

They continued along the lane until they came to an old woman sitting on a rock. At her feet was a huge basket. Inside were half a dozen wrapped parcels.

Gryf paused beside her. "Are you feeling unwell, mistress?"

The old woman shaded the sun from her eyes to look up at him. "Nay. Just a bit weary is all."

"Why don't you let me carry this home for you?" Gryf picked up the basket, then offered his arm.

The old woman looked surprised, then pleased as she stood and caught his arm, leaning heavily on him. "Aye, thank you. My home is up yonder a bit."

They passed through the village, admiring the tidy cottages and shops. Though many people smiled and waved at the old woman, all rushed past, too busy to stop and speak with her. For her part, she seemed content to permit Gryf to offer his arm and assist her on her way.

They continued along until they came to a big house at the very end of the lane.

As they approached, a big yellow dog came rushing out at them, barking furiously. At once Gryf stepped in front of the others to shield them from attack.

Seeing their fear the old woman said, "Dunna' be afraid of her, lad. She's just protecting what's hers. Come here, lass. Good girl."

The dog approached and licked the old woman's hand. Then, at a command from the woman, the dog stood very still, allowing Whit to pet her, as well.

"She's been my boon companion since my husband died," the old woman explained. "I don't know what I'd have done without her."

Feeling invigorated now that she was home, the old woman led the way inside her house. A house that was filled with the fragrance of bread baking and meat roasting. "Come in. The least I can do to thank you is to offer you some tea."

Gryf glanced at Darcy, and seeing her nod of agreement, stepped aside, allowing her and the boy to precede him. The dog, assured that all was well, returned to a low basket in the corner of the room. Poking over the edge of the basket were six furry yellow heads.

"Oh, Whit, look." Darcy pointed and the lad hurried over to stare at the litter of pups.

Darcy walked up beside him. "Aren't they precious?"

He nodded.

Turning to the old woman he asked, "Will their mother let me pet them?"

"She'd probably be grateful for the distraction. The lot of them have been climbing all over her from the moment they were born weeks ago."

As soon as Whit got down on his knees the puppies were tumbling over each other to get to him. Darcy and Gryf stood back laughing as he was pounced on by six balls of yellow fluff. Soon he was giggling and rolling around the floor, while the pups climbed over him, eager to lick his face.

The old woman set a kettle over the fire, then invited her guests to sit. "I'm Margaret MacInnis, and it's grateful I am for your help."

"You're welcome, Mistress MacInnis. My name is Gryf, and this is Darcy. The lad is named Whit."

Margaret MacInnis began to set the table with fine cups and a plate of scones. At once Darcy helped, filling the teapot when the kettle boiled, and fetching a little pot of fruit conserve from a side table.

"Whit," Darcy called. "Mistress MacInnis has scones."

She turned to their hostess. "The lad has a love for anything sweet."

He surprised them all by saying, "I'd rather stay here and play with the pups."

Darcy shot a quick look at Gryf, and saw his answering smile.

As Margaret MacInnis began to pour the tea she said, "You're a bit young to have a son."

Before Darcy could correct her she went on, "But then, so was I. Wed at thirteen, I was. Had five big strapping sons. Now all of them gone. And their father, as well." She glanced at Gryf. "You look a bit like him, you do. Tall, handsome of face. Are you a sailor?"

"Aye."

She turned to Darcy. "Then I'm sorry for you lass. You'll no doubt be widowed soon enough. It's the fate of all women who give their hearts to men of the sea. But at least you have the lad."

Darcy glanced at Gryf and saw the slight shake of his head, warning her not to bother setting the old woman straight. She thought about it a moment, then sighed in agreement and sipped her tea.

"Are you all sailing together then?"

"Aye. Aboard the *Undaunted*."

"Where is her home port?"

Darcy slathered conserve on a scone. "Cornwall."

"Ah. At least you're not English." The old woman's eyes danced. "I'd feared at first you might be, from your accent."

"But we are English, Mistress MacInnis."

Margaret MacInnis shook her head. "Nay. My husband used to say the Cornish were as fiercely independent as the Scots. And far enough from London that they're not under England's thumb. We're alike, the Scots and the Cornish. There's not a royal born who will tell us how to live our lives. We'd rather die than bend to the will of another."

The old woman looked over at Whit, still happily playing with the puppies. The big dog lay by the fire, eyes closed in contentment. "Have you friends here in the village that you've come to visit?"

Gryf shook his head. "Our ship is anchored in the

harbor, and we thought we'd just take a walk around your fine village.''

"Then you must stay for supper. It's the least I can do to repay you for your kindness.''

"That's too much work,'' Darcy protested.

The old woman gave her a long look. "Do you know how long it's been since I've had company for supper?''

At once Darcy regretted her words. She glanced at Gryf and saw his nod of approval.

She gave the woman a warm smile. "We'd be honored to stay for supper, Mistress MacInnis. But I hope you'll let me help you.''

"Aye.'' Margaret MacInnis pointed to the blackened pot that hung over the fire. "I've mutton roasting. I'll see to that, while you slice a loaf of bread. Mind, it's still warm from the oven.''

Darcy uncovered the bread and breathed in the wonderful fragrance. For the space of a moment she experienced such a wave of homesickness, she nearly wept. The feeling caught her by surprise. She could see in her mind's eye her beloved family sitting around the table. Grandpapa, Ambrosia, Bethany, Winnie and Mistress Coffey. Oh, how she suddenly missed them all. Desperately. The thought of their dear faces brought such a wave of tenderness.

She forced herself to work, slicing the bread, setting it on a platter, carrying it to the table. It occurred to her that Gryf looked more relaxed than he had at any time since she'd met him. He sipped his tea and chatted with Margaret MacInnis as though they'd known each other for a lifetime.

Sailors had that ability to make themselves at home

all over the world. With all sorts of strangers, who, in the course of an hour or a day, could become life-long friends. Gray had had such a gift. She closed her eyes against the pain of remembering.

"Gryf, you and the lad can wash up in that basin." Margaret pointed to a pretty bowl and pitcher on a stand.

"Come on, Whit. If you can tear yourself away from the pups long enough, Mistress MacInnis has offered to share her supper."

"It smells good." When the boy stood, the puppies made a mad dash for the big dog, who awoke from sleep to nurse her babies.

"Aye. It does indeed." Beside him, Gryf dried his hands on a square of linen.

When the two were seated, Margaret MacInnis handed Gryf a platter of meat swimming in rich gravy and a platter of potatoes mashed with turnips. When their plates were filled, she poured tea, then reached up in the cupboard and retrieved a decanter of whiskey.

"I've been saving this for company." She filled a tumbler and set it in front of Gryf. "My husband drank this only on special occasions. And this is a very special day for me."

Gryf tasted and felt the whiskey burn a path of fire down his throat. Then he smiled at the old woman and lifted the tumbler in a salute. "It's a special day for me, as well, Mistress MacInnis. And for my—" he turned to include Darcy and Whit "—family as well."

He saw the look of surprise on Whit's face, and the laughter that sprang to Darcy's lips. Then he turned to the old woman and gave her a dazzling smile before draining the tumbler and bending to his meal.

And what a meal it was. After Fielding's boiled meat and hard biscuits, this was a rare feast. Meat roasted slowly until it fell off the bone and melted in the mouth. Potatoes and turnips mashed together with rich cream and butter. Crusty bread to mop up the gravy. And as if that weren't enough, for dessert a heavenly confection of scones and pudding that tasted as if the angels themselves had prepared it in heaven.

When he was offered a second helping, Whit was forced to refuse. "I'm afraid if I eat one more bite I'll split wide open, Mistress MacInnis."

That had the old woman cackling with laughter. "My Robby used to say that very thing, lad. Oh, he was a fine big lad, he was. But even Robby couldn't eat two helpings of my scone pudding."

While she poured tea, the boy returned to the basket and ran a finger over the now sleeping pups.

"It looks like they've had too much to eat, too. They can't even open their eyes."

"Their mum'll be glad. Poor lass never gets any rest with the six of them pulling at her." Margaret filled a basin with hot water from the kettle and began to wash the dishes.

Beside her, Darcy dried, admiring the delicate pattern on the plates. "You've a fine home, Mistress MacInnis. And such pretty things."

"Aye. The MacInnis, rest his soul, used to bring me fine things from all over the world. Porcelain. Crystal. China. Lace. And my lads did the same." She lay a hand over Darcy's. "But it isn't fine pretty things that bring us joy in this life, lass. It's love. And family. And doing simple things together.''

She glanced over at the boy, still kneeling beside the basket. ''He's a bonny lad. And the way he looks at you and Gryf, there's no doubt how much he loves you. Treasure that love, lass. For it's a precious thing. And when the hard times come, as they surely will, the love is what will sustain you.''

Darcy was silent as she hung the linen cloth to dry. She had a lump in her throat that was threatening to choke her. But whether from the old woman's words, or from the thought of what she'd loved and lost, she couldn't be certain.

When she turned, Margaret MacInnis was standing beside Whit, looking down at the puppies.

''Which is your favorite, lad?''

He never even hesitated. ''That one. The smallest one.''

''Why, lad?''

He touched his finger to the soft ruff of its neck. ''The others kept pushing him aside. He had to fight to get anything to eat, but he kept trying until he finally made it.''

''He's a fighter, is he, lad?''

''Aye.''

''How would you like to take him with you?''

The boy's eyes went so wide, they seemed too big for his face. ''Do you mean it, Mistress MacInnis?''

''I do. That is, if your folks approve.''

Whit turned to Gryf and Darcy. ''Could I? Could I keep him?''

It was on the tip of Darcy's tongue to remind him

that a ship was no place for a puppy. But how could she possibly be the one to erase the joy in those eyes?

When Darcy held her silence, Gryf muttered, "Newt will have your head."

"Aye. That he will." Darcy knew the old man well enough to figure that, when he caught sight of a puppy, he'd probably let loose with every rich, ripe curse he'd ever learned. Still, she was the captain. And there were times when she simply had to remind the old man of that fact.

"If you want him, Whit, the puppy is yours."

"Do you mean it? Oh, you do. You do." He raced across the room and hugged her fiercely, then turned and hugged Gryf, before dancing back to the old woman to hug her as well.

She looked startled for a moment, then hugged him back. Laughing, she said, "His mum will have one less to feed now. And I'll be satisfied that the pup has someone who'll love him."

"I will love him, Mistress MacInnis." Whit picked up the sleeping pup and held him close to his chest. "And I'll take the very best care of him. I promise."

Darcy glanced at the growing shadows and said, "We'd best leave now. Newt will be waiting."

"Aye." Gryf opened the door and held it while Darcy and Whit stepped outside.

As he turned to say goodbye, Margaret MacInnis caught him in a warm embrace. "I thank you, Gryf, for coming to my aid. I'd been feeling like an old, foolish woman, far from home, and too tired to go on. But now, after your lovely visit, I'm feeling almost young again. I'm remembering all those years ago when I was wildly in love, and raising a pack of my own pups.''

"I'm glad.'' He returned the hug and pressed a kiss to her cheek. "You made our visit to Orkney more pleasant that we could have ever imagined. And you've made one little boy happier than I've ever seen him.''

"It's small enough payment for what you gave me.'' She took a step back, and with a twinkle in her eyes said, "Now if you've any sense in that head of yours, you'll take the lass home and make several more lads like that one, to fill your home with love and laughter.''

He gave her a wink. "I thank you, Margaret MacInnis. You're a wise woman indeed.''

As he and Darcy started back toward the wharf, Whit trailed behind, cuddling the pup inside his coat.

Darcy turned to Gryf. "What did Mistress MacInnis say to you when you were leaving?''

"I'll tell you sometime.'' He caught her hand in his and felt the quick jolt to his heart. And wondered why it had taken him the entire day to work up the courage to touch her.

Maybe, he reasoned, because with every touch, he felt himself being drawn ever more tightly into her web. As much as he might resent filling the shoes of another, he couldn't deny the envy he felt for a dead man who had inspired so much love and loyalty from this beautiful, beguiling woman. And try as he might, there was no way he could resist the pull of her charms.

Chapter Eleven

"It's about time." Newton was pacing the dock, hands behind his back, a frown furrowing his leathery brow. He jerked a thumb toward the waiting skiff. "The rest of the crew is already back aboard the *Undaunted*. I was thinking I might have to start searching the village for ye, cottage by cottage."

"Sorry, Newt." Darcy lay a hand on his arm. "We were having such a grand time, we just forgot."

"A grand time? Ye're out of breath." His concern grew as he studied her red cheeks, her hair flying in the breeze.

"We had to run to make it back in time. I knew you'd be waiting and wondering."

And worrying. But he didn't bother to admit that. He helped her into the skiff and picked up the oars, ignoring Gryf and Whit, who scrambled in behind him.

"Here, Newt. I'll see to that." Taking pity on him, Gryf took the oars from him.

The old man made no protest as he settled himself beside Darcy. Then he waited for his heart to settle, as well. He'd been pacing and worrying himself half to death over the lass. And she off having a grand time. But what did that mean? And just how grand had it been? Alarm had his heart racing again.

As soon as they were seated, Gryf began to row toward the ship in the harbor. From her vantage point Darcy watched the effortless way he bent to the task, arms barely straining as the oars cut through the choppy water. There it was again. That strange tingling deep inside whenever she looked at him. He was so strong. Almost as strong as...

"Where've ye been all afternoon, lass?" Newton's voice was sharp with concern.

She pulled herself back. She had to stop thinking like this. "In the home of Margaret MacInnis."

At the old man's questioning look she explained. "On our stroll through the village we met a sweet old lady who needed a bit of help. Gryf carried her basket and offered his arm. And she repaid his kindness by inviting us to share her supper."

"Ye've been at her cottage the whole time?"

"Aye. And what a lovely home it was. Big and cozy, and filled with treasures from around the world. Her husband and sons were sailors."

As she went on describing their afternoon, the old man breathed a sigh of relief. Not too much could have passed between the lass and Gryf if they were in the company of others the entire time. For that, he offered a word of thanks.

Still, he was grateful to have her back, and determined that she wouldn't leave his sight again. He'd spent the past hour tormenting himself on just how he'd break the news to her family that she'd run off with a man who reminded her of Gray Barton.

Gryf heard the old man's sigh and saw the pleasure that lit his eyes. He nearly laughed aloud. Newton was as transparent as the widow MacInnis's crystal. It was obvious that he'd been worried sick about Darcy's precious honor.

Not that he blamed him, Gryf was forced to admit. He'd seen the looks of admiration from the lads in the village as she'd walked beside Whit. Her beauty would be enough to turn any man's head. But what they didn't know, and he'd only begun to discover, was the surprising sweetness beneath that beauty. A sweetness that would make it difficult for any man of honor to take advantage of her.

A man of honor. Had he been one? Was he now? He supposed only time would tell.

"Here we are." Newt reached out and climbed the rope ladder to the deck of the *Undaunted*, with Darcy following.

When the old man turned around, Whit was just clambering over the rail, while holding one hand to his chest.

"Here, lad." He reached out a hand. "Have ye hurt ye'rself?" He'd been so concerned about Darcy, he hadn't paid any attention whatever to the lad.

"Nay, Newt. I was just holding on to my pet so he wouldn't fall." Whit reached inside his coat and removed the ball of fluff.

At the sight of it the old sailor took a step back, his eyes narrowing. "Is that a...dog?"

"Aye, Newt. Isn't he beautiful? Mistress MacInnis gave him to me. Darcy said I could keep him."

"She did, did she?" He whirled, pinning her with a look. "And who did ye think would clean up his messes? Or were ye thinking a puppy would just clean up after himself?"

"Whit promised to clean up after the pup." She stepped closer to the boy and brushed a hand over the soft yellow head. "Look at him, Newt. Isn't he adorable?"

"He's a dog, lass. And a baby one at that. They're always cute, for about a minute. Then they do what animals do. They chew what doesn't belong to them, and leave their...leavings where we can step in them." His voice rose. "I'll not have that animal aboard the *Undaunted.*"

The little boy stared from Darcy to Newt, then back again. He'd never seen the old man so quick to anger. He just hoped the captain was a match for her first mate.

Instead of anger, Darcy surprised him by smiling. "Would you like to row back to shore and accompany Whit to Mistress MacInnis's, Newt?"

"In the dark?"

"That's the choice you have. Take the puppy back home to its mother, or allow Whit to keep it aboard ship."

The old man stood glowering at her. "There's another choice, lass. We can toss this...creature overboard and let it sink or swim home."

Whit tightened his grasp on the pup, determined to fight anyone who tried to do such a cruel thing.

Darcy's voice remained carefully controlled. "You know that isn't a choice, Newt. Your heart is far too tender."

"Tender is it?" The old man felt his temper flare even higher. He'd had to keep it on a short tether while waiting and wondering all alone on the dock. Now that his worst fears hadn't materialized, he had the luxury of turning all his pent-up anger in another direction. "Would ye like to dare me, lass?"

Darcy stood facing the old man, not at all alarmed at his bluster. She'd expected as much, and had prepared herself for this confrontation. "The puppy was a gift from a sweet woman. It belongs to Whit now, and it'll be his responsibility to see that it causes no problems aboard the *Undaunted*." She turned to Whit. "Do I have your word on this, lad?"

"Aye, Captain."

The two of them turned to Newton, whose frown had grown more pronounced with each word. "Oh, aye. Easy enough for him to promise. The lad means it. But nobody remembered to tell the pup. Ye can bet all ye'r wages that this…adorable animal will cause more problems than it's worth." He turned away. Over his shoulder he called, "Just don't bother to ask me to set things right. It's in ye'r hands now, Darcy. Ye'rs and the lad's."

He stormed across the deck. When he disappeared below, Whit cleared his throat. "Thanks for standing up to Newt for me, Captain."

She turned. At the look of adoration in his eyes, she decided not to bother telling him how often she'd witnessed just such displays of temper in her childhood. "I hope I won't be sorry, Whit. Remember what you agreed to. The pup is your responsibility. Every mess he makes must be cleaned at once."

"I'll see to it." He set the puppy down on the deck and watched as it sniffed its new surroundings.

Gryf, who had remained silent until now, watched the pup's movements. "Did you give him a name yet, lad?"

"Aye. All the way here I've been pondering. And I've decided to call him Fearless."

"Fearless?" Gryf watched as a sudden gust of wind caused the ship to lurch.

With a yelp the pup raced back to squat at Whit's feet. When he stood up minutes later he left a trail of yellow across the lad's boots.

Unconcerned, Whit gently lifted the pup in his arms and tucked him inside his coat. "Fearless is going to become a sailor, just like me. And once he gets used to the pitch and roll of the ship, you'll see. He'll live up to his name."

Seeing the serious look in the boy's eyes, Gryf bit back a smile. "Aye. I've no doubt of it. Now you'd best get below and into your hammock. And hope Fearless doesn't miss his mother too much."

"How will I know if he's missing her?"

Now Gryf did smile. "He'll cry like a baby. And probably wake the entire crew from a sound sleep. If that happens, you'd best find a place to hide. Or one of them may do what Newt suggested, and throw Fearless overboard. And you along with him."

Darcy lay in her bunk and wondered what had awakened her. In the darkness she strained to hear anything out of the ordinary. But all she heard was the creaking of timber, and the moaning of the wind, along with the rhythmic slap of water against the hull.

Then she heard it. A sound like the bleat of a lamb. She was up and dressed like a cannon shot, and still slipping her arms into the sleeves of her seaman's coat as she headed toward the sound.

It wasn't coming from the crew's cabin, she realized, but from above deck.

She found Whit huddled in a corner of the bow, his blanket draped around his shoulders to ward off the bitter wind. Coming from his arms was the unmistakable sound of high-pitched whining.

He looked up in misery as she approached.

"I don't know what to do, Captain. Fearless won't sleep. And he won't stop crying. I've been out here for an hour or more, trying to make him stop. Was I wrong to take him away from his mama and family?"

"Nay, lad. You weren't wrong." She knelt beside him and touched a finger to the pup's head. "He's old enough to be weaned. But it's just the newness. He needs some comforting."

"I've tried walking with him, whispering to him. But nothing helps."

They both looked up as a dark shadow fell over them.

"Gryf." The boy looked crestfallen. "Did Fearless wake you, too?"

"It's okay, lad." The man hunkered down in front of him. "Crying a bit, is he?"

Whit nodded. "More than a bit. I was afraid if I didn't come topside, I'd have the whole crew after me."

Darcy looked over. "Whit's tried walking Fearless and whispering to him, and still the pup cries. Have you any ideas, Gryf?"

"Maybe he's hungry. I'll see what Fielding's got in the galley."

A short time later he returned with a handful of crumbled beef and a small bowl of water. After some coaxing, the puppy ate every crumb, then drained the bowl.

"Now," Darcy said, "You and Fearless need to get out of this cold."

"I can't go back to my hammock, Captain. If he starts to cry again, I just know he'll wake Newton. And on the morrow the old man will make me take Fearless back to shore."

"Aye. You're right. I've seen Newt after a bad night." She thought a moment. "You can sleep in my cabin. With the door closed, the crew won't hear if Fearless starts in wailing again."

The boy hung his head. "If the crew found out I spent the night with you, they'd call me a baby."

She took a deep breath, and calculated how many hours until dawn. "Then there's no reason to worry. You and Fearless will have my cabin to yourselves. I was getting up now anyway. I've...chores to see to."

The boy's eyes widened. "Truly?"

"Aye. Come on, now. I'll help you get settled."

She led the way down the steps to her cabin. Once inside she lifted the blanket from her bunk and helped the boy climb in. She settled the blanket around him and watched as the pup curled up in his arms and closed its eyes.

"Good night, Whit."

"Good night, Captain. Thank you."

She closed the cabin door and climbed topside, then walked to the rail and stared at the night sky.

When she felt the warmth of a blanket enfold her, she looked up to see Gryf standing behind her.

"I thought you'd gone back to sleep."

"And I thought you said you had chores to see to, Captain."

"I do." She sighed. "In just a few hours."

"I'd guessed as much. Chores are better done in daylight. But there are still some very good ways to use the darkness." His tone lowered seductively. "One of the best things in life is spending a pleasant night in the company of a beautiful woman."

"Ah." She laughed. "I can see that you haven't really recovered from your wounds. Your mind is still addled. For you see, the night is bitter, and the woman is—"

"The most beautiful creature I've ever met."

She struggled against the curl of pleasure at his words. "And how would you know, since you can't remember all the women you've met?"

He chuckled. "Don't try to argue with me, Darcy. I know a beautiful woman when I meet one."

The wind gusted, causing her to draw the blanket more tightly around her. "You were saying something about a pleasant night?"

"What's a little north wind when the company is so special?"

"I see you're daft as well as blind. Ah, well. How can I complain when you're paying me compliments?" She opened the blanket. "As long as you're sacrificing your sleep to keep me company, I think you'd better get in out of that wind."

"I don't think that would be wise."

"And why not? You're as cold as I am."

He stared at her for the space of a heartbeat, before accepting her offer and stepping close enough to wrap the blanket around his shoulders.

"There now." She turned toward him with a smile. "Isn't that better?"

"Aye." His tone lowered. "But infinitely more dangerous."

At the look in his eyes she turned away to stare at the darkened water. "Why didn't you want to tell Mistress MacInnis that we weren't wed?"

"And spoil all her romantic illusions? The dear sweet woman wanted us to be a family. Maybe, for a little while, she was reminded of her own youth and happiness. I didn't see the harm."

"You've a kind heart, Gryf." Darcy turned back to him and was startled to find his mouth inches from hers.

Before she could draw back, his lips were pressed to hers.

Her heart slammed against her chest. She tried to back up, but she was pinned inside the blanket. He drew it tighter, so that she was drawn firmly into the kiss.

His hands framed her face, and he drew out the kiss until they were both struggling for breath.

"I want you, Darcy." He spoke the words against her mouth, sending her heart racing out of control. His dark eyes focused on hers, and he watched the flare of passion as his words sank in. "I know it isn't wise. You're captain of this ship, and I'm a lowly seaman, without a past or a future. But there's no denying the attraction. And I'm tired of fighting it.''

''I can't...I don't...'' She put her hands to his chest to hold him at bay, and could feel the thundering of his heartbeat. It was as out of control as her own.

''Do you deny what you feel when we touch, Darcy?''

She swallowed. ''Nay. I can't deny it.''

''And this.'' He brushed his lips lightly over hers and felt the flare of heat all the way to his toes. ''Do you feel it?''

She had to grasp the front of his coat to remain standing. The mere touch of his mouth was enough to stagger her.

''I know your heart belongs to another, Darcy.''

''A-another? Who told...?'' Her tone hardened. ''What do you know?''

''Only that he's gone. And I'm here.'' He kissed her again, long and slow and deep until her head was spinning, and she couldn't form a single coherent thought. ''And I'd like to stay here. Just here, holding you. Kissing you. And maybe even helping you forget every other man you've ever known.''

''Gryf...'' She shuddered as he brought his lips down her throat and buried them in the hollow where her heartbeat was pounding with all the fury of cannonfire.

''You can't deny the attraction, Darcy. Nor can you deny your reaction each time we kiss.'' He ran his mouth up her throat and felt her trembling response.

''Aye. It's true.'' She closed her eyes as he nibbled his way to her chin. ''But that doesn't mean we must give in to our feelings.''

"Why not?" His tone was rough with need. "It's what men and women do. And whether or not you care to admit it, it's what you want, as well."

She couldn't deny it, not when her heart was there in her throat and her blood was pounding in her temples. Why was it this man's touch held the key to unlocking all this passion? What was it about Gryf that made her so weak, when she'd always been so strong?

He pressed kisses to her cheek, the tip of her nose, and then to her closed eyelids, before tugging on her lobe. Against her ear he whispered fiercely, "Say the words, Darcy. Tell me you want this too."

She shuddered. "I want…" Oh, how she wanted. But fear had her holding back. And fear was something she'd had little of in her life. It baffled her. Puzzled her. And had her questioning her every move. "I want time. This is all happening too quickly, Gryf."

With an oath he stepped back, and she felt the cold seep in where only moments before heat had been.

"I won't pretend to be a patient man, Darcy. There's a demon inside me, pushing me to take what I want." His eyes narrowed. His voice lowered. "So be warned. Don't allow yourself to be alone with me. Don't return my kisses, unless you want what I want. And when you do, if you do, I'll be here, waiting."

He turned up the collar of his coat and faced into the wind as he walked away.

Darcy stayed where she was, watching until he'd disappeared belowdecks. Then with a sigh she wrapped the blanket around herself and turned to stare at the ribbons of moonlight trailing the blackened water.

As a child she'd always thought of the *Undaunted* as a giant playground, where she could run around in circles, climb until she reached the very top of the mast, or hide where no one could ever find her. Now, suddenly, it seemed so small. No matter where she went, she was bound to bump into Gryf at every turn. And each time she did, she would feel this strange, aching need.

So what was she going to do about this? she wondered.

It wasn't enough to try to evade. Not this time. He'd issued a challenge.

And she had no idea how she would answer it.

Chapter Twelve

"**W**hit, ye thickheaded lout. Get over here now. And bring a rag."

At the sound of Newton's voice, the boy sighed and looked around for his pup, who came careening across the deck, tongue lolling, tail wagging joyfully.

The old man was swearing as he scraped something from his boot. Whit knew, without asking, what the pup had been up to. It had been the same for days. Every time Newton or one of the crew hollered, it had something to do with Fearless.

Gryf had helped the lad to barricade a small section of the deck with some overturned benches. Then he'd lined the space with some rags, in the hope that Fearless could be taught to use just that one section for what Newton called his leavings. The only problem was, Fearless dropped his leavings any place except there.

And, as the old man had predicted, the puppy was driven to chew everything he could sink his teeth into. The toe of a seaman's boot. The buttons off Fielding's coat, which had sent the cook into such a rage, he'd threatened to withhold Whit's meals unless the lad agreed to sew them back on at once. Worse, the pup had nudged open the door to the captain's cabin and had curled up on her bunk. Which wouldn't have seemed so bad, if only he hadn't chewed a hole through her blanket before taking his leave. But by far the most serious infraction had been yesterday, when Newton had discovered the puppy happily chewing through a newly mended sail, which one of the seamen had left unguarded on deck for only a moment. The old sailor had flown into a rage, and if Gryf hadn't come to his rescue, Newton might have made good his threat to toss the pup into the ocean. It took Gryf and Whit more than an hour to repair the damage. And every time Newton looked at the patch they'd put on the sail, he got angry all over again.

"Shark bait. That's all he's good for," the old man shouted as Gryf rescued the drooling puppy and carried it back to its owner.

Repentant, Whit hurried over to wipe down the deck, and even offered to clean Newton's boots, but the old man turned away with a snarl.

With a look of dejection, Whit walked over to where Gryf stood holding Fearless.

"Here, lad." Gryf handed Whit the puppy and a length of knotted rope.

"What's this?"

"Something for Fearless to chew on. And if you know what's good for you, you'll see that he's confined for the rest of the afternoon, until Newt has a chance to calm down."

"Aye. But how can I confine him? Captain Lambert won't let him stay in her cabin anymore. And every time I try to keep him in his corner, he just jumps clear of the barriers.''

"Then I suggest you try tying him up." Seeing the lad's sad face he softened his tone. "It isn't cruel, Whit. It's kind. He's a baby. He needs you to set limits. Make him a bed, and see that he stays in it for a while. Give him the rope to chew on, so that he has something to occupy his quiet time. He'll be fine. You'll see."

"I hope you're right. I'm afraid if he doesn't settle down pretty soon, someone will toss him overboard when I'm not looking."

Gryf chuckled as the boy walked away carrying the pup. For all the complaints about the presence of a dog aboard ship, they'd already seen considerable progress. Fearless was able to sleep through the night without whimpering, curled up in Whit's arms in the hammock. After being stepped on and bumped, he'd learned to keep out of the way of the seamen as they swabbed the deck or hauled cargo to the hold. And he'd stopped barking frantically whenever Whit climbed the rigging, though he still danced in gleeful circles whenever the lad returned to the deck.

And for all the crew's grumbling, Gryf had seen the cook, Fielding, slip Fearless scraps of meat from the galley when he thought no one was looking. The rest of the crew occasionally laughed at the dog's antics, especially when he slipped and slid across the rain-slicked deck. During the course of the day several of the seamen could be seen pausing in their duties to bend and scratch behind the pup's ear. And Darcy was teaching Fearless to sit up and offer a paw, in return for a treat.

Newton, however, hadn't softened at all toward the puppy. In fact, with each day, the old man seemed ever more determined to harden his heart against this fuzzy intruder. If he could, he'd even blame Fearless for the weather, which had taken a turn for the worse.

The wind out of the north stung the eyes and lashed the skin. Some mornings the deck was layered with a coat of ice, making walking from one side to the other impossible until a thin winter sun sent it washing over the sides of the ship in frosty rivers. The waters of the Atlantic were as dark as the storm clouds that rolled overhead.

Darcy made her way down the rigging and hurried to Newton's side. "There's no land in sight yet, Newt. It's been days."

"Aye, lass." He stared out at the angry waves. "And it could be a few days more. I'm thinking, since we've delivered the last of our cargo, that we ought to give some thought to heading back to Cornwall, instead of going on."

Home. The thought of it brought such a wave of homesickness, she had to close her eyes against the pain.

Her voice was dreamy. "I suppose we could. I went over the ledgers last night. We've made enough to pay the crew, and still show a profit. Our last delivery, to the Western Isles of Scotland, was by far our best yet."

"And well it ought. There aren't many ships' captains who would permit that much timber to be loaded in the hold when the seas are this rough. I thought we'd surely sink before we made land again. Especially when we sailed into that storm off the coast of Shetland.''

"But we made it, Newt. And a fortune, as well.''

"Aye.'' For the first time in days the old man smiled. "Ye drive a hard bargain, lass. I watched the harbormaster's face growing more purple with every one of ye'r demands, and thought ye'd bargained ye'rself right out of a job.''

She grinned. "There was nobody else willing to haul that timber, and we both knew it.''

He shook his head. "Maybe. But ye had me worried there for a moment. I thought we'd lost that cargo for sure.'' He waited for the space of several moments, hoping to keep his tone casual. "So. Will I be giving the order to turn the ship around and head for home?''

She needed only a moment to consider. "Aye, Newt. Give the order.''

Now his smile came. Quick and bright. "Ye'll not regret it, lass.''

As he walked away, shouting orders, Darcy turned to the rail and stared down into the foam left in their wake. She'd let Newton believe they were returning home because she'd made enough money to show a profit. And that was partly true. They did have money in their coffers. But the real reason she had decided to end this voyage was standing at the wheel, steering the ship at this very moment.

Try as she might, the confines of the *Undaunted* made it impossible for her to escape Gryf. No matter where she went, she could feel him watching her. Even her cabin offered no refuge. The image of him crept unbidden into her dreams. Visions of him holding her, kissing her and tempting her with forbidden pleasures, were driving her to distraction.

She needed to go home. To feel the love and warmth of her family. She craved her grandfather's humor, the common sense of their housekeeper and the sweetness of her old nurse. Perhaps she'd even seek the wise counsel of her sisters. After all, they'd faced these same temptations with the men they'd married. They would know what she ought to do.

Aye. The smile came finally, as she put her worries behind her. She wouldn't give Gryf another thought until she'd had time to lay all this before the people who loved her. Together they'd chart the proper course. Together. Her smile grew.

"Gryf says we're heading to Cornwall." Whit looked over at the captain.

The crew had gathered belowdecks to eat and to escape the bitter weather. Only Newton and a couple of sailors remained on deck.

Darcy nodded and drew closer to the heat of the brazier. Despite the gloves she'd worn while steering the ship, her hands were nearly frozen. "I think we'll all be happier when we can put into port. At least until spring."

"Is Cornwall your home?" the lad asked.

"Aye." Darcy nibbled a crust of bread, washing it down with hot tea. She could feel Gryf watching her. The very thought of it brought color to her cheeks. She'd promised herself she wouldn't give him another thought. But he was constantly on her mind. Tiptoeing across her heart.

"What's it like in Cornwall?" the boy persisted.

"It's lovely and green in summer, the meadows strewn with wildflowers. There are flocks of sheep on the hillsides." Seeing Whit's interest sharpen, she leaned back, smiling. "Our village, Land's End, is rather wild and primitive, with huge boulders along the shore." She closed her eyes a moment, seeing it in her mind. "When I was a little girl, I thought that giants had walked across the land, tossing boulders like pebbles in the sand."

The boy smiled at the image.

"Our home, MaryCastle, is built on a finger of land that juts into the Atlantic. My father built it for my mother so that she could watch for his ship whenever he went off to sea. There are those in the village who refer to it as Lambert's Folly. But Papa knew what he was doing." She gave a little laugh. "Oh, it was just the finest place to grow up. We never tired of swimming and sailing and playing along the shore."

Whit's eyes were round with interest. He idly petted the pup who lay snuggled on his lap, dozing. "Did you know, even then, that some day you'd grow up to be a ship's captain?"

"Nay." Her eyes clouded for a moment. "That was to be a privilege reserved only for my brother, James. He began sailing with Papa when he was only ten and two. But when James and Papa were lost at sea, my sisters and I made a pact to carry on."

Gryf sipped his tea and listened in silence. He loved the sound of her voice. Loved the cadence, the rhythm, the inflection. Her laugh was as lyrical as church bells carried on a summer breeze. The mere sound of it lightened his heart, though he knew not why. When she spoke, he could forget about the wind that howled above deck. Could forget about the cold that seeped into a man's very bones. Could forget the fact that he had no memories of his own childhood. Or of his life before the fire. Her voice reminded him of springtime. Of warm days and gentle nights. Of a fine mist blowing in off the ocean to add the sparkle of diamonds to skin and hair.

Had he once seen her like that? With mist-dampened hair and laughing eyes? Or was he imagining it?

A sailor stuck his head in the doorway, causing Gryf to blink away the image.

"Captain, Newt says it's your turn to take the wheel."

"Aye." She set aside her tea and started to stand.

Gryf sprang up, touching a hand to her arm. "Stay here where it's warm. I'll take your watch."

"Nay." She brushed aside his hand and hurried out the door, ignoring the warmth where he'd touched her. "I'll see to it myself."

She didn't want to be beholden to him. It would be far too easy to allow herself to accept his help, and then to look forward to it. She wanted, needed, to stand alone. To make her own way. It was as necessary to her as breathing. She had no intention of allowing any man, especially Gryf, to lull her into a false sense of security.

"Watch this, Fielding." Whit held up a tiny scrap of meat and ordered Fearless to sit. At once the puppy squatted down, his tail swishing furiously across the boards of the lower deck.

In the past few days the increasingly bitter weather

had sent the crew belowdecks whenever their watch ended. Along with gambling, the pup had become their main source of entertainment.

"Roll over, Fearless."

The puppy did as he was told, and was rewarded with the meat.

Whit took up a second scrap. "Fearless, beg."

The puppy obediently stood on its hind legs, waiting for a reward.

"That's pretty good, lad. Now watch this." The cook winked at the others, then stomped his foot.

At once the puppy cowered behind Whit's leg, sending the crew into spasms of laughter.

"I think we ought to start calling him Fearful, instead of Fearless. That dog's scared of his own shadow."

"He is not." Whit picked up the whining pup and cuddled it to his chest. "You just startled him."

"Aye. But then a lot of things startle Fearful. The wind. The sails flapping in the wind. Footsteps. He probably cowers at the sound of someone coughing. When is he going to live up to his name, lad?"

"Give him time." Whit pressed his face to the pup's neck, breathing him in. "He'll learn. Hasn't he learned not to chew?"

One of the crew nodded, then added, "It's a good thing, too, lad, or by now he'd be swimming back to Scotland."

The others roared with laughter.

"And hasn't he learned to drop his leavings only in his spot?"

"Aye, now. There's the best thing he's learned." Fielding looked to the others, who laughed and nodded. "It's a relief to be able to walk the deck at night and not have to worry about what we'll step in. Eh, mates?"

While the others chuckled, one grizzled sailor leaned close to whisper, "They're just having fun with you, lad. They all wish they could have a pet as fine as your Fearless."

Whit shot him a smile, before going off to his hammock for the night. As the pup snuggled against his chest, he found himself thinking about the old sailor's words. Aye. Fearless was his. Only his. Nobody else could ever claim the pup for their own. For he would know, and Fearless would know, that they belonged together.

It was the most wonderful feeling in the world to have something that belonged only to him.

He rubbed a hand over the pup's coat and felt such a welling of love in his heart for this small, helpless creature. And vowed that he'd do whatever it took to keep him safe.

Newton held the wheel steady as the *Undaunted* carved a path through the black water. The moon was a thin yellow sliver in the midnight sky. The stars looked as though they'd been carved from ice. An occasional snowflake drifted on the night air, a harbinger of the storm that lay in wait just ahead.

The old sailor heard the sound of footsteps and turned to see Gryf walking across the deck toward him.

"Figured ye'd be asleep with the rest of the crew, Gryf."

"I slept for a few hours. Now I'm awake, and thought I'd spell you for a while."

"I'll be glad for the break." The old man blew on his hands, wrapped in a length of wool. "Don't think I can feel my fingers any longer."

"Fielding left a brazier of hot coals in the galley with a pot of soup. That ought to warm you before you go to sleep."

"I thank ye." As he turned over the wheel, the old man saw Gryf glance up to where Darcy hung by one hand at the top of the rigging. Following the direction of his gaze he muttered, "I tried to persuade her to go below and let one of the others take her watch, but ye know the lass. Stubborn, she is. Always has been."

"Some might call it dedicated."

"Some might." Newt turned to give him a long look, before walking away.

Gryf stood listening to the sound of the old man's peg leg tapping against the wood of the deck. When the footsteps faded, he lifted his head. Darcy had climbed so high she was no longer visible. But he knew she was up there, at the very top of the mast, peering into the darkness, searching for any light that might signal land, or a passing ship.

A short time later he caught sight of her, halfway down, and moving with all the agility of a dancer. When she landed on the deck she seemed surprised to see him.

"What happened to Newt?"

"Nothing. I offered to spell him for a while. I figured it's too cold tonight for his old bones."

"That was nice of you, Gryf."

He shrugged off the compliment. "Maybe I had other reasons for wanting him out of the way."

She would have laughed, except for the roughness of his tone. She chanced a quick glance at his face, and found him watching her with an intensity that had her heart beating overtime.

He reached out. Her cold hand was engulfed in his big, warm palm and she felt the surge of heat all the way to her heart. "You've been avoiding me, Darcy."

"Aye." There it was again. That sudden jolt, and then the unsteady bumping of her pulse. "And for the best of reasons."

He gave her a quick, dangerous smile. "Could one of those reasons be this?" He brought his hand to her throat and his smile grew at the way her heartbeat stuttered.

"You know it is. Gryf, I don't think—"

"There you go again." He drew her close and pressed his lips to her temple. "Thinking. All I want is to warm you."

"Warm?" She tried to laugh, but it came out on a sigh. "One touch and my skin's on fire."

"That's even better." He dragged her firmly against him and slipped his hands inside her coat. She knew he could feel the way her breath was already hitching. And when his mouth came down on hers, she couldn't breathe.

"I've been thinking about this all day." The words were muttered against her lips. "About you. And the way you'd taste." He took the kiss deeper until she felt her head spinning and the deck swaying beneath her feet. "I could go on like this for hours."

At the moment, she hoped he would. Though she knew it was dangerous, she wrapped her arms around his neck and sighed with the pure pleasure of it.

"And here I thought the only thing on your mind was the fish you and Whit caught for our supper."

"Fishing was just an excuse, so I wouldn't have to talk. That way I could concentrate on how many ways I could find to be alone with you tonight." He changed angles and kissed her again until he felt her sigh and open to him.

Need was a hard, tight ball in his gut that had him pressing her back against the wheel as he bent to skim his mouth along her throat.

"Gryf, I—" She shuddered as he parted her coat and brought his mouth to her breast.

Despite the layers of clothes, she felt her nipple harden. Desire was so quick and unexpected, she had no defense against it. She nearly cried out, but the sound became a low moan of pleasure as his hands moved over her, torturing them both.

She'd never known anything like the feelings she was experiencing. An ache that started deep inside her, then seemed to curl through her veins, causing the most unexpected yearning. A yearning to lie with him here on the cold, hard deck and let him take her wherever he chose. A desperate, driving desire to touch him as he was touching her. To make him tremble as she was trembling. To make him ache for her as she was aching.

It never occurred to her to stop. She had no will left. No thought, except to take and give until they were both sated.

She opened herself to him, letting him taste all the

passion, all the hunger. And was rewarded with a low moan as he took them both higher.

Somewhere in the distant edge of her mind Darcy heard the sound of hurried footfalls. A moment later Gryf muttered an oath against her lips, before drawing the lapels of her coat together and taking a step back. Out of the corner of her eye she caught the blurred image of Whit and Fearless stepping onto the deck.

"Can you believe it?" the boy called. "Fearless woke me up to let me know he wanted to…drop his leavings on deck."

"That's…good news, lad." Darcy was surprised at how difficult it was to speak. She was grateful that Gryf continued to keep his hand at her shoulder. Otherwise, she feared, she would probably slip bonelessly to the deck.

The pup raced off to his favorite place, then returned on the run. The boy cleaned the spot before picking him up and heading toward the steps.

"Are you coming below, Captain?"

"Aye. In a moment."

When Whit disappeared Gryf drew her close, but this time she kept her hand against his chest to hold him at bay.

"What's wrong?" His voice was rough with need.

"I had a moment to clear my mind. I'm going below with the crew."

His hand tightened at her shoulder. "Don't go, Darcy. The lad's gone now. Nothing's changed."

"Aye. Something has." She drew in a deep breath. "I think it's fortunate Whit came along when he did. It made me realize I'm not ready for this, Gryf."

"You seemed ready enough a moment ago."

"Aye. Your kisses have a way of doing that to me. But now..." She shook her head. "I'm not ready. Who knows? Perhaps I'll never be."

Without another word she made her way below-decks.

When he was alone he lifted his face to the sky and gulped in the frigid air until his breathing returned to normal.

As he counted stars he found himself wondering if his blood would ever cool. Or if this need for her would ever loosen its grip on his heart.

Chapter Thirteen

Darcy awoke with a light heart. Newton had said they were only a day away from Cornwall. Another day and she'd be home. Oh, she didn't know if she'd be able to stand the waiting. She slipped out of bed and dressed quickly, eager for the day to be over.

On deck, storm clouds layered the sky, blocking the morning sun. Fog settled around the *Undaunted* like a thick, dark blanket. It was impossible to tell if it was daybreak or dusk. An eerie silence had settled over the Atlantic. No seabirds wheeled and cried overhead. The voices of the sailors aboard ship seemed to bounce back at them whenever they spoke.

"I don't like this, lass." Newton stood at the rail, trying vainly to see through the heavy curtain of frost and mist. "There's no way to navigate. By the time this fog blows away, we could find ourselves miles off course."

"We've already lowered the sails. We're barely moving."

"Aye, but the ocean current will keep pulling us, lass."

"Should we drop anchor, Newt?"

He shrugged, deep in thought. "I think it's best if we keep drifting."

"Why?"

He idly rubbed his leg, feeling the phantom pain that often came when the weather changed. "If we were a pirate ship, lass, this would be the perfect time to attack our enemies. They wouldn't even see us coming."

"But their advantage is also ours, Newt. We could slip past them without even being seen."

"Aye." He paced, turned, paced some more. "But I can feel them, lass. In my bones. They're close by. I know it."

Darcy shivered. She'd always trusted the old man's instincts. There was no reason to doubt him now. "I could climb the rigging."

He shook his head. "'Twould do ye no good. In fog this thick, we're running blind."

"At least we can make it impossible for them to hear us if they're nearby. Give the order to the crew that they're to remain silent until this fog lifts, Newt."

"Aye, lass." He nodded and went belowdecks, returning minutes later trailed by a string of silent, somber seamen, who lined the deck, watching and listening.

But there was only the strange, eerie silence, that seemed to stretch on endlessly. And the slap of waves against the hull.

Suddenly, without warning, the *Undaunted* shuddered, sending half its crew tumbling about like puppets. Darcy picked herself up and caught her breath at the sight of a ship's mast looming over their deck like a ghostly spectre. The pirate ship had rammed them broadside, leaving them crippled and helpless to escape.

Chaos reigned on deck as Darcy shouted for the crew to uncover the cannons, and to retrieve their weapons and pass them about. Then she went in search of Whit and Fearless. She found them in the galley with Fielding.

"Lad, take your pup and go to my cabin at once. Lock yourself in. Remain there until I say otherwise."

"What's happened, Captain?" Fielding, retrieving pots that had been tossed around, looked up sharply. "Have we run aground?"

"Worse. We've been rammed by a pirate ship. We need you topside, Fielding. As for you, Whit, go now and do as I say."

"Aye, Captain." The boy picked up the puppy and started out, then paused and turned. "Do you think it's my uncle's ship?"

"I know not, lad. But, no matter what you hear, you're to stay locked safely in my cabin. Do you hear?"

"Aye, Captain."

She saw the terrified look on his face and her heart went out to the boy. Then she pulled herself back to the task at hand.

She tucked a knife at her waist and another in her boot, then started up the steps. Even before she reached the deck, she could hear the shrieking, the cursing and shouting, and could make out the shadowy figures of men swinging from ropes across the deck.

With screams guaranteed to send shivers along

their spines, the pirates swarmed across the deck of the *Undaunted,* cutting down all in their path. Though Darcy's crew struggled valiantly, they were no match for these cunning, desperate men, who were slashing and cutting, and laughing like madmen with every victory.

"Watch your back, Darcy." Gryf's warning had her whirling just as a sword blade sang past her head.

In one quick motion she tossed her knife and watched it land in her attacker's chest. The man gasped and released his hold on his sword as he tried desperately to rid himself of the pain. But it was too late, and he fell to the deck in a pool of his own blood.

Darcy stepped over him, grabbing up his sword as she did. Seeing Newton dueling with several grizzled pirates, she leapt into the fray to even the score. The two stood back to back, driving the pirates toward the rail. With one quick flash of blade Darcy sent one of the men overboard, and watched the other fall on his own weapon.

Convinced that he wouldn't be getting up to fight again, she turned toward the old man. "Can you handle this one, Newt?"

"Aye, lass. See to Fielding."

She turned. The cook was sweating profusely as he tried to fend off the blade of a vicious swordsman. Darcy could see the pirate's strategy. He intended to back his opponent against the cannon, where the smoke and heat would work to his advantage. Though her crew had loaded and fired their cannon, they'd been caught off guard, with no hope of discharging a volley.

"Fielding." She stepped up beside him and saw his look of gratitude.

"I'll be—" The pirate gave a laugh of delight. "My mates told me there was a female aboard this ship, but I didn't believe them."

"And now you can boast that you were bested by that same female." Darcy's blade flashed and she began slowly driving the pirate across the deck.

His laughter quickly faded as he tasted her skill. Each time he lunged, she was able to dance aside, avoiding his blade. For every thrust of his weapon, she managed to parry. After several minutes, she bore not a single wound. But the pirate had been cut in half a dozen different places. And the loss of blood was beginning to weaken him.

"I think it's time you joined your shipmates." She brought her blade to his chest, leaving him but two choices. Stay and face certain death, or take his chances on the swirling water.

He jumped, landing with a cry of desperation in the foaming waves below.

"Darcy." When she turned, Gryf leapt to her side to save her from an attacker. But in so doing, he took the blade meant for her. Blood streamed from his shoulder, soaking the front of his tunic.

Enraged, Darcy drove the swordsman back and ran him through, then turned back in time to see Gryf fighting three more pirates. She rushed to his side and engaged first one, then the other, until both men had fallen. Then she turned in time to see Gryf drop the third man before leaning weakly against the rail.

"Go below, Gryf."

"Not until these cutthroats are routed."

"You're too badly wounded to be of any use. Go below, I say."

He gave her that quick, dangerous smile. "Aye, Captain. In a while."

"Gryf…" She saw him straighten and raise his sword. By the time she'd turned, he'd sent an attacker falling backward, the hilt of his sword still buried in the pirate's chest.

Gryf met her look. "You were saying, Captain?"

She bent and retrieved his sword, then handed it to him. "Stay close. I need you to guard my back."

"Aye, Captain. It's such a lovely back, it would be a shame to see it marred." He stumbled after her as she hurried to join in yet another fight.

For what seemed hours the battle went on, as the crew of the *Undaunted* stood up to the band of pirates determined to take possession of their ship and its bounty. But though they fought bravely, they were outnumbered five to one. The pirate ship had taken on fresh recruits, who were eager for blood. The element of surprise had further weakened the resistance of Darcy's crew.

As the fighting dragged on, Darcy and her men could feel their strength waning.

Though Darcy had sustained several minor wounds, they were nothing compared with some of the others. She feared for her crew. Newton had been dueling with men half his age. Gryf was hanging on despite a gaping wound to the shoulder that was obviously draining him. Several of the crew lay moaning against the rail, holding torn strips of cloth to bloody wounds. The deck was spattered with their blood. Were the wounds minor or deadly? There wasn't even a moment to see. Like a swarm of angry bees, each time one pirate was driven overboard, two more stepped up to take his place.

And each time the pirates looked as though they might begin to fall back, their captain's voice would order them to pick up the slack.

Darcy glanced across the distance that separated their two ships. Wylie York kept himself above the fray, remaining aboard the *Sinner,* and watching from the safety of the ship's wheel.

"Come on, mates." His voice boomed through the fog and mist. "Are you going to let a female and her lowly crew best you? Put some muscle into this, so we can be on our way."

"Coward," Darcy shouted. "Are you afraid to face our swords yourself?"

"Afraid?" His voice came bouncing back like a hollow echo. "You're the ones who'd best fear for your lives. For we're not leaving until every sailor aboard your ship is lying in his own blood."

"Someone needs to silence that lout's roar." Newton backed an opponent against the rail and gave the pirate a choice to die or leap to safety. As so many others had done, the man jumped over the rail and landed in the frothy waves below, hoping one of his shipmates would throw him a lifeline.

"I agree." Gryf, leaning weakly against the rail after defeating yet another opponent, looked to Darcy. His face was ashen, and she could see the pain he was struggling to ignore. "Let me try to take him, Captain."

"Nay, Gryf. You'd be inviting death. Besides, you're needed here."

"Then I'll go, lass." Newton turned away. Just then a blade slashed the old man's good leg, sending him sprawling on the deck.

"Newt!" Darcy was by his side, dropping to her knees. "Hold on, Newt." In one quick movement she tore the scarf from her neck and began wrapping it around the old man's leg to stem the river of blood.

"Behind ye, lass."

Before she could react Gryf was there beside her, plunging his sword into the man who'd been about to attack. The pirate dropped to the deck, but not before sending his own sword into Gryf's side. With a grunt of pain Gryf dropped to his knees and struggled to remove the weapon.

Three more pirates stepped over their dead comrade and lifted their swords. Darcy picked up Newton's weapon and in one smooth motion got to her feet, facing her attackers.

"Now, isn't this interesting?" The voice sent shivers along Darcy's spine as she found herself looking into the feral eyes of Wylie York. "I've been hoping I could do battle with the famous female."

"But only if the odds are in your favor." Instead of backing away as he'd expected, this bold little female faced him without flinching. "I see you waited until my crew was too weakened by battle to be a threat to you."

"That's how I got to be captain of my ship. By calculating the odds. Now—" he motioned to the pirates standing on either side of him "—hold that man." He pointed to Gryf. "I wouldn't want him to try to be a hero."

At once the two pirates grabbed Gryf, holding him

when he tried to fight back. For good measure two more dragged Newton aside and stood over him, in case he attempted to stand.

Wylie York motioned to two more pirates. "Now hold the woman. I intend to teach her a lesson."

With Gryf and Newt forced to watch helplessly, the pirate captain lifted his sword to the neckline of Darcy's shirt and expertly slashed it open.

"Well, now. Isn't this interesting?" He stepped closer, his eyes narrowed on the expanse of lovely flesh, covered only by a sheer chemise. "It seems a pity to hide all this beauty under such drab clothing. Why aren't you warming some Englishman's bed, woman?"

"Because I'd rather be sailing the seas, cutting out the hearts of pirates like you."

He threw back his head and roared. "Oh, my. Such an outspoken female. If you'd been my mate, I'd have seen to it that you learned your proper place."

"It's fortunate for you that you aren't my mate. For I'd have plunged my blade into your heart the first time you touched me."

His eyes narrowed. "A word of warning, woman. You're still alive only because I've permitted it. And when I give the order, you'll die, just like all the others who litter this deck."

"Then give the word. I'd rather die quickly than have my men watch this game you play."

"Would you now?" He laughed again, a chilling, high-pitched sound that sent ice along the spines of all who heard. "But you see, woman, the game has just begun. And I'm the one making all the rules."

He turned to his men. "How many of you would care to sample the woman's charms?"

"I would, Captain." A lean young pirate chuckled, showing a gap where his teeth had once been.

"Aye," called another, with a missing arm. "Count me in, Captain."

An old pirate, with long black hair and a face badly scarred from battle shouted, "It's been a long time since I've seen one as lovely as this female."

The others nodded in agreement until their voices were a loud roar of approval.

Wylie York turned to her. "You see? Now I suggest you show them just what they'll be enjoying." He pressed the tip of his sword to her heart. "Let's remove the rest of these clothes."

Before he could cut through the ribbons of her chemise, Whit suddenly dashed on deck and raced to Darcy's side. "Don't touch her, Uncle."

At the gleam in the pirate captain's eyes, Darcy felt a wave of horror. This was the one thing she'd most dreaded. She'd hoped, prayed, that the lad would follow orders and stay hidden.

"Go back, lad." Her voice rang with all the righteous anger she could muster. "I ordered you below-decks."

"Nay, Captain. It's me he wants. Not you." Though he was trembling violently, Whit lifted his chin. "So come and get me, Uncle." He opened his hand, revealing a knife. "But before you do, before you touch me or my captain, you'll have to fight me."

"Now what do you think you're going to do with that? Stick me?" York grinned at the circle of pirates, who joined in his laughter. "You sniveling little coward. You don't have the courage."

"You think not?" Whit's voice trembled, mirroring the fear that was in his eyes.

"Look at you. You're shivering like a leaf in the wind."

"Aye. I may be afraid. But I'd rather die than ever let you touch my captain."

"Your death can easily be arranged, little fool." The pirate captain lunged, and Whit surprised even himself by standing his ground and slashing out with the blade of his knife. It bit into the pirate's arm, sending him jumping back.

At the sight of his own blood, York's eyes narrowed. His smile was wiped from his face. "Now you'll have to suffer before you die, boy. You think I beat you the last time? That was nothing compared with what I intend to do to you this time. I'll beat you and stomp you until there's nothing left but a pile of stinking, rotting flesh."

As he advanced, he heard a snarl, seconds before small sharp teeth were imbedded in his ankle. He gave a yelp of surprise and looked down to find a yellow puppy latched onto his leg.

"Fearless! Nay!" Whit shouted.

"Fearless? This useless cur? Is he yours?"

"Aye." Whit's eyes were round with surprise and fear.

"A pity." The pirate captain gave a vicious kick, sending the pup flying across the deck with a yelp. "That's one more thing you'll have to pay for, boy."

As Wylie York advanced, the pup came charging

back, teeth bared, and a low growl issuing from its throat.

This time the man picked up the pup and slammed it against the rail of the ship, where it gave a series of yelps before falling strangely silent.

"You've killed him!" Tears streamed from Whit's eyes as he stared at the still form of his pet, lying in a heap on the deck. When Whit turned back to his uncle, he could hardly see through the flood of tears. "I promised him I'd always take care of him. And now you've killed him."

"Well, just so you don't have to miss him too much…" With his sword uplifted, York started toward the boy. "I'll allow you to join him. You and I are going to settle this thing between us once and for all, you miserable little whelp." His eyes glittered with madness. "Do you know why I beat you? Why I hated you? Because you look just like your mother. A pretty thing she was, but thought herself too good for the likes of me. She told me she'd never let me touch her. But I showed her. I took her by force. And when I was through with her, she knew she was no better than a tavern wench. But when I went off to sea, she ran away. It took me some years to find her, and when I did, it was too late. She was more dead than alive. She boasted that she'd beaten me. But I wasn't through with her yet. When I learned that she had a son, I knew I'd found the perfect vengeance." He laughed. A high, shrill sound that left no doubt of his madness. "And here you are. A sniveling little coward who ran away just like his mother."

The boy's chin lifted. "At least now I understand. You hate me because of my mother."

The pirate captain lifted his head and hooted with laughter. ''Nay, little fool. I don't hate you because you're your mother's son. I hate you because you're mine. And I'm about to do to you what I should have done to her, so that you'd have never been born.''

Even the pirates, accustomed as they were to violence, seemed shaken by the venom in their captain's voice. And by the madness in his eyes.

Darcy watched in horror as Whit swiped a dirty hand at his tears and faced this man who claimed to be his father with nothing more than the small knife.

Once again the boy managed to inflict a minor wound, which only added to Wylie York's fury.

''That was your last chance, boy. Now you can join your mother.'' York thrust his sword with all the strength he could muster.

It pierced the lad's chest and sent him reeling backward, where he lay on the deck beside the body of his pet.

At the horror of the scene before her, Darcy heard a long, piercing scream, and realized it was her own voice. The sound went on and on as she stared at the sight of the little boy and the puppy, lying in an ever-widening pool of blood.

Grief and rage poured through her, filling her with an unbelievable well of strength. Added to that was the shock of the pirates, who seemed caught in the grip of panic at the sight of their captain attacking his own flesh and blood.

In a frenzy Darcy twisted free of the hands holding her and charged toward the pirate captain with nothing more than her bare fists.

With a laugh Wylie York pulled his sword from

the boy's small body and lifted it over his head. "Come on, woman. This ought to be interesting, since it isn't even a contest."

Darcy braced herself for the pain she knew would come. But before York could bring his weapon down, he suddenly stiffened.

Feeling the white-hot thrust of pain in his back, he whirled. And found himself staring at Gryf, who was leaning weakly against the rail. Like Darcy, he'd taken advantage of the moment to break free of the pirates who'd been holding him.

"I'll regret to my dying day that I wasn't able to save the boy. But I'll gladly welcome my own death, rather than allow you to harm the woman." Gryf's voice was oddly hollow, and all who watched could see what it cost him to continue standing, as blood poured from his wound. "England's ships need never have to fear you again, York."

As the pirate captain dropped to the deck, Gryf held himself upright for another minute, before sinking to his knees. He was helpless to defend himself against the pirates who, after a moment's hesitation, took up their weapons.

With a cry Darcy reached into her boot and tossed her knife at the pirate who was about to attack Gryf. Then, propelled by a fierce black rage, she plucked a sword from the deck and proceeded to drive the rest of the pirates over the rail one after the other. When at last there was only silence, she looked around at the carnage as if in a daze.

Newton and Gryf were kneeling over the lad, struggling to stem the flow of blood.

"Is he—?" She couldn't bring herself to speak the word. It was too hideous to imagine.

Gryf shook his head. "Not dead. There's a heartbeat, however faint. But the wound is grave."

Darcy dropped down beside him, unaware of the tears that streamed down her face to mingle with the blood. "We need to get him to my cabin."

"Aye, lass." Newton pulled himself up to the rail and stared around at the destruction. "And we must assess the wounds of the others, as well."

"I'll see to them." She wrapped her arms around the old man and closed her eyes a moment. "Are you all right, Newt?"

"I am." He touched her hair, then drew her face up so that he could look into her eyes. "And you?"

She nodded. "Oh, Newt. What a terrible mess I've made of things."

"Here now." He took a deep breath. "We're in this together, lass. We'll see it through. First we'll deal with the wounded. Then we must get the lad some help, as quickly as possible."

"Aye. But how? Where? He needs much more than we can give him aboard ship."

"Aye." Newton looked up at the thin streams of sunlight that had broken through the fog. There on the distant horizon was a dark shadow that could only be land.

He lay a gnarled hand against her cheek. "Pray our courageous lad lives long enough for us to take him to the best place of all, lass. Home."

Chapter Fourteen

"Has he moved, Gryf?"

Darcy returned from above deck, where she had assessed the damage. Now she stood peering at the pale lad lying so still on her bunk.

"Not yet. But he's still alive." Gryf scrubbed his hands over his face in a gesture of weariness. "Darcy, he needs more than I can give him."

"Aye. And more than I can give him, as well. Our best hope is to keep him alive until we make land."

She pointed to her chair. "Sit here and I'll have a look at your wound."

"It's nothing. See to the others."

"I'll see to you. Sit."

"How much damage is there?" Gryf sat and watched without emotion as Darcy cut away his shirt and began to bathe his shoulder.

Once again she was jolted by the scars that criss-crossed his back. No wonder he didn't complain about this wound. He was no stranger to pain.

"No one is dead. But every member of the crew

has at least minor wounds. Fielding is tending them, beginning with the most serious.''

''And the *Undaunted*?''

''We're taking on water from the damage sustained when the *Sinner* rammed us. Several of the crew will have to remain in the hold to bail at all times until we make shore. We managed to pry the two ships apart. The *Sinner* is quickly sinking, but we unlashed its skiff and set it in the water, in case there are any survivors. So far we've seen none. I doubt any could survive the frigid waters for more than a few minutes.''

She continued bathing his wound until it was clean. ''We salvaged what we could from the pirate ship. A good many weapons, including another cannon. In the hold we found gold and jewels, and something even better.'' She reached into her pocket and retrieved a flask of whiskey.

''Ah, now, there's what I need.''

Before he could reach for it she snatched it away. ''Nay. I'll let you drink some after I use it.'' She poured a liberal amount on his wound and heard his hiss of pain. ''Sorry. But it was necessary. Now...'' She tilted the flask to his mouth and watched as he took a long pull.

After a moment he lowered it. ''Is there more for the others?''

''Aye. Several jugs of ale, in fact. Enough for all the crew to deaden their pain.''

Gryf glanced over at the small, still figure on the bunk. ''If only we could deaden Whit's pain as easily.''

She finished dressing Gryf's wound, then crossed

to the boy and touched a hand to his forehead. She bit her lip to keep it from trembling. She was, after all, captain of this ship. She needed to be strong for her crew. But there was a horrible fear growing inside her. A fear that the lad was beyond help. "He's burning with fever."

"Aye." Seeing the fear in her eyes Gryf stood and gathered her close. "Don't despair, Darcy. Hold on to the thought that he's young and strong."

"But he was so brave. And if he'd stayed here in my cabin, he would have been safe."

"Perhaps. But by coming above deck and facing his worst nightmare, he also saved the rest of us. It was the bold action of Whit and Fearless that gave us that one small opportunity to fight back."

"And by doing so, he may have sacrificed his own life." Without warning the dam burst and the tears started. Once she allowed herself to give in to the weakness, she sobbed as though her heart would break.

Gryf knew what it cost her to give vent to her emotions. And though his own heart was heavy, he held her and whispered words meant to soothe. He prayed they would soon make land. For despite all his fine words meant to comfort, he knew the lad's wounds were grievous. Whit's chances of surviving were growing dimmer with each passing hour.

"Here, mates. Lend a hand." Despite the wound to his leg which had him pausing between each step to catch his breath, Newton worked as quickly as possible, determined to spare Darcy the gruesome task of disposing of the dead. Using a tattered remnant of sail from the *Sinner*'s mast, the seamen lifted each of the bodies from the deck of the *Undaunted*. While Newton whispered a prayer he'd learned at his mother's knee, the dead pirates were consigned to the sea.

He saw the sailors' questioning looks and gave a negligent shrug. "Whether saints or sinners, we all deserve to have a prayer spoken as we leave this world."

As the last body dropped into the waves and slipped out of sight, the exhausted sailors made their way to their quarters.

Alone on deck, Newton stared up at the thin winter sunlight, wishing it would erase this chill from his bones. He'd never felt so cold or so weary. It wasn't the weather. It wasn't even the battle, though it had been fierce. It was watching the lad, trembling with fear, standing up to his worst nightmare. Not only standing up, but fighting back with all the fury of a seasoned warrior. Aye, that was what stayed with the old man. The image of a little boy standing alone, willing to fight to the death, for the sake of his captain.

With a sigh the old sailor turned away, and nearly stumbled over the small yellow ball of fur that lay unmoving at his feet.

"Here, now. What's this?" He bent down to lift the pup. Better to dispose of it now, before Darcy had a chance to see it all broken and battered. "'Twould break her heart," he muttered.

As he straightened, he could feel the blood that had congealed, matting the dog's coat. His fingers probed beneath the fur, searching for the source of the cut. He could find none. As he probed further, he felt a

slight trembling motion. It was little more than a rip-
ple of hide.

A heartbeat? Not likely, he thought as he knelt and
carefully lay the pup on deck before beginning to
probe further.

He searched the pup's body from nose to tail, but
could find no cut. And then it occurred to him that
the blood was Whit's. The lad had fallen beside his
pet.

With his face so close to the dog's, Newton felt the
tiniest bit of warmth. Breath? Could the dog be
breathing still, after all he'd endured?

His eyes widened as he moved his hands over the
small body again. Aye. There. A faint heartbeat. And
an occasional shallow breath.

It wouldn't do to get Darcy's hopes up. The pup
had taken a terrible blow. Still…where there was
breath, there was hope.

He decided quickly. He'd watch the pup while they
made their way home. If Fearless didn't survive, he'd
dispose of him without the knowledge of the others,
to save further pain.

He cradled the dog against his chest, and made his
way to the galley, since it was the warmest spot
aboard ship. He'd wrap the pup in a blanket and place
it near the brazier for heat. And leave the tiny creature's future up to the fates.

The sunlight lasted less than an hour before the
clouds blew in, and with them, the icy rain. Though
no one said as much, the sailors were relieved to let
nature cleanse the deck of all reminders of the bloody
battle.

Despite their wounds, the crew's spirits were high, knowing that they were growing closer to land with every hour. The thought of a snug fire and shelter from this bitter storm had them sighing with eagerness. The knowledge that they would stay put for more than a day had them dreaming about a wench to warm their beds and perhaps even cook them a meal in the bargain.

The only dark cloud on their happiness was the courageous lad who lay in the captain's cabin, fighting for his life. Hour after hour, the sailors stopped by the cabin on their way to the galley to warm themselves. They would stand in silence and watch as Darcy and Gryf took turns kneeling beside the bunk, bathing the lad's fevered body. Then they would leave, as somber and serious as if they'd attended Whit's funeral.

In the galley they spoke in hushed tones about his extraordinary courage in the face of such evil. By the time they reached the channel leading to port, the tale had taken on the importance of a legend.

Newton sent a crewman to Darcy's cabin.

After a respectful knock, the sailor opened the door. "Newt says he'll need you to bring the *Undaunted* through the shallows, captain."

"Aye." Pressing a hand to the small of her back, Darcy straightened and turned from the bunk. She'd been beside Whit for hours, praying the lad could hang on until they reached shore.

At the door she turned. "You'll stay with him, Gryf?"

"Aye. I'll not leave him."

She followed the sailor above deck and took the

wheel, while several sailors climbed the rigging to watch for hazards. This channel, one of the most dangerous in all of Cornwall, was littered with rocks and the hulks of several ancient ships that had been dashed upon them.

"Hazard to port, Captain." The warning was shouted from the top of the mast.

Darcy turned the wheel slightly, and the big ship eased past the rocks lurking just below the surface. She had to pull her thoughts back from the lad lying so deathly still in her cabin. With a whispered prayer, she forced herself to focus on the task at hand.

"Hazard to starboard, Captain." A second sailor, high in the rigging, cupped his hands around his mouth to give the cry.

Again she made the adjustment, and the ship moved steadily toward land.

"Shallows dead ahead, Cap'n."

"Lower the sails," Newton shouted, and the crew began working feverishly, lowering sails until the *Undaunted* slowed to a crawl.

"Prepare to drop anchor."

Half a dozen sturdy seamen snapped to attention.

"Prepare to lower the skiff."

The deck of the *Undaunted* was suddenly swarming with sailors eager to go ashore.

As the skiff was lowered Newton crossed the deck and lay a hand on Darcy's. It was as cold as ice.

She gave him a thin smile, though her face felt stiff and frozen. "I'll go below and bring up the strongbox. The crew will want their pay."

"Leave it, lass. I'll see to it. Ye and Gryf have but one job now. Ye must take the lad ashore at once."

"But the ship. The crew..."

"Don't ye worry. They'll all be fine. Now go."

Darcy turned to see Gryf coming up the steps, with a blanket-clad Whit in his arms. The sailors watched in respectful silence. Several of them touched a hand to the lad's head, or called out words of encouragement as he was carried past.

"Thank you, Newt." Darcy pressed a kiss to his leathery cheek. "I'm sorry to leave you with all this...."

"Go, lass. I'll join ye at MaryCastle soon enough."

She nodded and followed Gryf down the rope ladder to the waiting skiff.

As the sailors rowed across the choppy waters toward the beach, her heart began to beat overtime. She stared hungrily at the lights in every window of the fortress that stood on the finger of land jutting into the Atlantic.

Home. She had to swallow several times to dislodge the lump in her throat. She had an almost overpowering urge to weep. Instead she held herself together, though by the merest of threads. And feared, as the skiff bumped the shore, that at any moment she might embarrass herself by falling apart.

"Here, now. What's this?" At the sound of the front door being opened, Mistress Coffey looked up from the dinner table, where she was pouring tea.

When she caught sight of Darcy stepping through the doorway, she spilled the tea and had to grasp the teapot with both hands to keep from dropping it altogether. "Oh, my sweet heaven."

The others who were gathered around the table followed her direction and turned toward the doorway, then let out a series of shouts.

"Darcy. Is it you, lass?" Geoffrey Lambert nearly knocked over his chair as he leapt to his feet.

"Aye, Grandpapa."

"We weren't expecting you." Bethany hurried over to hug her little sister. "Why didn't you send us a missive, so we could have been watching and waiting?"

"There was no time."

"Of course there wasn't." Ambrosia drew her close and kissed her cheek. "As sailors, we all know that there are few opportunities to send missives home when you're in the middle of the ocean. We—"

She stopped and stared beyond Darcy to the man who remained in the shadows, holding something in his arms.

Her eyes widened. "Gray! Oh, my. Isn't this wonderful?" She turned to the others. "Look, Grandpapa. Bethany. It's Gray. Oh, Darcy. No wonder you've come home to us. You've found him. Where? How?"

"Nay." As the others gathered around him, Darcy had to shout to be heard over their excited voices. "This isn't Gray. His name is Gryf. He signed aboard the *Undaunted* in Wales. And the lad in his arms is named Whit. He's been badly wounded."

"Wounded?" Winifred Mellon pushed her way past the others and touched a hand to the lad's forehead. "Oh, sweet heaven. He's burning up."

"Aye." Darcy turned to the housekeeper. "We must get him into a bed, Mistress Coffey."

"Indeed we must." The housekeeper beckoned.

"Come, Libby." She shouted to their maid. "Libby. We'll need to make ready Bethany's old room."

As she led the way upstairs, Gryf followed, with the others trailing behind.

"How was the lad wounded?" Riordan Spencer, Ambrosia's husband, asked.

"A sword through his chest."

That drew gasps from everyone.

"I hope you caught the bastard who did this." Bethany's husband, Kane Preston, the Earl of Alsmeeth, swore under his breath.

Behind him trailed Noah, the lad he and Bethany had adopted as their son.

Kane suddenly turned and caught the lad's hand, as though realizing just how precious he was.

"Aye, Kane. It was a pirate captain named Wylie York."

"I know of him." Riordan Spencer exchanged a look with Geoffrey Lambert. "One of the most hated pirates on the high seas. He and his band of cutthroats have been terrorizing English ships for years."

"He'll terrorize them no more. He lies at the bottom of the ocean, along with his crew."

"That's my girl." Geoffrey patted Darcy's arm as they stepped into the bedroom. "The king will be glad to hear the news."

"As will every English sea captain," Riordan muttered.

"Put the lad here." Mistress Coffey, all business now, turned down the blankets and waited until Gryf had deposited his burden in the bed. Then she lifted a candle to study the lad. At the sight of his chest she covered her mouth with her hand to stifle her gasp.

The tiny body was covered in linen. Little rivers of blood oozed through the dressings. The boy's flesh was drained of all color. He looked as pale, as frail, as a corpse.

"How could anyone do such a thing to a child? What kind of monster was this pirate captain?"

"The worst kind, Mistress Coffey." Darcy smoothed the hair from Whit's forehead and lowered her voice. "Wylie York was Whit's father, though the lad never knew it until their last encounter."

Ambrosia shuddered and leaned her head on Riordan's shoulder.

Bethany and her husband clasped hands and drew Noah closer, as if to shield him from such horrors.

Geoffrey Lambert cleared his throat and had to swallow several times.

It was tenderhearted Winifred Mellon who pulled herself together and took charge. "You must all leave now, while I see to the lad."

"Nay." Both Darcy and Gryf issued a protest in the same breath.

"Just for a little while." The old woman kept her tone soothing. "I know you'll want to stay with him. But I'd like to examine the lad's wounds. You can put the time to good use. Perhaps you could bathe and change. You'll need to eat something to keep up your strength." She turned to the others. "Ambrosia and Bethany, you may want to save your questions for the morrow. And Geoffrey, these two young people look as though they could use some ale before they do anything else."

"Aye. Good thinking, Winnie." The old man led the way down the stairs.

In the parlor he poured a tankard of ale and handed it to Gryf. As he did, he tried not to stare. But it was impossible to look away at the one so like Gray.

"I believe I'd like one of those as well, Grandpapa."

"Forgive me, Darcy." The old man tore his gaze from their houseguest and smiled at his granddaughter, before filling a tumbler with ale and handing it to her.

"What is the lad to you, Gryf?" he asked.

"A friend, sir."

"I see. Then, to ease your mind, I'll tell you that Winnie has a healing touch. If anyone can bring your young friend through this, it's our sweet Winnie. Isn't that so, girls?"

Ambrosia and Bethany nodded, too overcome to speak.

Mistress Coffey bustled into the room. "Cook has kept our dinner hot. It's ready in the dining room."

Darcy shook her head. "I couldn't eat a thing. If you don't mind, I'd like to go up to my room." She turned to the housekeeper. "Where would you like Gryf to sleep?"

"I have Libby preparing James's old room right now." She turned to their guest. "Would you eat something before you retire?"

He shook his head and set down the tankard. "Thank you. That's very kind. But if you don't mind, I think I'd like to go up to my room as well. Perhaps I'll rest for an hour or so. And then I'd like to sit with the lad."

"Of course. Of course." The housekeeper was all business as she hurried from the room, to inform

Cook that her efforts had been in vain. From the looks of the others, no one had an interest in eating now.

Gryf shook hands with the men, and nodded at the women, before following Darcy from the room.

Ambrosia and Bethany, like their grandfather, tried not to stare. But the resemblance between this man called Gryf, and the young lad they'd all known, was simply too remarkable to ignore.

They waited until Darcy and Gryf were out of earshot. Then they began whispering and speculating among themselves.

Chapter Fifteen

"This is my room." Darcy led the way up the stairs and pointed to a closed door before moving on to the room beside it. "And this was my brother's room." She smiled at the little housemaid who was just walking out the door. "Libby, this is our guest, Gryf."

"Welcome, sir." Like the others, the maid couldn't seem to tear her gaze from the man's face. "Let me know if you have need of anything."

"Thank you, Libby." If Gryf noticed the maid's probing looks, he gave no indication. Perhaps he was simply too weary. Or perhaps his mind was too preoccupied with thoughts of the lad.

While Darcy remained in the doorway, he stepped into the room and glanced around at the comfortable bed, and then at the night table, upon which rested a basin and inviting pitcher of steaming water.

It was obviously a seaman's room. The desk was still littered with charts and maps. A sea chest stood on one side of the room. Hanging on the wall were assorted remnants of ancient sailing vessels.

Seeing the direction of his gaze, Darcy smiled.

"James could never resist bringing home anything that washed up on shore. These were his treasures. They came from all over the world. They held a special fascination for him. Even when he was very young, he would roam the shore, picking up flotsam and jetsam from ships that had wrecked. He used to say that one day he would sail around the world, and bring us back treasures from every country he visited."

"Did he get to follow his dream?"

She shook her head. "He died far too young."

As soon as the words were out of her mouth, she realized what she'd said. Thinking of the lad who lay fighting for his life, she felt a sudden shaft of fear. Death, at least in this house, wasn't some distant worry. The cold hard reality of it had been felt by everyone who dwelled within these walls.

Gryf saw her sudden pallor and closed the distance between them. He took her hand in his, then looked down in surprise. "You're freezing."

"Just—" she shook her head "—afraid."

"Don't, Darcy." He drew her close. "Don't dwell on those things you can't control. Just hold a good thought."

"Aye." She took a step back, breaking contact, and nodded toward the far wall. "My brother's clothes are still there in the wardrobe. I'm sure some of them will fit you."

"You won't mind?"

She shook her head. "It would please me. Please all of us, if you can make use of them."

She turned away and made her way to her own room, where Libby had already set up a tub.

With a sigh Darcy stripped off her clothes and sank into warm, fragrant water. At any other time, after a voyage such as the one she'd just made, she might have been tempted to linger for an hour or more. To soak away the grime of the voyage, and allow the warmth to seep back into her bones. But her mind wasn't on her own comfort now. All she could think of was Whit. He had to come out of this. To survive. To live. He couldn't let his cruel, heartless father win.

She washed quickly and scrubbed her hair before stepping out of the water and wrapping herself in a thick towel. Dressing in a simple gown of pale-pink wool, she ran a brush through her tangles, leaving her hair damp and curling around her face. With her feet encased in soft kid boots, and a shawl around her shoulders, she hurried from the room and made her way to Whit's side.

Gryf was already there, seated in a chair pulled beside the bed. For a moment she felt a jolt at the sight of him dressed in her brother's clothes. He was broader across the shoulders than James, and the shirt strained across the muscles of his chest. His dark hair and beard still bore traces of glittering water droplets from his quick bath. His hand was clasping the lad's, and his voice was low and soothing as he crooned words of hope to one he hoped could hear.

"Come on, Whit. Hold on, lad. We're all here for you. Stay with us, Whit. Fight, boy."

On the other side of the bed, Winifred Mellon was on her knees, holding a cool cloth to Whit's forehead.

"I'll do that, Winnie." Darcy took the cloth from the old woman's hands and helped her to her feet. "You need your sleep."

The old woman studied her by the light of the flickering candles. "As do you, child."

"Don't worry about me, Winnie." She squeezed the old nurse's hand. "Just being home again has restored me more than even a night's sleep. Go now and rest awhile."

"Aye." Miss Mellon touched a hand to Darcy's cheek and kept her voice to a whisper. "You must be vigilant, child. This lad is nearing a crisis. I fear if his fever climbs, he'll not make it."

Darcy closed her eyes a moment against the wave of pain that nearly swamped her. Fear, so alien to her, felt like a band around her heart. A band that was slowly tightening, until she could hardly breathe.

She forced in a deep breath. "We'll get him through this, Winnie."

When the old woman was gone, she dipped the cloth into a basin of cold water. Then, pulling up a chair beside the bed, she wrung out the cloth and pressed it to Whit's forehead. And whispered a prayer that she wouldn't have to lose another loved one to the whims of man and sea.

"How does it go?" Geoffrey Lambert stepped into the room and seemed surprised to see so many gathered around the bed.

"His fever refuses to give up its hold." The housekeeper set down a fresh basin of water and strode away carrying an empty pitcher.

One by one the other members of the family had given up their attempts to sleep and had crept into the room to hold a silent vigil around the lad's bed. Ambrosia and Riordan sat side by side, clasping hands.

Bethany and Kane, who had decided not to return to their home for the night, paced from one side of the room to the other, pausing often to exchange a look or a silent shake of their heads. Miss Mellon continued to check the lad's dressings for any sign of fresh bleeding. And Mistress Coffey bustled in moments later with tea and biscuits, hoping to keep everyone's spirits high. Even the maid, Libby, returned frequently with fresh water, or fresh candles for the night table. Each time she took a moment to pause and study the boy who lay so pale and still in the bed, she would walk away shaking her head in dismay.

"The lad's a fighter, Grandpapa." Ambrosia gave her grandfather a weak smile and patted the chair beside hers.

When he took a seat she linked her fingers with his, needing his strength even as she sought to share hers.

They watched as Darcy continued to sponge the boy's face, neck, torso, in a valiant effort to stem the fever that held him in its grip.

On the other side of the bed, Gryf kept the boy's hand in his and continued to croon words of comfort.

"Come on, lad," he muttered. "You've been through bad times before. We both have. Don't give up now. Think of that fine big ship you intend to captain one day. And think of all the exotic lands you've yet to see. There's a whole grand world just waiting for you, Whit. Don't leave it yet. Don't leave me, lad. We made a pact, remember?"

Darcy felt her eyes fill and had to blink frantically. There was no time for tears. While she wrung out the cloth yet again, she found comfort in the thought of a little boy, beaten beyond recognition, who had been redeemed by the love of a man whose own suffering had wiped out any memory of his past.

There had to be a good reason for the love that had developed between these two. Would the fates be so cruel as to bring them back from the ashes, only to separate them again? Would the angel of death snatch away the lad who had brought this man so much joy?

As if in answer, she touched a hand to Whit's forehead and let out a cry of dismay. "The cool water isn't helping. I think he grows worse."

Gryf brought his hand next to hers on the boy's skin and nodded in agreement. His eyes narrowed with worry. "Aye. His flesh is on fire."

While the others gathered around the bed the boy's breathing grew ever more shallow, until he was struggling for each painful breath.

Darcy looked to her old nursemaid. "Winnie, what can we do?"

"We've done all we can, child." The old woman drew an arm around her shoulder. "The only thing we can do now is pray. And ask the Almighty to spare the lad any more suffering."

The hour stretched into two, and then three, and still Whit's fever climbed. Darcy continued sponging his body with cool water. Gryf continued whispering words in the hope that some of them might penetrate the deep sleep that held the lad in its grip.

As the family remained circled around the bed, they found themselves listening for each shallow breath he took, and breathing with him.

Even while Gryf urged the lad to fight, Darcy fretted that he might be asking too much of Whit. How much should a lad have to endure in this life? Perhaps he was too weary of the fight, and wanted only to put an end to the struggle.

The thought of his cruel past brought fresh tears to her eyes. But she gamely blinked them aside and clung instead to a thread of hope. If a strong spirit was enough to survive, then surely Whit would make it. The lad had endured so much pain. Had risen above so many heartaches. And had survived with his heart and his smile intact.

If only, she thought, he would give some sign that he even knew they were there. The thought that he might feel all alone in his suffering brought fresh pain to her heart.

She didn't bother to look up when the door to his room opened yet again. So many family members had gathered around, the little room was crowded. That brought a measure of comfort to Darcy. She only wished the lad could open his eyes to see how many people cared about him.

It wasn't until she heard thc tap of Newton's footsteps that she glanced over. He was crossing the room, his gaze fixed on the boy in the bed. In his arms was a small, blanket-clad bundle.

"Has the lad rallied?" he asked in hushed tones.

"Nay." Gryf glanced up, then returned his attention to Whit.

"In fact," Mistress Coffey said in an aside, "we fear the lad is failing quickly. His fever refuses to break, despite Darcy's best efforts. And he seems to have slipped into his own world, where he can no longer hear us."

At the old woman's words, Darcy felt her heart constrict. *His own world.* She wanted desperately to penetrate that world which held Whit in its spell. If only they could find a way to bring him back. To penetrate the wall that separated him from them.

"What did you bring, Newt?" Darcy was surprised at how difficult it was to speak over the lump that seemed to have lodged permanently in her throat.

"The lad's pup."

"Fearless?" Darcy's head came up sharply. "But isn't he——? I thought he was——"

"I thought so, as well," the old sailor said. "But he seems to be a fighter. Like the lad."

"He's alive?" For a moment Darcy was speechless. "Why didn't you tell us?"

The old man shrugged. "I was afraid he might not make it, and I didn't want to get ye'r hopes up for nothing." He walked to the bed and uncovered the yellow ball of fluff, setting it beside the boy. "In fact, I'm still not sure the pup will make it. He hasn't eaten a thing since he was separated from the lad. But I thought the two of them ought to be together now. In case…" He shrugged. "I just thought they might be a measure of comfort for one another."

He leaned close and lifted the boy's hand to the puppy's head.

At the touch of it, the pup sniffed, stirred and opened its eyes. Seeing Whit, Fearless struggled to stand. Too weak to manage, he crawled closer and began to lick the lad's face.

After a few moments there was a flicker of movement behind the boy's closed eyes. Seeing it, those around the bed went suddenly silent. As the puppy continued to lick Whit's face, the boy's eyes opened and he heaved a sigh that seemed to well up from deep inside.

His hand moved over the dog once, twice, before a smile touched his mouth. He moved his lips. And though no sounds came out, he formed the pup's name.

Mistress Coffey gave a cry and covered her mouth with her hand as she fled the room in tears. Geoffrey Lambert comforted Miss Mellon as she wept into a handkerchief. Ambrosia and Riordan fell into each others arms, laughing and weeping, while Bethany and Kane kissed.

Darcy and Gryf stood stiffly on either side of the bed staring down at the lad with matching looks of disbelief. They had been prepared for the worst. And now that their worst fears had been banished, they seemed unable to fully grasp their good fortune.

Newton seemed the only one unaffected by the miracle he'd just witnessed. He continued to watch as the boy's hand moved over the pup's head.

Finally Whit found his voice. It was no more than a feeble whisper, but the mere fact that he could speak at all had everyone amazed.

"I just knew Fearless would never leave me." His eyes were troubled as he looked up at the old man. "I'm sorry for all the naughty things Fearless did aboard ship, Newt. I know he sorely tried your patience."

"That he did." Newton sank down on the edge of the bed and ran a hand over the puppy's soft coat. "But don't trouble ye'rself about such things, lad. He's just a baby. He'll learn in time."

"Do you think so?"

"Aye, lad. And do ye know why?"

"No, sir. Why?"

"He has a fine teacher." The old man winked. "Ye'll teach him good and proper, won't ye, lad?"

As Newton stood the boy caught his hand. "Thank you, Newt. For taking care of Fearless for me."

"Ye'r welcome, lad. Now ye and the pup had best get some rest. Ye've both got a fair piece of mending to do."

"Aye, sir."

As the old sailor walked from the room, Darcy ran after him. While the others watched in silence, she threw her arms around his neck and hugged him fiercely. "You saved his life, you know."

"Ye mean the pup?"

"Nay, Newt. I mean Whit. It was having Fearless returned to him that brought him back from the edge of an abyss. It was the pup that gave him the will to live." She pressed her cheek to his. "And you tried to be so hard-hearted toward that dog."

"Dogs don't belong on ships." He saw the glint of mocking laughter in her eye and looked away. "Most dogs, anyway. But that one's a scrapper, all right. I watched him fight for every breath."

"Just like Whit."

"Aye." He nodded and glanced over at the dog, curled up beside the boy. "Ye were right, lass. They belong together." He took a step back and looked her in the eye. "It doesn't happen often. But for some few, it does. They discover that other half of their own heart. And when it happens, there's no sense fighting it."

She watched him walk away.

And when she turned, she saw Gryf studying her with a thoughtful expression.

It occurred to her that the old man had no longer been talking about the boy and dog.

What he'd just done, Darcy realized, was given a sign that he approved of this stranger who had already won her heart.

Chapter Sixteen

"All right now, little sister." Ambrosia's voice broke the stillness of Darcy's room.

It was late afternoon. Ambrosia and Bethany had forced Darcy to leave young Whit to Winnie's capable hands, while she caught up on her sleep. Once she knew that the lad had passed through the crisis, she'd slept for more than twenty-four hours. Hours in which they'd tiptoed into her room, then out again, eager for all the details of her journey, and yet unwilling to disturb her rest.

Now, as they burst into her room and found her up and about, they settled themselves on the bed and faced her.

The two older sisters glanced at one another and grinned before Bethany said, "We want to hear everything."

"About the voyage?" Darcy slipped into a simple wool gown and began running a brush through her hair.

"Nay, you silly goose. We'll hear about the voyage

later. Right now we want to know all about Gryf. Starting with the first time you met.''

Darcy laughed. ''You're not about to waste any time on other things, are you?''

''Nay. They're unimportant next to this. Now tell us,'' Bethany demanded.

Darcy sighed, needing to talk about Gryf as much as they needed to hear. She was only too happy to share with her sisters. ''It was in a small Welsh fishing village. I thought him slow-witted because he moved so slowly. Later I learned that he was recovering from severe burns.''

''Burns?'' The two sisters glanced at each other.

''Weren't you immediately struck by his resemblance to Gray?'' Bethany nudged Ambrosia's elbow.

Darcy avoided their eyes. ''I might have been. For a moment.''

''A moment?'' Ambrosia took the brush from her hands and began pinning Darcy's hair back with combs. She studied her sister's reflection in the looking glass. ''Don't try to tell us you don't still see the resemblance.''

''Perhaps. A little.''

''A little?'' Bethany flounced closer. ''Darcy, except for the beard and the hair, he could be Gray's twin.''

Darcy pulled away and walked to the window, keeping her back to her sisters. ''Aye. I thought so in the beginning. But now I'm convinced I was wrong. Once I got to know Gryf, I realized he's...different, somehow.''

''In what way?'' Ambrosia arched a brow at Bethany.

Darcy shrugged. "There's a boldness to Gryf. A toughness, that is completely unlike Gray. The way he—" She turned to face her sisters, and they saw something in her eyes they'd never seen before. It was the look of a woman who was completely perplexed by a man. Or bewitched by him. "The way he looks at me, sometimes. And the way he touches me. Gray never touched me in any way except with gentleness."

"Is he cruel or rough?" Bethany looked alarmed.

"Nay. It isn't that. But there's a...boldness in Gryf that I never sensed in Gray. An impatience."

"Has he kissed you?" Bethany watched her sister's pale cheeks suddenly flood with color.

"Aye."

"Well? Does he kiss like Gray? A woman can tell these things."

Darcy's blush deepened. "That's what has me worried. Gray always kissed me with gentleness. He always let me chart my own course. But Gryf..." She looked away, but not before her two sisters saw her discomfort. "With Gryf I have no stars by which to navigate. I feel...lost at sea."

The two sisters shared a knowing smile.

"And you love him." Bethany touched a hand to her sister's shoulder.

Darcy's head came up. Without looking at either of them she whispered, "Aye. And I feel so...guilty about it."

"Guilty? Why in the world should you feel guilty for loving someone?" At Ambrosia's outburst, Bethany shot her a dark look.

"Aye. Guilty. And why not?" Darcy's voice lowered to a whisper. "What kind of woman am I that I can grieve the loss of the only boy I ever loved, and then, just months later, give my heart to another man?"

Bethany led her young sister to a chaise and gently pressed her to sit. Then she knelt before her and took her hands. "You just answered your own question, Darcy."

"I don't understand." Darcy shook her head, sending the golden curls flying. The same curls her sister had just smoothed.

"You grieved the loss of the only boy you ever loved. Gray was that boy. And now you've lost your heart to a man. From what little I've seen, Gryf is definitely not a boy, but a man. And he'll expect to be loved, not by a girl, but by a woman."

She squeezed Darcy's hands. "You're the only one who can decide if he's the right man for you. And if you're woman enough for him."

Darcy closed her eyes. "I'm so confused. I was hoping the two of you could help me."

Ambrosia walked over to lay a hand on her sister's shoulder. "If it's any comfort, I felt the same way with Riordan. Lost and confused, and thoroughly miserable."

Bethany nodded. "It was the same for me with Kane." She leaned close and pressed a kiss to her sister's cheek. "But don't fret, Darcy. You and Gryf will find your way through these turbulent seas."

Darcy shook her head. "I'm not so sure."

"I am." Bethany grinned at her older sister. "Come, Ambrosia. Let's go give Mistress Coffey a hand. And leave our little sister here to contemplate her future.''

''What future?'' Darcy looked as lost as she had when she was five, and had wandered away from her nursemaid and older sisters. After more than an hour of climbing over boulders, and wading through the shallows, she had arrived home to MaryCastle, her knees scraped, her boots and the hem of her gown soaked, and her face streaked with dirt. But there had been no tears shed. Even at such a tender age, she hadn't permitted herself to wallow in pity. She had simply squared her little shoulders and found her way home.

Just as she had then, her lips formed the most perfect pout, bringing delighted laughs to both her sisters.

''You'll figure it out,'' Bethany called cheerfully.

''Aye. You always do.''

With giggles, Ambrosia and Bethany danced off, closing the door behind them.

In the silence of her room, Darcy began to pace. But all she could think of was Gryf, the look of him, the feel of his arms around her, and the pleasure she found in his kisses.

Annoyed with the direction of her thoughts she flounced out of her room and decided to spend the morning with young Whit. Now that the lad was out of danger, she would be able to relax and enjoy his company without any of the confusion she felt in Gryf's presence.

Of course, if Gryf should happen to be visiting the lad as well, all the better. She could bask in the glow of his company without appearing to have planned it.

* * *

"And that's all you know of Gryf, Newt?" Ambrosia and Bethany had cornered the old man in the shed, where he was busy gathering the tools needed to repair the *Undaunted.*

After prying out of Newton as much as he could tell about Gryf's history, the two sisters turned to each other excitedly. "Despite the fact that it was a tavern fire instead of a ship's fire, I still think there's a chance he could be Gray. Don't you think he bears a remarkable resemblance, Bethany?"

"Aye. If he were to shave that beard…"

"Exactly what I was thinking. And if we were to cut his hair and comb it the way Gray always did…"

"Ye two are playing a dangerous game," the old man grumbled. "If ye care about ye'r sister, ye'll not even think about such things."

"But we do care about her, Newt." Ambrosia grinned at Bethany. "We've just come from her room, and we can see that she's feeling lost and confused, and wildly in love."

"And ye think the two of ye can steer her through uncharted waters, do ye?"

"We'll just give them both a nudge." Bethany rubbed her hands together. "Now if there's anything more you can tell us about Gryf…"

"If there is, I'll keep it to myself. I'm warning ye, lasses. If ye love ye'r sister, stay out of her love life and let her sort these things out herself."

"Oh, Newt." The two young women caught hands and started toward the house, their heads bent close, their faces animated.

The old man turned away, muttering a few ripe

oaths. Obstinate females. Never could take directions. But this time, their meddling could very well do more harm than good. He only hoped they didn't go too far. There were two very fragile hearts involved in their little scheme. Hearts which might, with just a tiny fall, shatter beyond repair.

"What's this?" Gryf returned from working on the *Undaunted* to find Bethany and Ambrosia standing beside his night table. "Sorry. I must have walked into the wrong room by mistake."

As he started to back out, Ambrosia caught him by the hand. "You made no mistake, Gryf. We saw you coming across the beach and thought we'd fetch up a basin of hot water, in case you wanted to shave your beard."

He looked from one to the other. "Why would I want to shave?"

"Spoken like a true sailor." Ambrosia chuckled. "Papa always returned from the sea with a beard. And Mama always had the razor sharpened, and the water heated, so that he could remove his beard before kissing her."

Bethany joined in the laughter. "Aye. She said it tickled too much, and spoiled the pleasure of his lips when they kissed."

Gryf didn't know whether to be amused or annoyed. "Your mother said that, did she?"

"Aye." The two sisters nodded their heads in unison.

"And whose lips will be pleasured if I should happen to shave my beard?"

"Well..." Ambrosia glanced at her sister. "We can't say her name. But there's a certain ship's captain who seems to spend a great many hours alone at night on the widow's walk.''

He'd seen Darcy up there on the balcony last night, pacing in the darkness. And he'd been tempted to go to her. But something held him back. A fear that he might intrude upon some deeply held private grief. ''What does your sister do up there?''

Bethany shrugged. ''Perhaps she dreams a woman's dreams, and waits for a certain sailor to come and claim her heart.''

He idly picked up the razor and touched a thumb to the finely honed edge. ''Is there anything else your mother used to ask your father to do when he returned from the sea?''

''Aye.'' Ambrosia could see that he was entering into the spirit of this with more enthusiasm than she'd hoped. ''Mama always asked him to put aside his sailor's clothes and put on the garb of an English gentleman.''

''I see.'' He turned and met their curious looks. ''Do you think that's something a certain ship's captain would ask of a lowly seafarer?''

''I think she would be pleased, though she'd never ask it herself.'' Bethany caught her sister's hand and led her to the door. ''I'm sure Mistress Coffey has need of our help in the dining room. Will we see you below stairs shortly, Gryf?''

''Aye.'' He turned away and studied his reflection in the looking glass. ''I'll be down in time for supper.''

''Darcy.'' At the shrill voice, Darcy turned to see Edwina Cannon racing across the entryway, arms outstretched.

Like a doe facing a hunter's sword, Darcy froze. Her first inclination was to turn and run in the opposite direction. But there was no escaping Edwina when she set her mind to it.

Darcy was caught in a bear hug while that high-pitched voice screeched across her nerves.

"I just heard the news that you'd returned, and had to see for myself." Edwina held her a little away and studied her carefully. "Well, you certainly look better than you did the last time I saw you."

"Aye. I'm feeling better, as well." Darcy extricated herself from the young woman's clutches and took a deliberate step back. "It was kind of you to come all this way just to greet me, Edwina. But if you'll excuse me…"

"It was no bother. Besides, Mistress Coffey has invited me to stay for supper."

Darcy nearly groaned aloud. An entire meal spent in this woman's company would give her indigestion for a week. Still, she couldn't see any way to evade her, without being openly rude. Something Winnie would never allow, even if Darcy could bring herself to attempt it.

"Come along, then, Edwina. Grandpapa's probably waiting impatiently to eat."

In the dining room the others were already seated.

"Ah." Geoffrey Lambert settled himself at the dining table and glanced around with a sigh of satisfaction. "It does my heart good to have my family back with me. Even if it's only for an occasional meal."

"You needn't worry about missing Riordan and me, Grandpapa." Ambrosia filled her plate and dug in. Her appetite had become monstrous lately. "Even though we'll be moving into our own home soon, Riordan would much rather enjoy Mistress Coffey's meals than try to tolerate anything I might cook."

Beside her, her husband gave a snort of laughter. "In fact, Ambrosia decided to fix breakfast this morrow. Kane and Bethany were ready to head back to Penhollow Abbey rather than swallow that congealed mess she referred to as eggs. And I threatened to leave on an around-the-world cruise if she decided to try cooking another meal. In fact, that's the real reason why we're building right next door. So we can always enjoy a decent meal at your home."

While Edwina giggled, Darcy shook her head. "I see some things never change. We always used to beg Mistress Coffey not to let Ambrosia help Cook in the kitchen. In fact I recall the time…" Her voice trailed off and she stared at the man standing in the doorway as though he were a ghost.

"I thought I'd shave." Gryf saw the way her face drained of color as she continued looking at him.

The others were staring, as well.

To fill the sudden silence he advanced toward the only one at the table he hadn't met. "Good evening. My name is Gryf."

"Gryf?" Edwina's voice had risen an entire octave, until it resembled the squeak of a nest of mice. "I'm Edwina Cannon. A good friend of the Lambert family."

"Do you live in Land's End?"

"Aye." She continued staring at him as he took the seat beside Darcy. "And you live…?"

"Here. At the moment."

Edwina's eyes lit as they always did when she found herself in the company of a handsome man. In her eyes, any unmarried man was fair game for her flirtations. "Has anyone told you that you look very much like—"

"You look—" alarmed, Bethany tried desperately to interrupt, before this fool ruined everything "—so handsome." Bethany nearly choked on her tea, but she had spoken the truth. He was a commanding presence, despite the puckered scar that ran from the tip of his ear to beneath his jaw.

As she and Ambrosia had suspected, his resemblance to Gray was even more pronounced than ever. The same full lower lip. The same square jaw.

Still, Darcy had been right about one thing. Except for the physical resemblance, he seemed quite different from the boy they'd all known. There was a toughness in this man. A hardness in the eyes. And a look of danger about him that had never been present in Gray Barton.

"I agree with Bethany." Ambrosia filled her plate with a second helping and attempted to fill the silence before Edwina could say something foolish or embarrassing. "You look...dashing."

Gryf gave a slight nod of his head before accepting the platter from Darcy's hands. As their fingers brushed, he felt her pull back as though burned.

He glanced at her plate. "You're not eating?"

She shook her head. "I'm...not hungry. Besides—" seeing Libby just passing through the dining room with a tray, she got to her feet and took it from her hands ''—I promised young Whit that I'd sit with him while he ate.''

''But what about me?'' Edwina wailed.

''I'm sorry, Edwina. But thank you for coming by. I'll...see you the next time I'm in the village.''

As she hurried away Darcy could feel Gryf watching her. And though she wanted to turn back for one last look, she squared her shoulders and continued out of the room.

Upstairs she took in several quick breaths to calm her heartbeat, before stepping into Whit's room. The puppy, lying on the pillow beside the lad, yawned and got to its feet to lick her hand as she settled the tray beside the bed.

When she removed the cover, Whit's eyes rounded in surprise.

''Look at all this food. Is it all for me?''

''Of course. For you and Fearless.'' She handed him a bowl of broth laced with bits of beef and vegetables, and was delighted to see him quickly drain the entire bowl.

''What's this?'' He poked a finger at the plate heaped with meat and potatoes, and several slices of warm, crusty bread.

''Mutton. And this,'' she said, lifting a glass, ''is goat's milk. Very rich, and very good for you.''

He sniffed, tasted, then emptied the entire glass. Afterward he divided his dinner into two plates, one of which he offered to the pup.

When both plates were cleaned he glanced at a bowl of mush on the tray. ''Is that gruel?''

''Nay. Cook's very special custard. She must think

highly of you to go to the trouble of making it, for it requires hours of preparation. Go ahead. Taste.''

When he did, he suddenly smiled. ''I've never tasted custard before. Are you sure it wasn't made by angels?''

Darcy laughed. ''I'll be sure to tell Cook what you said. If you're not careful, you may have to eat her custard morning, noon and night.''

''Not that I'd complain, Captain.''

''I think,'' Darcy said gently, ''now that we're on land, you ought to call me by my given name. Can you do that?''

He looked surprised and pleased. ''Aye.'' He decided to try it out. ''Darcy.''

Seeing her smile, he offered her some of the custard.

''Nay. It's for you and Fearless.''

Again he divided the food into two bowls, and soon both were empty, as he imitated the puppy and licked around the rim.

''Judging by that appetite, I'd say you and Fearless will soon be up and around.''

''Do you think so, Cap—Darcy?''

''Aye.'' She touched a hand to the dressing at his chest. ''How does your wound feel, Whit?''

''It still hurts to breathe. But not nearly as much today. Gryf promised me that as soon as I'm strong enough—'' He looked up as the door opened and gave a delighted laugh. ''Gryf. I was just talking about you.''

''And I was just thinking about you, lad.'' He glanced at the tray of empty dishes. ''Did you eat all that? Or did someone help you?''

"Just Fearless. Darcy didn't want to eat a thing. I was going to tell her what you promised. You said as soon as I'm strong enough, I could go down to shore and watch the men as they work on the *Undaunted.*"

"Aye. That's a promise, Whit." Gryf took a seat beside the boy's bed, across from Darcy, and began scratching behind the pup's ears.

Darcy tried not to stare at his face. But the temptation was too great. When she did, she found him looking at her in a way that had her heart stuttering.

She picked up the tray and stood. "Well, I'll leave you two alone to visit, while I take this down to the scullery."

"Will I see you again before I go to sleep?" Whit called.

She paused in the doorway. "Aye. If you'd like."

"I would. And so would Fearless."

"Then I'll stop back before I go to my room."

She left quickly. But even downstairs she couldn't escape the image of Gryf that seemed frozen in her mind. An image of another. And yet, for all the similarities, she felt more confused than ever. Why was she attracted, not by the physical resemblance, but by their emotional differences?

Though she'd spent her childhood loving one sweet boy, it was a dark, rough, mysterious stranger who was suddenly laying claim to her woman's heart. And that knowledge had her more mystified than ever.

Chapter Seventeen

"You're still awake?" Darcy slipped into Whit's room and was surprised to see him sitting up in bed, with Fearless snuggled up beside him.

Except for quick trips outside, which their housekeeper demanded in no uncertain terms, the puppy hadn't left Whit's side since their loving reunion.

She peered through the flickering candlelight and realized that Gryf was sitting there as well, half-hidden in shadows.

"I was waiting for you," the boy said almost accusingly.

"I'm sorry, Whit. I was in the parlor with my family, and the time just seemed to slip away." She sat on the edge of the bed facing him and caught his hands in hers. "When you're feeling stronger, you'll be able to join us in the parlor. You'll love listening to Grandpapa's tales. He's had some fine adventures as a ship's captain traveling all over the world."

"Do you think he'd mind telling me about some of his adventures?"

"Mind?" She laughed. "He'll be delighted to have

a fresh audience for his stories. Now—'' she leaned close and pressed a kiss to his cheek ''—it's time you and Fearless got to sleep.''

His smile bloomed. ''Will I see you on the morrow?''

''You will, indeed.'' She stood. ''Sleep now, Whit. And if you need anything, just ring this bell on the night table.''

''You mean you'll come, even in the middle of the night?''

''Aye. No matter what the time, if you're in pain or need anything at all, just ring.'' She gave a quick glance toward Gryf and felt that little thrill that always curled along her spine at the knowledge that he was watching her. ''Good night, Gryf.''

His voice sounded even deeper than usual. ''Good night, Darcy.''

As she walked out, the boy looked over at the man. ''Can you believe that, Gryf?''

''You mean about the bell?''

''Nay. She kissed me.'' The boy touched a hand to his cheek. ''My mother used to kiss me like that. I can still remember how it felt when she held me. Sometimes I can even recall how she smelled. Like a field of wildflowers after a rain.''

Gryf was jolted by the boy's words. They perfectly described Darcy, as well.

He leaned near and closed a hand over the lad's, then blew out the candle. In the darkness his voice was gruff. ''Darcy was right. It's time to sleep now, Whit.''

''Aye. Thanks for sitting with me, Gryf.'' The lad

watched as the man moved like a shadow across the room.

Gryf closed the door and started down the hall toward his room. What he needed, he mused, was a solid night's sleep. What he wanted was another matter.

Aye. What he wanted. It was the same thing he'd wanted since he'd first beheld Darcy Lambert in that tavern room in a village in Wales. Only now it was much more than lustful desire. It had become love. And it had come sneaking up on him like a thief in the night.

Without taking time to think it through, he followed a sudden impulse and climbed the stairs to the attic. From there it was another flight of stairs to the widow's walk.

As he stepped outside, he caught sight of Darcy. She was standing as still as a statue, staring out to sea.

He breathed in the needles of cold, sharp air and started toward her. "Can you see them?"

His voice, low and deep, sent tremors along her spine. The rusty sound caused by the burns to his throat had begun to smooth out, leaving a tone as rich and deep as velvet.

Though she'd heard his footsteps, she kept her face averted. "See what?"

"The phantom ships that are said to sail while the world sleeps."

"I've heard of them. But I've yet to see them."

"I thought that might be what draws you out here."

She shook her head. But still she refused to look at him. "It's an old habit. I can't seem to break it."

"Maybe you're still looking for him."

"Who?"

"The lad you loved and lost."

She did turn then. "Who told you?"

He shook his head. "It doesn't matter. I hate seeing that sadness in your eyes." He caught her chin, staring down into her eyes. "I'd do anything to take it away. To take you away. From the pain. From the memories."

She reached a hand to his chest. "Don't, Gryf."

"Don't what? Love you? It's too late for that. Much too late. As for touching you..." He caught the hand she held to his chest and lifted it, palm up to his mouth, to press kisses there, sending a series of tremors spiraling through her. "I can no more keep from touching you, kissing you, than I can stop the waves from battering the shore."

Then his mouth was on hers, though he didn't know how it happened. And his hand was fisted in her hair as he drank her in like a man who was parched and dying of thirst.

She meant to stop him. God knew she'd meant to. But the minute his lips covered hers she was lost. Needs so long denied took over her will. The need to have his hands on her until she quivered and trembled. The need to have his mouth moving over hers, until they devoured each other. The need to forget all the rules she'd set for herself. And for him.

Her heart was pounding. A wild primal beat that had the pulse throbbing in her temples.

This wasn't like before. It was unlike anything

she'd ever experienced. This was raw, primitive. A hunger that gnawed. A need that ached and clawed to be free. It rocked her simple, comfortable world and sent it spinning out of control like a ship caught in the grip of a hurricane.

"Unless you tell me right now to stop—" his voice was a low whisper of need that only added to the feelings of danger and excitement "—it'll be too late, Darcy."

When she didn't respond he drew her head back and stared down into her eyes. "Do you understand what I intend?"

She met his gaze without blinking. "Aye. It's what I want, as well."

For the space of several seconds he continued to stare at her. Then, keeping his eyes open, he covered her mouth in a kiss so hot, so hungry, she could do nothing but hang on as the world seemed to dip and tilt before it slipped away.

Without a word he scooped her into his arms and carried her down two flights of stairs. At his room he kicked in the door and then slammed it shut before setting her on her feet. Before she could recover her breath his mouth was on hers, sending her pulse rate climbing even higher.

"You need to know." He kept his eyes steady on hers as he pressed her back against the closed door. "I can't make you any promises. I could wake tomorrow to remember a past that could cause us both pain."

"I don't care—"

"You have to care." He cut off her protest. "I

want you to be forewarned, Darcy. There could be things in my past that would come between us.''

"I know you, Gryf. You're too fine to have done anything wrong. You haven't killed anyone. Or stolen from anyone. You're not a man with a wicked past.''

His eyes narrowed. "Those aren't the only unknowns. Think about this. There could be a wife and family out there, waiting for my return. Would my love for you be more important than doing the right thing by them?''

She sucked in a breath at the razor that sliced her heart.

Hearing the sound, seeing the pain in her eyes, he straightened and took a step back. "It's as I feared. You haven't thought this through." He sighed. "This isn't right. For either of us." He reached around her to pull open the door.

Her hand closed over his, stopping him. She stared at their two hands. "You're right, Gryf. I haven't allowed myself to think about another woman having a prior claim to your heart. It's too...painful." She looked up at him, and saw the same need in his eyes that burned in hers. "But what if you never regain your memory? Should we be doomed to a life apart, even though we love each other?''

"Do you know what you're saying?" He tipped up her chin and stared deeply into her eyes. "Are you willing to risk dishonor with a man who can offer you no future?''

"No future?" She smiled then, and lay a hand on his cheek. "I was the one with no future. I'd lost all hope of ever loving again. And then you came into my life and all the pain, all the suffering of my loss no longer mattered to me. You're all that matters to me, Gryf. Just the way you are. With a borrowed name and a forgotten past. All I ask is that you love me. If not forever, at least for now.''

He closed his eyes a moment, wondering if she had any idea what she had just offered. Hope, to a man who'd had none. A lifeline to a man who'd been drowning.

He dragged her close and pressed his face in her hair, breathing her in. "Heaven help us, Darcy." The words were torn from his lips. "For I haven't the will to deny your gift to me."

And then his hands were on her, rough with impatience. And his mouth, that incredibly soft mouth, was savaging hers as needs tumbled over each other in a quest to be satisfied.

He ran hot wet kisses over her face, down her throat, until, on a moan, she arched her neck, giving him easier access. When he encountered the bodice of her gown he nearly growled in frustration. With a desperate need to feel her flesh, he brought his hands to the neckline and tore it aside. As the remnants fluttered to the floor, he caught the ribbons of her chemise, freeing her breasts.

Her body was so delicate. All soft curves, with flesh as pale as moonlight on water. For a moment all he could do was stare as desire slammed into him. And then he touched her. The merest touch had her trembling. When he cupped her breasts in his hands and followed with his lips, he felt the shudder that rippled through her.

As he pleasured himself and her, he felt the air thicken, and his breath back up in his lungs. How long he had wanted to touch her like this. To feel her, pressed to him, warm flesh to warm flesh. To fill himself with the taste of her.

Fearing that her legs would fail her, Darcy clutched his waist to keep from falling. As she did, she tugged aside his tunic, needing to touch him as he was touching her.

All that hard, corded muscle seemed to tighten even as she moved her hands over him. The flat planes of his stomach. The hair-roughened chest. Even the ridges of scars along his torso were arousing. The thought of what he'd endured, and the strength he'd needed to do so, made her heart swell with love for him.

The feel of her hands on his flesh was the sweetest torture. The thought of taking her now, hard and fast, had the blood pounding in his temples.

Instead, he took a moment to toss aside the rest of his clothes, where they joined hers in a heap at their feet. Then he caught her hands and dragged her down until they were kneeling.

"Darcy." He framed her face with his hands, and brought his mouth to hers. "You're so beautiful, you take my breath away."

She sighed and moved in his arms, loving the way emotion deepened the timbre of his voice, a voice that sent tiny splinters along her spine. But as his kisses continued, she could feel her breath coming harder, faster, and her blood heating until it flowed like liquid fire through her veins.

The bed was just steps away. But it was too far. He couldn't bear even a moment without his mouth on hers.

Still kissing her he lay her down, using their clothes as a cushion against the hard floor. Then he drew her into the circle of his arms. The need was fierce now, driving him beyond reason.

With lips and fingertips he moved over her, taking her on a dizzying ride. Her hands clutched him as he took her up, up, until she reached a sudden, unexpected crest. He watched her eyes stare blindly as she was swept over. And then, before she could recover, he took her again until her head fell back, and she moaned with pleasure.

He could feel her, hot and wet, and knew that she was ready. But still he held back, wanting more. Wanting all.

There was so much he wanted to tell her. To give her. For so long he'd watched this strong, independent woman climb the rigging of her ship with all the agility of a dancer. Now he wanted to take her that high. And even higher if possible. He had a desperate need to posses. To make her his. Only his. To watch her lose all control, and know that he was the reason.

And so he continued to kiss, to caress, to soothe, until she clutched at his waist, her eyes wide and focused only on him.

But when she touched him the way he was touching her, and kissed him back with such wild abandon, he found himself caught in his own trap.

Need struggled inside him, desperate to be free. There were no whispered sighs, no gentle pleasures, only an urgency that could no longer be held in check.

He knew he was rough when he covered her body with his and savaged her mouth until they were both dragging air into their lungs. He dug his fingers into her hair and watched her eyes as he entered her.

He heard her gasp and covered her mouth with his, swallowing the sound. For the space of a heartbeat he went completely still, ashamed of the fact that he could be hurting her. She was, after all, a maiden. But it was Darcy who sighed with the pure pleasure of it, and began to move, drawing him in deeper, stealing his will to be gentle.

There was no denying the need that climbed and built, sensation after sensation, until it had become a monster, struggling to be free.

Her body arched. Her fingers clung, her nails scraped his flesh, as she felt herself moving with him, climbing with him.

He felt himself straining and marveled at her strength as she kept pace with him. His hands sought hers, their fingers joined. Their eyes opened, steady on each other as they reached the very peak.

They were suddenly hurled into the frenzy of a hurricane. Whirling. Twisting. Hurtling. And then, as they reached the eye of the storm, they exploded, shattered and drifted back to earth.

He lay perfectly still, his body pressing into hers, his mouth buried against her throat, willing his heart-beat to settle. If he were to die this very moment, he'd die happy.

He wondered idly if he'd ever felt like this before. Was it possible to experience something this incredible and have it wiped completely from his mind?

Not likely, he thought with a sigh. If he could, he'd stay like this, just this, for the rest of the night. Even the thought of lifting his head seemed too much effort. Still, he had to try.

"Am I too heavy?"

"Aye." The word was little more than a whisper. "But I don't mind."

"Here…" He rolled to one side and drew her into the curve of his arm. It occurred to him that she fit as though made for him. "Better?"

"Aye." She fitted herself against him, and he could feel the flutter of her lashes against his cheek. "Much better."

"I'm sorry I was so rough."

"Mmm. Were you?"

He chuckled. "I guess I wasn't as rough as I'd feared."

"Not that I noticed. But then, I was…preoccupied. Next time, I'll try to pay more attention."

"Next time?" He shot her a look. "What makes you think we'll do this again?"

"Because we both enjoyed it too much to walk away now."

"You seem quite sure of yourself, Captain Lambert."

"I'm certain about what I felt. As for you…" As she started to roll aside he drew her back and kissed her, lingering over her mouth until she felt the heat begin to rise again, and with it, the desire.

"Oh, I enjoyed myself as well, Captain. So much, I think we ought to try it again right now."

"Can you? I mean, can we?"

He found himself laughing at the look of astonishment on her face. "We can. All it takes is this…."

He brought his lips to her throat, then lower, where his tongue made lazy circles around her breast.

Seeing the way her eyes darkened, he began, with lips and tongue and fingertips, to slowly drive them both mad.

It took but a touch to turn their simmering passions into another blazing inferno.

With sighs and moans and sobs they slipped once more into the dark world of forbidden pleasures. A world made just for lovers.

"I'm going to have to give my compliments to Mistress Coffey." Gryf bit into cold mutton and closed his eyes at the pleasure.

"Aye. She rules the kitchens with an iron hand and sees that Cook prepares all of Grandpapa's favorite foods." Darcy took the morsel he offered, and swallowed it down with ale from the tankard they shared.

Outside their window, the midnight sky was awash with glittering stars. Moonlight spilled across the bed in a golden arc.

While Gryf had added a log to the fire, Darcy had padded downstairs and returned with food. Now she sat beside him in the bed, her cloak tossed carelessly aside, unmindful of her nakedness.

"I couldn't eat a thing at supper after you left," he admitted.

"Why?"

"Because I realized how foolish I'd been to shave off my beard."

She touched a hand to his chin. "It wasn't foolish. You look…handsome. Why did you decide to shave?"

"Someone suggested I might look more... appealing to you."

"Who suggested such a thing?"

Seeing the fire in her eyes he shrugged. "I can't recall."

She saw the hint of a smile on his lips, and her own blossomed. "That's a fine excuse, Gryf. You can use it whenever you don't want to admit to something."

"Aye. That's what I've been learning. At first I was so damnably furious at the fates that had stolen my memory. But now I've decided it may be quite convenient at times."

They shared a laugh and he leaned back against the nest of pillows in the big bed. "I love looking at you, Darcy. The way you look in moonlight. In sunlight. In no light at all."

"And I like looking at you. With or without a beard."

"That's comforting. How about without clothes?"

"That's even better."

They both laughed. But after a moment he sobered. "I was trying to hide the fact that I was serious. Don't my scars offend you?"

"Offend me?" She touched a hand to the scar on his chin. "Nothing about you offends me, Gryf. But it hurts me to think about the pain you've suffered."

"It no longer matters. Just think. If I hadn't wandered to the village of Timmeron, and you hadn't been in need of sailors aboard the *Undaunted,* we'd have never met."

When she said nothing he took the tankard from her hands and drew her down into his arms. Against her temple he murmured, "And I'd have never experienced such happiness."

"I'm happy, too. Oh, Gryf. So happy." She lifted her face to him and waited for his kiss.

When his mouth covered hers, she wrapped her arms around his neck and felt once again the quick sexual tug deep inside.

Would he always have the power to arouse her like this? With a single touch, a single kiss? And what would happen if his memory should return, and he was forced to leave?

She nudged the thought aside and allowed herself to sink slowly into that deep well of desire. For now she would take all the love, all the happiness, he offered and store it up in her poor, battered heart. And if on the morrow she had to face fresh heartache, she prayed she would have the strength, the courage, to deal with whatever the fates had in store.

Chapter Eighteen

"Has anybody seen Darcy?" Miss Mellon's voice, outside Gryf's closed door, had the two lovers stirring.

"Isn't she in her room, Winnie?" Geoffrey Lambert sounded sleepy and grumpy now that his rest had been disturbed.

"Nay. She's already up and about. And her bed made, as well. Where could the lass go this early in the morning?"

Hearing the voices outside the door Darcy sat up, shoving golden curls out of her eyes, and tugging frantically on Gryf's shoulder. "Wake up. Oh, Gryf, what are we to do?"

"We?" He grinned at her. "I didn't hear my name mentioned. I think you're the one they're discussing."

She picked up a pillow and slammed it against his head. "You've got to help me. How am I to slip out of here and back to my own room without being caught?"

"Caught?" His smile grew. "You sound like a naughty child." He squinted up at her. "Have you been naughty, Captain Lambert?"

"How can you laugh at a time like this?"

"Because, my love—" he dragged her down and pressed kisses all over her face until she was giggling "—I feel far too good this morrow to frown. And apparently you do, as well."

"Aye. I do." She wrapped her arms around his neck and kissed him back.

A mistake, she realized, when his laughter faded and his eyes took on that dark, wolfish look she'd learned to recognize. All through the night they'd love, dozed, then loved again. Each time they'd learned a bit more about each other, until now they were as comfortable as old lovers.

But the lazy comfort soon gave way to a blazing wave of need as his hands moved over her, and he drew out the kiss until they were both gasping.

"Gryf." She pushed against his chest. "I really must…"

"Aye. You must." He pressed her into the bed linens and began running nibbling kisses down the length of her body.

"Gryf. You can't—We can't—" Her hands gripped his head. And then, before she could utter another protest, she made a sound that might have been a cry or a sob.

She felt a flash of dizzying lights exploding inside her head as he slowly drove her mad. And as her whole world tilted, she found herself spinning once more out of control.

Mistress Coffey's voice was sharp with disapproval as Darcy and Gryf entered the dining room. "We've been waiting to break our fast. Where have the two of you been?''

''I…wanted to look in on Whit.'' Darcy took her place at the table and avoided her sisters' eyes.

''That takes only a moment or two. You've had your family waiting for nearly an hour.''

''Gryf wanted to take Fearless outside.''

''That would account for another minute or two.''

As the housekeeper circled the table pouring tea, Bethany winked at Ambrosia and decided to come to her sister's rescue. ''You ought to be grateful, Mistress Coffey. You know how you worry about the pup making a mess.''

''Aye.'' The old woman frowned. ''The lad's room is beginning to smell like a barnyard.''

''It can't be helped,'' Geoffrey Lambert interjected. ''There's no way we can separate that lad from his dog. I'm thinking it's Fearless that has the lad healing so quickly.''

Darcy sat back, relieved that the focus had shifted to Whit and Fearless. Now, perhaps, the others would forget about her and Gryf for a while.

While the conversation swirled around her, she glanced at Gryf. Sensing her, he turned and gave her a knowing smile.

Across the table Newton ate in silence and watched the two of them with a sinking heart. There was no denying that look of intimacy. It was as he'd feared. They'd crossed the line. He sighed. It was bound to happen, he supposed. Now all he could do was hope the lass didn't have to endure another heartbreak. He had no doubt she would survive, no matter how much pain was inflicted. He wasn't at all certain about himself. Each time she suffered, he took another knife to the heart.

"Newton." The housekeeper's voice was highpitched with frenzy. "I need help with this sideboard."

Gryf looked up as he descended the stairs. The old man had the face of a man going to his own hanging. "What's wrong, Newt?"

"Mistress Coffey always gets herself worked up like this when we're having visitors. Move this. Fix that." He shrugged. "As if they ever notice all that's been done."

"Who's coming to visit?"

"The young vicar and his wife. You'd think it was the king himself the way the old biddy barks her orders."

"Newton," came the housekeeper's voice, even louder. "I need you now."

"You see?" With a shake of his head the old sailor started toward the dining room.

Gryf couldn't help grinning as he turned toward the parlor, where the rest of the family had gathered before dinner. Whit was ensconced in a nest of pillows and quilts on a chaise, listening intently to Geoffrey Lambert relating a tale from his seagoing days. In a chair beside him sat Noah. With Bethany and Kane visiting MaryCastle frequently, the two lads had become fast friends

Whit looked up as Gryf entered. "You should have been here, Gryf. Captain Lambert and his crew once fought off three pirate ships at one time."

"And beat them all, I have no doubt." Gryf accepted a tumbler of ale from Darcy and gave her a long, lingering smile, remembering the tryst they'd enjoyed in her room not an hour ago.

"Aye. He sent them all to Davy Jones's locker."

"You've become quite a seafarer, lad," Geoffrey remarked. He tried not to dwell on the way their houseguest was looking at his granddaughter. But the attraction between Gryf and Darcy was so dazzling, a man would have to be blind not to notice.

"I'm going to go to sea like you did, sir." Whit stroked the puppy who lay nestled on a pillow beside him. "And some day I'll be captain of my own ship."

"A noble endeavor." The old man turned to Gryf. "The lad was telling me that you're a natural at sea."

Gryf sipped his ale. "I feel comfortable aboard ship. I like to think I was a sailor before my accident."

"Do you recall nothing of your past?"

"Nothing." Gryf met the old man's questioning glance. "I've been told by those who've witnessed such things, that my memory might return in bits and pieces, or it might be lost to me forever."

Ambrosia turned a nervous glance on her sister. Before she could put her thoughts into words, the sound of a horse and carriage could be heard approaching.

They streamed out of the parlor and hearded toward the front door just as Libby opened it to admit a tall, handsome young man and a beautiful woman, each carrying a child in their arms. Behind them trailed half a dozen more children.

There were warm greetings all around as the three

Lambert sisters greeted the young woman who had married the former deacon in their village. There was an even warmer reunion between Noah and the children he'd once lived with, before his adoption by Bethany and Kane.

Before Darcy could handle the introductions, the young vicar turned to Gryf with an outstretched hand. "Gray Barton. I say. Nobody told me you'd been found. Look, Jenna. It's Gray, home from sea."

As the young woman hurried toward him Gryf held out a hand. "Sorry. I seem to be confused with him a great deal. My name's Gryf. I signed aboard the *Undaunted* in Wales."

"Gryf." The young couple shook his hand and offered their apologies.

To ease their discomfort he turned his attention to the children. "Are these all yours?"

"Aye." The young bride blushed. "That is to say, they are now. When Ian met me, I was operating the Mead Foundling Home. Now that he's vicar at the Mead chapel, and we run the foundling home together, the children really belong to both of us."

"Gryf would understand that, since he has befriended a homeless lad himself. Come on," Darcy called. "I'd like you to meet him."

As their guests followed her to the parlor, Gryf could feel them studying him just the way Darcy's family did, when they thought he wasn't looking.

Once in the parlor they were introduced to Whit, who in turn introduced Fearless. The pup became instantly popular with the small children, who gathered around to pet him and exclaim over him.

"Dinner is ready," Mistress Coffey announced.

They filed into the dining room and found it transformed. The table, which usually held no more than ten, had now been extended to accommodate twenty. Crystal and silver glittered under a chandelier aglow with dozens of candles.

"It looks like a splendid royal ball," one of the children said with a trace of awe.

"It does indeed." Geoffrey Lambert held a chair for Winifred Mellon, while around the table the others took their places. "Mistress Coffey, what's the occasion?"

The old housekeeper beamed as Gryf carried Whit to a chair beside Noah.

"It's the lad's first time downstairs with the family. And since we have company here, as well, I thought it the perfect opportunity to make Whit feel welcome."

"You're...doing this for me?" The boy's eyes widened, and for a moment he feared he might embarrass himself by blubbering like a baby. No one had ever made him feel so warm or so welcome. And these kind people did it all so naturally. In the short time he'd been at MaryCastle he'd already begun to feel as if he'd always belonged here.

Seeing his distress, Darcy drew attention from him by saying, "And what better way of welcoming Whit than by introducing him to all these smiling faces. As you take your places, children, why don't each of you tell a few things about yourself."

For the next few moments the children explained how they happened to end up at the Mead Foundling Home, and into the loving care of Vicar Ian Welland and his wife.

Gryf leaned over to whisper, "Well done, my dear."

Darcy beamed, while Noah related his own childhood. "Before I was adopted by my new parents—" the smile he gave to Bethany and Kane had everyone swallowing a lump in their throats "—I used to live at the Mead Foundling Home, as well."

"You did?" Whit couldn't hide his surprise.

Noah nodded. "Before I found a home in Mead, I was a pickpocket, living on the streets. But at Mead I always had a place to sleep and enough to eat."

"And now you're the son of an earl."

Noah laughed as he picked up his fork and began to eat. "Being the son of an earl isn't the important thing. Being the son of a man who loves me is."

Darcy saw Whit glance across the table at Gryf before he followed suit and began to dig into his own meal.

She swallowed back the lump in her throat, and worried that it might become a permanent affliction. Lately there'd been so many times when she'd been nearly reduced to tears. But at least this time they were indeed happy ones.

"How are the repairs going on the *Undaunted*?" The vicar, content after such a fine meal, sat in the parlor sipping tea and enjoying the sounds of the children, seated around Whit and Fearless.

"With winter upon us, we're in no rush to finish." Geoffrey Lambert accepted a tankard of ale from the housekeeper. "But she'll be seaworthy in plenty of time for her spring cargo run."

"And your new house, Riordan?" The vicar smiled. "Will it be ready by springtime, as well?"

"It had better be." He glanced at Ambrosia, and she blushed and looked away.

Watching them, Darcy thought how perfect they were together. They were so blindingly happy with each other. And every day was like a new and special gift.

It was the way she'd been feeling with Gryf, since they'd finally admitted their feelings for each other. She couldn't wait to slip away to his room. To spend the night in his arms. She glanced over and could see him watching her. As if, she thought with a jolt, he were reading her mind.

She smiled, and he returned the smile, then gave her a wink that had her heart tumbling in her chest.

At a burst of laughter from the children, the vicar said, "It's a shame we have to leave. They're having such a grand time."

"Why not stay the night?" Geoffrey Lambert glanced toward the housekeeper for approval. "We have plenty of room."

"I do thank you." The vicar shook his head. "But I'll be leading a service in the chapel on the morrow. And we have a long ride ahead of us back to Mead. I'm afraid we really have to leave."

Kane caught Bethany's hand. "We ought to return to Penhollow Abbey, as well." Seeing the frown on Geoffrey Lambert's face he couldn't help laughing. "I'm not taking your granddaughter away forever. Just for a few days. I really do have some work to see to from time to time."

"Of course you do." The old man shrugged. "But

I've been enjoying having all my girls back with me.''

"And you'll have them again by week's end. I promise.'' Kane caught Noah's hand. "Come on, son. It's time we went home.''

With hugs and handshakes all around, they prepared to take their leave.

Gryf lifted Whit from the chaise and carried him to the front door, so that he could bid goodbye to his new friends.

"You must come to Mead soon, Gryf.'' Ian stuck out his hand. "And bring Whit and his puppy. The children would be so proud to show you around.''

Gryf accepted the vicar's handshake. "We'll be there. I promise.''

Everyone gathered in the doorway, waving and shouting as two carriages started away.

When they were gone, Geoffrey Lambert turned away and looked at his two remaining granddaughters. "I'm glad your home isn't yet completed, Ambrosia. I rather like knowing that you and Darcy are still here under my roof.''

As he started up the stairs, Ambrosia turned to Newton. "I don't know why Grandpapa should feel so sad about our leaving. Even when Riordan and I move out, we'll be living right next door.''

"Aye. So ye say, lass.'' The old sailor gave her a gentle smile. "But ye must forgive ye'r grandfather. He sees the lot of ye all grown-up and living on ye'r own. And he knows ye'll never be his little girls again.''

"I don't know about the others, Newt. But I'll always be his little girl.'' Darcy reached up to kiss his cheek. ''And yours, too.''

As she followed the others up the stairs, the old man touched a hand to his cheek. Then, not in the mood to have the evening end so soon, he slipped into his coat and made his way to the village tavern, where he could sip a pint with the sailors.

The best part, of course, was knowing that when the stories had been told and retold, he could return to the comfort of home and hearth here at MaryCastle with the family that had become his own.

Chapter Nineteen

"Newton Findlay." Mistress Coffey stood in front of the door, arms crossed over her chest, eyes narrowed in challenge. "Just where do you think you're taking the lad?"

Newton was carrying Whit, who in turn cradled Fearless in his arms.

"I promised the lad he could go down to the beach and watch us make some repairs on the *Undaunted*."

"It's far too soon for that boy to be out of doors."

"He's been taking his meals with the family now, and spending his evenings in the parlor."

"Aye. But that's not the same as being outside. He could take a chill."

"I'll see he's kept warm."

"I won't have it. The lad needs at least another week indoors."

"Cap'n." The old sailor turned to Geoffrey Lambert, who was just coming out of his study. "What say you? Is it too soon to take the lad down to the shore?"

"I don't see why, as long as you don't let him get too tired."

At that the housekeeper exploded. "I expected as much. The two of you always stick together. You probably talked it over before you even showed your faces."

The two old men winked at each other and walked past her.

When they were outside, Whit looked up at the old sailor. "How do you do it, Newt?"

"Do what, lad?"

"Stand up to Mistress Coffey's temper?"

"I'd had years of practice, lad." He sighed. "It feels like a hundred years or more." Newton placed the lad and his pup in a wooden cart that had been lined with pillows and blankets. When they were bundled against the cold, he hauled them along the sandy beach until they reached the crew of men working on the ship, which was anchored in the shallows.

"Ye'll tell me when ye're tired, lad?"

"Aye, Newt."

As the old man walked away, Whit leaned back and watched the men crawling over the ship, sawing, hammering, and sealing the hull of the *Undaunted* with hot pitch.

Catching sight of him Gryf turned from the timber he was sawing to saunter over. "So. You must be feeling a good bit stronger this morrow."

"Aye, Gryf." Whit stroked the head of his pup, who began dozing in the thin winter sunshine. "I wish I could work alongside you."

"It can't be helped, lad. You'll lend a hand the

next time there's work to be done. By then you'll be feeling fit.''

"I hope so. I like being close to the ship."

"Do you miss it, lad?"

"Aye. But I can see the mast from the window of my room. And at night, when I close my eyes, I can hear the sound of the ocean. I'd almost believe I was still aboard ship."

"I've noticed the same thing. Darcy once told us that the villagers call their home Lambert's Folly. But I think her father was a wise man. Being a man of the sea, he needed to be able to hear the slap of waves, and feel the pull of the tide. I'd want the same for myself if I were to build a home." He turned to study the fortress that loomed over the beach. "It's a fine sturdy structure."

At a shout from one of the sailors, Gryf looked up. "I'd better get back to work. Don't stay out here too long, Whit. The sun's warm enough if you're working. But that air has a bite to it."

"Aye, Gryf. I won't stay long."

A short time later Darcy walked down to the shore and found the boy and dog sound asleep, snuggled inside their quilts. With a laugh she went in search of Newton.

"Newt. If you don't mind, I think I'd better take Whit and Fearless back home."

The old sailor nodded. "I was thinking the same, lass. Ye don't mind seeing to it?"

"Nay. You stay here." As she walked away she caught sight of Gryf and another sailor hauling a massive timber across the beach.

Despite the chill in the air, Gryf was shirtless and

sweating from his labors. The sight of all those muscles sent a thrill along her spine. She chided herself for her weakness. After all, they had been spending every night together, until they knew each other's body as intimately as their own. Still, the sight of him gave her such pleasure.

He'd left his bed this morrow with a quick kiss on her lips. He'd been up before dawn, and down at the beach working with the crew assigned to make repairs to the ship. Since he took his midday meal with the men, the only time she saw him was in the evening, when he joined her family at dinner, and afterward, in the parlor, where Newton and Geoffrey Lambert regaled them with tales of the sea.

And then, of course, there were the nights. She shivered. Such delicious nights. She'd never known such happiness. Being held in his arms, being loved all through the night, was the sweetest thing she'd ever experienced. And waking beside him, sharing whispered secrets and carefree laughter, made her heart feel lighter than she would have believed possible.

All the pain and anguish of the past months had begun to disappear, thanks to the love she now shared with Gryf. And slowly, gradually, she was beginning to believe that their newfound happiness could endure.

Still, though she was loath to admit it, except in the deepest recesses of her heart, something was missing. She'd thought she would be satisfied just knowing she had Gryf's love. He had warned her, after all, that he could make her no promises. Not as long as his memory of the past eluded him. But in her heart of hearts she knew that she wanted more. She wanted what her sisters had. A vow. A union. A promise of unending love.

She started hauling the cart with the sleeping boy and pup toward the house. When she felt a hand on her shoulder, she turned to find Gryf standing behind her.

"You looked so warm and snug and sweet this morning when I left you."

She dimpled. "I'd have been warmer if you'd stayed."

"You don't know how tempted I was to do just that." He framed her face with his hands and stared down into those blue eyes, feeling his heart swell with love.

He glanced down at the sleeping lad. "It looks like we wore him out."

"Aye." She laughed. "Just being in the air is enough to tire him. But it's so good seeing color back in his cheeks."

"Aye. Though I must admit, I'm loving the color in your cheeks, as well." He kissed her hard and quick, then kissed her once more, lingering over her lips before walking away.

She watched him, wondering how it could be that a simple kiss from him could make everything seem all right. In fact, even the frugal winter sun seemed warmer now, because of Gryf.

With a light heart she resumed hauling the cart, while her mind was already conjuring images of what they would do later tonight when they were alone.

* * *

"Here, Libby." Ambrosia and Bethany stopped the little maid in the upper hallway and relieved her of an armload of bed linens.

"We'll see to these," Bethany assured her.

When the maid was gone, the two sisters shared a conspiratorial smile before knocking on Darcy's door. When she opened it they bustled inside, and began to help her make up the bed.

"Where's Libby?" Darcy began stuffing pillows into fresh cases.

"She has so much extra work these days, while Riordan and I wait for our house to be finished." Ambrosia snapped a sheet and watched it drift over the bed, before she bent to the task of tucking in the edges.

Bethany took up the slack on the other side of the bed. "Not to mention the fact that Kane and Noah and I seem to spend as many nights here as we do at Penhollow Abbey."

"Poor Libby. And pity Mistress Coffey. And now I've brought more work home with Gryf and young Whit."

"They aren't complaining. In fact, I think Mistress Coffey is secretly enjoying the fact that we're all here. I know Grandpapa is." Ambrosia stood back to admire the freshly made bed, before walking to the window, where she stood a moment, watching the workmen swarm over the *Undaunted.*

Then she turned. "It does my heart good to see you looking so happy these days, Darcy. After the news of Gray's accident, we feared we might never again see you smile."

"I am happy." Darcy plumped the pillows, then turned to see both sisters watching her closely. "What is it?"

"It's just—" Bethany looked to Ambrosia for support, then plunged ahead "—now that Gryf's wounds are healing, we think he more nearly resembles Gray than ever."

"Bethany, please…"

Her sister cut off her protest. "Let me finish, Darcy. Shaving off his beard was a start. But we both think, if you should cut his hair, the transformation would be complete. Of course, we could be wrong. In which case, Edwina would win."

"Edwina would win what?" Darcy stared from one sister to the other. "What sort of wager have you made with that silly twit?"

"Please, Darcy. We didn't mean any harm…." Bethany turned to Ambrosia for support.

"Aye. We simply mentioned the resemblance between Gryf and Gray. And when we mentioned Gryf's hair, Edwina said it wouldn't make any difference. And said she would wager that lovely mother-of-pearl comb you've always admired, against Bethany's favorite blue sash, that she was right."

"You didn't agree?" With her hands on her hips Darcy turned to Bethany.

Her sister gave a mock sigh of distress. "It matters not. Kane promised to buy me a new sash the next time he goes to London."

Darcy was shaking her head. "How could you be so foolish as to fall into Edwina Cannon's little trap?"

Bethany touched a hand to her arm. "Don't fret,

Darcy. It was just a silly wager. We meant no harm by it.''

Ambrosia reached into her pocket and withdrew a comb and a pair of scissors. ''I'll just leave these on your dresser, in case you decide you'd like to call Edwina's bluff.''

With Darcy glowering, the two sisters beat a hasty retreat.

''Well?'' Bethany whispered as they descended the stairs.

Ambrosia merely smiled. ''I've never known Darcy to be able to ignore a challenge. Especially if she thinks it comes from Edwina.''

''Aye. That part was positively inspired, Ambrosia.''

Her sister smiled. ''Why, thank you.''

The two women covered their mouths to stifle their giggles.

''Is Whit asleep?'' Darcy looked up as the bedroom door opened.

Gryf nodded. ''His eyes closed the minute his head hit the pillow. I'm sure all that fresh air had something to do with it.'' He crossed the room and wrapped his arms around Darcy's waist, drawing her back against the length of him. ''I'll have to thank him in the morning. He's just given us more time for each other.''

He ran his hands down her arms, then held up her hand. ''What's this? Scissors? Were you thinking of cutting out my heart?''

''Nay. Not your heart, my love. Your hair.''

''You want to cut my hair?'' The beginnings of a smile touched his lips at the thought of having her run her fingers through his hair. "Is this a family tradition?"

"Something like that." She turned. "You don't mind?"

He shrugged. "If you'd like to cut my hair, I'm more than willing to let you."

She breathed a sigh of relief. For some strange reason, she'd expected an argument. "First you'd better remove your tunic."

While he did that, she studied the width of his shoulders, the muscles of his back. It was always such a surprise to her to see that taut, muscled body, and to feel that quick flash of heat.

She spread several towels around the floor, then positioned a chair in the center of them, facing a tall looking glass. When he straddled the chair, she draped a towel around his shoulders.

She picked up the comb and began moving it through his dark hair. It was the most purely sensual feeling she'd ever experienced, causing a tingling in the tips of her fingers that went all the way to her toes.

As she worked she could feel him watching her in the mirror.

"How much do you intend to cut?"

She shrugged. "I'll let you decide. Tell me when you think I've sheared enough."

"Aye." He watched as dark hair drifted past his shoulders to land on the towels at his feet.

At first her movements were awkward, hesitant. But after a few minutes she became more confident. The more she cut, the bolder she became, until her fingers were flexing and the scissors were flashing.

He couldn't help chuckling. "I believe you're enjoying yourself, my love."

"I am. And you?"

"Aye." Gryf closed his eyes, loving the feel of her fingers against his scalp. Had any woman ever done this for him before? Wouldn't a man remember such pleasure? Could the mind actually blot out such memories? How cruel that he couldn't even recall a single touch, a kiss. The simplest of pleasures had been lost from his memory.

Her movements stilled. The scissors suddenly dropped from her nerveless fingers. Struggling for calm, she remained standing as still as a statue.

He heard the way her breath seemed to catch in her throat. At once his eyes snapped open.

The first reflection he saw was his own. It was his face looking back, and yet not his face. He looked like a stranger. The removal of the beard had been shocking enough. But now, with his hair shorn, he hardly recognized himself.

Then he caught sight of Darcy's reflection. Her face had drained of all color. He stood, kicking aside the chair, grasping both her hands in his.

"Who do you see when you look at me, Darcy?" His voice was tight and angry. His eyes hot and fierce.

"I see..." Gray. His name played through her mind, mocking her. His image floated before her until she blinked furiously and tried to focus on the man who was facing her.

She swallowed and tried again. "I see you, Gryf."

"Nay. I think not." He hauled her closer to the looking glass, and caught her by the shoulders, so that he was standing directly behind her. Their reflections peered back at them, mocking them.

"Look at me, Darcy." His voice was entirely too calm. Too controlled. "Who do you see?"

She swallowed and said nothing.

"I understand. At least you've finally chosen honesty. Your silence speaks more than words." He released her and crossed the room to pick up his tunic. As he pulled it on he said tiredly, "I've been so blinded by my love for you that I've refused to see the obvious."

"Please, Gryf…"

"Nay." He held up a hand, then began backing toward the door. "I love you, Darcy. Desperately. I don't know if I've ever loved like this before. But I know what is in my heart. And it's called love."

He studied her bowed head. His voice lowered. "And you claim to love me. But what you really want is to love me and the lad you lost. You want me to be both Gray and Gryf. And for a short time, I thought I could play the game, out of love for you. I allowed myself to bare my face, and my scars, knowing you were seeing, not me, but another. But now I see the folly of such playacting. It's there in your eyes. When you see me, you see the one you lost. But I can't be him, Darcy. Not even for the woman I love." He picked up his heavy coat and opened the door. Then he turned for one last look. Whatever pain he felt was masked by anger. His words were flung like daggers that landed with deadly accuracy in her heart. "Don't wait for me. I won't be back. I can't be the man you wanted."

She couldn't think of a single word to offer in her

own defense. For the truth of it was, everything he'd said was true. She could offer nothing to refute his claim. And it hurt. Oh, how it hurt.

All she could do was stare at him, eyes wide, jaw clamped, as he stormed out of the room.

She heard the sound of his footsteps as he stomped down the stairs. Heard the front door open, then slam shut behind him. The sound seemed to reverberate through her mind until she pressed her hands to her ears to muffle it.

And then there was only silence.

It was the loneliest sound she'd ever heard.

Chapter Twenty

"Oh, Newt." Bethany, out of breath, found the old sailor in a shed, carefully sorting through a pile of tools. "Thank heaven we've found you. Ambrosia and I have been searching for you everywhere. You must help us, Newt."

"Aye, lass." He continued sifting through the pile, without looking up. "How can I help?"

"You must go to the village and find out where Gryf is staying."

"Where he's staying?" The old man lifted his head to study her. "Why wouldn't he be staying here at MaryCastle?"

"Because he left last night. He and Darcy had a terrible fight, and he told her he was leaving."

The old man returned his attention to the tools. "I heard the slamming of doors. The stomp of footsteps. A lovers' spat. It happens. They'll get together when they come to their senses."

"You don't understand. Darcy said Gryf was deeply wounded because he thinks she wants him to be Gray. And all because she cut his hair. But it wasn't her fault. It was mine.''

"And mine," Ambrosia cried as she came huffing up behind Bethany.

At that the old man got to his feet and turned on them with an oath. "Ye couldn't let it alone, could ye? Ye had to poke and prod, and bully the lass into doing things better left undone. Didn't I tell ye not to meddle?''

"Aye. You did." Ambrosia's eyes were red-rimmed, and it was obvious that she'd been weeping. "But we had no idea Gryf would become so enraged. Oh, Newt, Darcy said she's never seen him so furious. She truly believes he's gone for good. We're not sure she'll ever get over this. Her poor heart is broken beyond repair. She's even sadder than when she heard about Gray's accident.''

The old man tossed aside the tools in his hand and turned on his heel. "I'll go to the village. But I don't see what I can do to help.''

"Tell him that it wasn't Darcy's fault, Newt. Tell him it was our fault." Bethany was openly sobbing now, as the enormity of the situation washed over her. "And tell him how sorry we are that we meddled.''

Newton started away, then returned to gather the two young women close for an awkward hug. "Here now. Ye're not to blame.''

"We are," Ambrosia sobbed. "We meddled, just like you said.''

"Aye. Well, if it's any consolation, I've meddled a time or two myself.''

The two young women sniffed and wiped at their eyes.

"Just tell him, Newt." Bethany's voice was little more than a husky whisper over the tears that choked her. "And ask him to give Darcy another chance."

The old man started toward the village of Land's End, wondering what in the world he could possibly say that would change the mind of a man who might be still simmering in the stew of his heated temper.

He sighed. For all his lectures to the lasses, he was about to meddle again. He only hoped it didn't make things worse than they already were.

"Sign here." The bewhiskered ship's captain shoved a parchment toward Gryf, who scratched his name and handed back the quill.

"We leave on the morrow. First light. Any man not aboard will be left behind without pay."

Gryf nodded and trailed a cluster of sailors who had also signed aboard the *Jenny Mae,* a cargo ship bound for India. As they filed into the tavern and ordered drinks, he climbed the stairs to the attic room he'd rented the night before.

Inside he sank down on the edge of the cot and stared at the ships in the harbor. It had been the most miserable night of his life. He hadn't thought anything could ever be worse than the night he'd awakened to find his flesh burned, his body scarred, and his mind blank. That had seemed like a nightmare. But this...this was real. A pain that would haunt him for the rest of his life.

Perhaps this seemed worse because he could remember it so clearly. The shocked look on Darcy's face as she'd studied his image in the mirror, and then the pained expression in her eyes when she realized that he was leaving for good.

For good.

Aye. It was for the best.

Why, then, did it hurt so much?

With a savage oath he got to his feet and headed down the stairs. There was no point in hiding in his room and making himself even more miserable. He may as well join his future shipmates in a round of drinks. It wouldn't make anything right again. But it might help dull the pain a bit.

Halfway down the stairs he saw the old man in the doorway. For a moment he was tempted to scurry back up the stairs and hide out in his room. Then he swore and continued down.

A tavern wench sidled over just as Newt reached his side.

"Whiskey." Gryf pulled out a chair and settled himself at a battered wooden table.

"The same." The old man sat across from him.

"Did she send you, Newt?"

"Nay. The lass doesn't know I'm here. 'Twas her sisters who sent me. It seems they feel they meddled in Darcy's life, and prodded her into cutting ye'r hair." He studied Gryf. "Ye do resemble him even more now, ye know."

Gryf pounded a fist on the table and swore. "I don't give a damn who I look like. I can't be someone I don't even know. It's hard enough just being me."

The old man fell silent.

Ashamed of his outburst, Gryf's voice lowered. "Don't you see, Newt? I have nothing on which to draw this man I am now. No memory of my childhood. No image of my parents. My brothers and sisters. No notion of friends I may have had. Women I may have loved." His voice trembled with emotion. "Children I may have fathered."

"I know it's hard, lad."

"Hard?" Gryf's eyes narrowed. He waited until the wench set the drinks in front of them and walked away.

He picked up his drink and drained it in one long swallow, then slammed the tumbler onto the table.

The wench returned to refill it. As she walked away he closed his hand around the glass, and stared at the man across from him.

"I've been fooling myself, Newt. And Darcy, as well. I have no right to a woman like her. No right." He picked up the glass and drained it. "I lay awake all night thinking about her. About us. I'm all wrong for her." His voice rang with emotion. "She's all that's good and decent and fine." He shook his head to add, "And I don't know who or what I am. I could be a murderer. A thief. A womanizer."

Before the old man could interrupt he added quickly, "She has a family that loves her. Friends who'll stand by her. Good friends like you and Winnie and Mistress Coffey. She'll be fine. You'll see." He couldn't stop the pain that crept into his voice as he added, "A year from now, she won't even be able to remember my name."

He signaled for the serving wench, and she returned yet again to fill his glass.

Newt continued watching him, without lifting his own glass to his lips.

"And what about the lad?"

"Whit?" Gryf experienced a wave of pain and clenched his teeth against it. "I've watched him with Darcy and her family. The boy's blossoming under their care."

"And so ye intend to just turn ye'r back on him? Abandon him?"

"I'm not abandoning him." Gryf's voice was more passionate than he'd intended as he lifted the tumbler and drank. "I'll send money for his care. And when I find a place to settle, I'll send for him. If he still wants to join me, I'll make a home for him."

"Do ye hear ye'rself, man?" Newton fixed him with a look. "Ye're the most important person in that lad's life. Ye're the father he never had. His friend and protector. And now ye're leaving him. Without a word."

"I can't go back there, Newt. I can't see him. Or Darcy."

"Why? Are ye afraid?"

"Nay. I just don't want to hurt them."

"They're already hurt and, if I know the lad and lass, struggling not to let on just how much. But they're hurting. And they'll go on hurting, for as long as ye're away from them. What ye're really saying is, ye're afraid to see the hurt in their eyes. For ye're the one who put it there. Ye're afraid to see what ye've done to them."

When Gryf said nothing in his own defense, Newton stared down at his drink for long silent minutes. Then he lifted his head and shoved the drink across the table toward the man seated there.

"Ye drink it, Gryf. Maybe it'll give ye the courage ye're lacking. For I've just realized that ye're afraid.

Oh, ye put up a brave front. But inside, ye're afraid. And ye've a right to be. It's true, ye may never remember ye'r past. Ye'll be denied the things we all take for granted. As ye said, ye'll be a man with no childhood memories. No image of ye'r mother and father. No notion of the friends ye may have cared about. Or women ye've loved.'' His voice lowered. "But at least ye have the most important things of all. The things we all yearn for in this world. Ye have a woman who loves ye, regardless of who or what ye may be. A grand woman, with the heart of a warrior. And a lad who adores ye. A lad who'd be proud to be ye'r son. And ye have a family that will stand by ye, Gryf.'' He shoved back his chair and got to his feet, staring down at the man's bowed head. "And whether or not ye care about such things, ye still have a friend, Gryf. A friend who'd be proud to sail with ye, and fight alongside ye." He turned and walked away.

Gryf downed the whiskey in one quick swallow, and saw the serving wench staring toward him with a hopeful smile.

"Newt. Wait." Before the old sailor could reach the door, Gryf caught up with him and clapped a hand on his shoulder. "Stay a while. I...could use a friend. Just until my ship sails."

When the old man made no effort to resist, Gryf led him back to the table, and signaled to the serving wench, who returned to fill their tumblers.

Newton stared at the amber liquid in his glass, debating the wisdom of what he was about to do. A wiser man would probably head back to MaryCastle to comfort the lass. But, as Gryf had said, he needed a friend.

Newton knew how it felt to be a man alone and in need of a friend. There'd been many a time in his life when he'd felt the same.

Casting aside his conscience, the old man lifted the tumbler to his lips and drank deeply.

"Newton Findlay." Mistress Coffey opened the front door, then drew back, sniffing the air with a look of disgust. "You're drunk."

"Aye. That I am." The walk from the village in the predawn light had his head pounding, his stomach churning. And though he was none too steady, he stumbled across the threshold to see the entire Lambert family standing on the stairway, glowering at him.

He lifted his head and stood very straight and tall, striving for a little dignity.

"Did you see him, Newt?" Darcy pushed past the others and hurried to his side.

"Aye, lass. I've been with him all night. I suppose I shouldn't have, but I thought maybe I could persuade him to come back."

"He isn't coming back, is he, Newt?"

"Nay, lass." He saw her recoil as though he'd struck her, and he reached out. But she evaded his hand. Her eyes looked a little too wide. The color on her cheeks a little too high.

"He's even now leaving on a ship bound for India."

"You saw him board?"

"Aye." Ashamed, he ducked his head and wished the floor would stop moving.

"What about Whit? What is he supposed to do?"

"He said he'd send money for the lad's keep. And when he finds a place to put down roots, he'll send for him." He looked up. "He's a sad, lost soul, lass, who loves ye and the lad, but doesn't feel worthy of ye."

"By heaven, he isn't worthy of them," Geoffrey Lambert shouted. "The scoundrel. I should have gone to Land's End myself, and defended my granddaughter's honor."

"Don't, Grandpapa." Darcy went to the old man and drew her arms around him. "I understand how you feel. You've always been able to give me whatever I wanted. And this time, you can't. It's out of your hands. And out of mine. I know that hurts you. But I'll—I'll survive. We all will."

"Darcy, I'm so sorry." Ambrosia touched a hand to her sister's arm, reeling with guilt. "This was all my fault."

"And mine," Bethany added. "If we hadn't meddled…"

"Nay. This wasn't your doing. It was mine. All mine. And Gryf was right. I did want him to be Gray. Or maybe I wanted Gray to turn into Gryf. I don't know what I wanted. All I know is, he's gone." Darcy could feel the tears starting, and knew she had to escape before the others saw her make a fool of herself. "I'm going…up on the widow's walk for some fresh air."

Feeling like a coward, she fled. Leaving her family to stare helplessly after her.

* * *

The sails of the *Jenny Mae* fluttered in the early morning breeze. From her position on the widow's walk, Darcy could even make out some of the crew bustling around the deck. Which of them was Gryf? she wondered. The one just climbing the rigging? The one standing near the rail, staring toward shore?

She'd promised her grandfather she would survive. But right now, this very moment, she had to admit to herself that she'd lied. Her heart was broken into so many pieces, there was nothing left of it. If she'd thought the loss of Gray was painful, the loss of Gryf was twice as bad. She'd loved him. Not just innocently, as a child loved a hero. But completely, absolutely, as a woman loved a man. She'd given everything there was to give. Trust. Honesty. Pride. And he'd taken it all, leaving her with nothing. Nothing but tears.

They came now. Big wet tears, rolling like rivers down her cheeks, soaking the front of her gown. She hated them. Hated the weakness they represented. But there it was. Despite all her fine attempts at being a tough sea captain, she was turning into a whimpering, foolish female, wasting tears over a man. A man who didn't even have the decency to care about the hearts he'd trampled before walking out.

She let the tears flow like rain, without bothering to try to stop them. There was no one here to see her humiliation. And no longer any reason to put up a brave front.

She gave herself up to the misery, burying her face in her hands while her whole body shook.

"Don't do that. I can't bear it." The deep voice behind her had her whirling.

"Gryf." She wiped at her eyes, convinced that she had imagined him. "What are you...? I thought..." She pointed to the ship. "Newt said he saw you go aboard."

"I did. And I thought I could go through with it. But the idea of sailing to India, while you were here..." He shook his head, still shaken at the sight of her crying. It twisted the knife that was already imbedded in his heart. "You've always been so brave. I didn't mean to make you cry."

"You didn't." She wiped furiously at her eyes. "I'm not crying."

"Aye. I can see that." He would allow her her dignity.

He cleared his throat. "Not that anything's changed, Darcy. I still believe I have no right to your love. And no right to ask you to share my life, when I have no idea what my future will be."

"Do any of us know the future, Gryf?"

Her question had him pausing. It was so like her to cut through all the unimportant details to the very heart of the matter. "Nay. But at least most people have knowledge of their past." He chose his words carefully. "I love you, Darcy. More than life itself. I'd be the happiest man in the world if you'd agree to marry me." When he saw the way her lips pursed to reply he held up his hand in warning. "But if you do, you need to accept the hard, cold fact that some day I may remember my past. A past that might include things we'd rather not know about. Perhaps even a wife and family."

She nudged aside the fear that trickled along her spine. She wouldn't think about that now. She'd save such thoughts for long winter nights, when the wind howled, and the soul was filled with trepidation. Right now she would cling to what he offered. For it was the only thing she truly wanted.

"I'm willing to take that risk, Gryf. But you must take the same risk."

He shook his head. "Darcy, for me there is no risk. I love you. Desperately. But I don't want to cause you even more pain in the future."

She faced him, the tears drying on her cheeks. "I love you so much, Gryf. I want us to be together, for as long as we can. And if the day ever comes that we have to part, I'll at least have these memories. And so will you."

"Oh, Darcy, my love." He opened his arms and she stepped into them.

Just then they heard the sound of cheering, and turned to see the entire family, as well as young Whit, gathered around the stairway, shamelessly listening to their every word. Even Geoffrey Lambert, who had been ready to engage Gryf in battle for her honor, was now smiling and cheering.

While they continued calling out words of cheer, Darcy whispered in Gryf's ear, and he nodded.

He lifted a hand to silence the family, then turned to Whit. "You heard me ask Darcy to be my wife, lad. Now she and I would like to ask you if you'd care to be our son."

"You mean it?" The boy's eyes went round with surprise.

"Aye, lad."

"You mean forever? The way Noah is Bethany and Kane's son forever?"

"That's what we mean, Whit."

"But what if you decide to leave us? I heard you tell Darcy that you might have another family somewhere."

Gryf shook his head. "I have no answer for that, lad. If my other life intrudes, I'll have to deal with it. Until then, I'll be the best father I can be to you. Is that enough?"

"Enough?" Overcome, the lad buried his face in his puppy's neck to hide his tears of joy.

Geoffrey Lambert cleared his throat. There was entirely too much weeping going on here. He needed to take charge of the situation. "I'd say this calls for a celebration. Mistress Coffey. Fetch a decanter of ale and bring it to the parlor."

At that, Newton groaned and held a hand to his head.

While the others hurried down to the parlor, Gryf caught Darcy's hand and held her back.

"Wait, love. Before I face the entire Lambert family, I need this." He drew her into the circle of his arms and kissed her long and slow and deep, until they were both sighing as they struggled to catch their breath.

When they finally came up for air, he caught her hand and led her toward the stairs. "All right, love. Now I'm fortified enough to face the celebration downstairs. But promise me we'll find some time later today for a more...private celebration."

She drew him back and gave him an impish smile.

"I know my family well enough to know they won't miss us for at least an hour."

"Right now? You're sure?" His smile grew.

"Aye."

He lifted her in his arms and carried her toward his room. His heart had never felt so light. As if the burden he'd carried all these long months had suddenly been completely erased. And it was all because of this woman in his arms, he realized. He may be a man with no past. But old Newt was right. He had everything that mattered. A woman who loved him. A most amazing woman. In fact, in the entire world, he doubted there was another one quite like her.

He had a feeling that from this day on, his future with Darcy Lambert would be anything but ordinary.

Epilogue

❧❧❧❧❧❧

The church in Land's End was quickly filling with villagers who had come to witness the marriage of Darcy Lambert, youngest granddaughter of Geoffrey Lambert, and the mystery man who'd won her heart. Some who saw him were convinced that he was Gray Barton, for they'd known the lad all his life, and this man bore a striking resemblance. But there were others who said he was too bold, too dangerous in appearance, to be the sweet lad they remembered.

The old vicar, Thatcher Goodwin, had invited the young vicar, Ian Welland, now living in Mead, to assist in the ceremony. He was especially pleased that the young vicar's wife, Jenna, was skilled with a harp and had a voice like an angel. Their presence would add a great deal to the solemnity of the occasion.

Darcy stood in a small knave of the church, fidgeting as her two sisters and Mistress Coffey circled her, making final adjustments to the gown that was as delicate as the gossamer wings of a butterfly.

"Oh, you look just like your mother did when she wore this." The housekeeper tightened the white satin sash around Darcy's tiny waist. "She looked just like a queen in this gown. And so do you."

"Thanks to you, Mistress Coffey. I don't know how you've managed to keep it in such excellent condition, considering that I'm the fourth in our family to wear it."

"The last. But certainly not the least," came Geoffrey's booming voice as he and Miss Mellon entered.

"Grandpapa. Winnie." Darcy started forward to accept their kisses.

"Doesn't Darcy look splendid, Grandpapa?" Bethany draped a wispy white veil over her sister's head and stood back so they could all admire her.

"Aye, you do, lass." The old man gathered her close and pressed a kiss to her cheek. "I still can't believe my youngest granddaughter is about to be wed. Are you as happy as you look, Darcy?"

"I've never felt such joy, Grandpapa." She circled her arms around his neck and kissed him, then turned to her old nursemaid. "Have you taken care of the altar, Winnie?"

The old woman beamed. "Wait until you see it, child. At first I wasn't certain just what to do. There are no wildflowers in the middle of winter. So I gathered tree branches laden with berries, and a few birds' nests, and adorned the altar with them."

Darcy clasped the old woman's hands. "Oh, Winnie, I can't wait to see it."

Geoffrey's eyes twinkled as he looked at the old woman. "I must say that I've never seen the altar looking lovelier. What you did was simply inspired, my dearest."

At his use of the endearment, everyone in the room

fell silent. The three sisters glanced at each other with matching looks of surprise.

It was Darcy who asked, with a grin, "Grandpapa, does that little slip of the tongue mean that your intentions toward Winnie are more than friendship?"

The old man had the look of a sly rogue as he caught Miss Mellon's hand in his. "Aye. I never thought I'd say this. But now that my granddaughters' futures are secure, I think it's our turn. I've asked Winnie to be my wife. And she has graciously consented."

"Oh, Winnie." The three sisters gathered around her to share hugs and kisses, before turning to their grandfather to do the same.

In the midst of all the fuss Riordan and Kane entered the room and joined in the celebration.

After congratulating the old couple, Riordan caught his wife's hand and drew her close to whisper in her ear. She looked up, eyes moist, and nodded.

He cleared his throat. "I guess this is the perfect time to share our news, as well. Ambrosia and I are going to have a new little seafarer to add to the family tree."

At the news, everyone started hugging and kissing once more until Mistress Coffey, overcome with all the excitement, burst into tears.

"Oh, it's all I've hoped and prayed for." She wrapped her arms around Ambrosia, her lips trembling. "I simply can't wait to hold another baby, and breathe in that wonderful baby scent. And pamper you, my dear, the way I pampered your mother all those years ago. It's been far too long."

Ambrosia lay her head on the old woman's shoulder while her own eyes filled with unexpected tears. "Oh, Mistress Coffey. Aren't we just the luckiest people in the world?"

"Aye, child. That we are."

Darcy and Bethany clasped hands and watched the tender scene with the happiest of smiles.

"Well, now." It was prim Miss Mellon who took charge of their overflowing emotions. "I think it's time we all went into church and took our places." She hugged Darcy, then caught Geoffrey's hand, and the two led a procession from the room.

When the last of them took their leave, Darcy looked up to see Newton standing in the doorway.

"Newt. My, don't you look fine."

He gave a look of disdain at the fancy breeches and fine coat the housekeeper had forced on him. "I don't know why the old biddy cares how I dress. One look at you, lass, and the entire congregation will be blind to all else."

"Oh, Newt." She stepped close and wrapped her arms around his neck.

He put out a hand to stop her. "Careful, lass. I'd hate to spoil such perfection."

"You're my dearest friend, Newt." She pressed her cheek to his. "And the finest first mate I've ever sailed with."

"Ye're not bad ye'rself, lass."

"Especially since you taught me everything I know."

"Aye. And a more apt pupil I never had." He cleared his throat. "Are ye happy, lass?"

"Aye, Newt. Completely."

He held her a little away and stared into her eyes.

"And what about the worry that some day Gryf's memory might return?"

She shrugged. "I'll deal with that when it happens. But I've decided not to burden myself with what might be."

"That's good, lass." He patted her arm, then stepped back. "I think ye'd better let ye're husband-to-be come in for a minute or two. Else he'll wear out the floor on the other side of this door."

"You mean he's pacing?"

"Like a caged panther, lass." He gave her a quick smile. "I'm sure ye'll find a way to calm his nerves."

He opened the door and stepped out, calling, "Ye'r bride's waiting for ye, mate."

A moment later Gryf walked in. For the space of several seconds he couldn't seem to find his voice. He simply stared at the vision in white as she walked toward him.

"Are you disappointed, Gryf?"

"Disappointed?" He shook his head. "I'm just… speechless. You're so lovely, it frightens me."

"Is that why you're frowning?" She touched a fingertip to the little line between his brows, hoping to tcase away his nerves. Instead, his frown grew.

"Ah. I see what's wrong." Her laughter bubbled up. "It's because I chose to spend my last night before the wedding with my two sisters, in the big bed we'd shared as children. Don't be jealous, Gryf. It was so special for the three of us. We talked long into the night. We laughed and cried together as well, before we finally drifted into sleep. It was, after all, our last night together as sisters. I promise you, the rest of my nights will be spent with you."

"Darcy, I understand your desire to share one last night with your sisters. But I must admit, my own sleep was disturbed. I suppose because I've grown accustomed to finding you in my arms."

"Then, if you're not upset about my sharing the night with my sisters, what could be giving you such a fierce look? Are you having second thoughts?"

"Of course not. But you might." He turned away, as though choosing his words carefully.

Darcy's heart flew to her throat, threatening to choke her. She clutched her hands together to keep from reaching out to him.

"I can see that something is troubling you, Gryf. Can you tell me what it is?"

He turned. "Aye. Something happened last night, Darcy. While I was walking along the shore. It was just a flash of memory. But it was very sharp. Very clear."

She caught her breath, terrified to hear. Equally terrified not to.

"I glanced at the *Undaunted's* white sails in the darkness, and suddenly saw myself aboard a ship. A ship going down in flames."

"A ship..." Darcy covered her mouth with her hand.

"I was in flames with it. My flesh was on fire as I sank beneath the waves. Then I was swimming until I could no longer move. There was a compelling reason why I kept pushing myself toward shore, though it's lost to me now. I recall lying in the shallows, thinking I would drown. Hoping I would, because the pain was so unbearable. Then strong arms lifted me from the water and dumped me into a cart. I remember each bump and rut in the road causing such pain. Then the movement halted, and I was carried into a darkened room that smelled of stale whiskey and unwashed bodies. Later there was screaming and shouting, and the acrid smell of burning wood. And then only silence.''

Darcy was looking at him with a look of astonishment. ''Do you realize what this means, Gryf?''

He nodded. ''It could mean that I wasn't burned in the tavern fire as I'd first believed. I may have been taken there after having been burned somewhere else. Likely on the ship I saw in that first sudden flash of memory.''

''Oh, Gryf.'' Her smile bloomed. ''This is what I'd dreamed of. Hoped for. If we can find proof that you were aboard the *Carrington*...''

''I know what you're thinking, Darcy. But there's more. And it has me deeply concerned. It won't make you nearly as happy as that other memory.''

''More?'' At the tone of his voice her smile faded. She had a quick slice of fear.

''Aye. I was excited about this bit of memory, no matter how brief. And I was agitated as well, I suppose, trying to remember more. Perhaps that's why my sleep was disturbed. But carly this morning, just before I awoke, I had another small flash of memory.''

Darcy caught his hands. ''Tell me about it.''

He shook his head. ''I don't think you'll want to hear it.''

Again she felt the quick rush of fear. Again she had to shrug it aside. ''I want to hear, Gryf. I need to. No matter how painful.''

He took a deep breath and turned his back on her to walk to the window, where he kept his face averted. "I was battling a fierce storm. As I neared shore I carried a little girl in my arms. There were people around us, but I continued carrying the girl until we lay in front of a warm fire, where she fell asleep in my arms."

He turned to her with a bleak look. Seeing the way she'd begun weeping, he closed his eyes against the pain. "You see, Darcy? It's the very thing I most feared. It probably means that I have a daughter somewhere. A daughter who is still grieving for her lost father."

Darcy's tears continued, which only added to his burden. "You see? This is the very thing I never wanted to do to you. Even on the most important day of our lives, on a day when we should be gloriously happy, my past is intruding. I remember a daughter, and on the day when we ought to be wed, I must instead break your heart."

"Nay, Gryf. That isn't why I weep." She crossed the room and caught his hands in hers. "These are tears of joy." Her voice caught in her throat. "Listen to me. I know who that girl is. The girl in your memory."

"You know her?"

"Aye." She took in a long, deep breath. "It was me."

"You? Darcy..." He began to shake his head in denial.

"Gryf, the scene you recalled happened when I was five and you were ten and three. You saved me from a storm, and carried me home. And from that day on, you were my beloved hero. Oh, my darling. Don't you see? This tiny bit of memory proves beyond a doubt that you're my own Gray. I'd always thought so in my heart. But now I have absolutely no doubt that it's so."

"How can you be so sure?"

"You recall something that happened to me when I was five. And you recall a ship's fire, that claimed the lives of most of your shipmates. I can't believe this is mere coincidence."

He closed his eyes a moment, trying to clear his thoughts. When he opened them, he pressed his lips to her forehead. "Can it be? Can it be true that my past is slowly returning?"

"Oh, Gryf." Her tears were coming faster now, and she didn't bother to hide them. "I believe in my heart that you are my Gray. My first love. And my last."

"And there's no reason why we shouldn't wed?"

"None at all."

He stared down at her. "If all of this be true, what name should I use for my vows?"

Despite the tears in Darcy's eyes, her smile was radiant. "It matters not to me, my darling. Gray was the boy I've loved for a lifetime. But Gryf is the man I love now. And will love for all time."

They both looked up as Geoffrey Lambert paused in the doorway. "In case the two of you haven't noticed, the music has started, and the vicar awaits the happy couple. But before you start up the aisle, there's a young lad out here who's been waiting impatiently to see you."

Whit stood in the doorway, looking stiff and awkward in the new suit Mistress Coffey had made for him. His shaggy red hair had been neatly trimmed, and his new shoes were polished to a high shine. From inside his coat a yellow head poked its way out to stare around uncertainly.

For the space of a heartbeat all the lad could do was stare at Darcy. Finally, his voice trembling slightly, he whispered, "You look more beautiful than a queen."

She dimpled. "Thank you. And you look as handsome as any prince, Whit."

"Will I..." He tried again, swallowing back his nerves. "Will I have to say anything?"

Gryf shook his head. "Not a thing. But you will have to keep Fearless tucked inside your coat. If he should get loose, the vicar will have your head."

"Aye." Darcy laughed. "Not to mention Mistress Coffey, who will be mortified."

"I'll keep him quiet." Whit took a halting step closer. "When do I become..." He took a deep breath. "When do we become a family?" There. He'd said the word aloud. A word that both elated and terrified him.

Darcy opened her arms and drew him close, pressing a kiss to the top of his head. "We're already a family, Whit."

"You mean I can call you Mama and Papa?"

Darcy felt the sting of tears. When had she become such a crybaby? "Aye, Whit. We'd be honored if you choose to call us that."

"Come on, son." Gryf caught the boy's hand. "I think it's time we got up to the altar and made it official." He leaned forward to brush his lips over

Darcy's, before turning to her grandfather. "Darcy has something to tell you, sir."

The two men shook hands, then Gryf and the lad hurried out.

The old man turned to her with a puzzled frown. "What's this, lass? Tears?"

"Aye, Grandpapa. But they're happy tears." Darcy put her hand on her grandfather's arm and walked with him from the knave into the aisle.

She could see Gryf and Whit standing at the altar, waiting for her. With a rush of words she turned to her grandfather and told him of Gryf's flash of memory.

"Ah, lass." He closed a hand over hers. "This is the answer to all our prayers."

"Aye. Oh, Grandpapa. What a grand wedding gift I've been given this day. This man is the other half of my heart and soul. And now that he's come back to me, I'm whole again. And so happy, Grandpapa. So very, very happy. "

As they started up the aisle, she remembered the words Gray had whispered on that day so very long ago. *I promised your father I'd always look out for you, Darcy, no matter what.*

She closed her eyes and whispered, "Oh, Papa. No man has ever worked so hard, or sacrificed so much, to keep a promise."

Aye. He'd gone through the fires of hell and back. But he'd kept the promise made to a man when he was a mere lad. And, she vowed as she placed her hand in his, and spoke the words that would make them one, she would do no less. For he was her hero, her lover, her one true love. The man who had always owned her heart.

A love like theirs was destined to last for all eternity.

*   *   *   *   *

Harlequin® Historical

PRESENTS
SIRENS OF THE SEA
The brand-new historical series
from bestselling author

Ruth Langan
Join the spirited Lambert sisters in their
search for adventure—and love!

THE SEA WITCH
When dashing Captain Riordan Spencer arrives in
Land's End, Ambrosia Lambert may have
met her perfect match!

On sale January 2001
THE SEA NYMPH
Middle sister Bethany must choose between a
scandalous highwayman and the very proper
Earl of Alsmeeth.

In June 2001
THE SEA SPRITE
Youngest sister Darcy loses the love of her life
in a shipwreck, only to fall for a man who
strongly resembles her lost lover.

Harlequin® Historical

MONTANA MAVERICKS

Bestselling author

SUSAN MALLERY

WILD WEST WIFE

THE ORIGINAL MONTANA MAVERICKS HISTORICAL NOVEL

Jesse Kincaid had sworn off love forever.
But when the handsome rancher kidnaps
his enemy's mail-order bride to get revenge,
he ends up falling for his innocent captive!

RETURN TO WHITEHORN, MONTANA, WITH

WILD WEST WIFE

Available July 2001

And be sure to pick up
MONTANA MAVERICKS: BIG SKY GROOMS,
three brand-new historical stories about Montana's
most popular family, coming in August 2001.

HARLEQUIN®
Makes any time special ®

*Harlequin truly does
make any time special. . . .
This year we are celebrating
weddings in style!*

A Walk Down the Aisle
WEDDING CELEBRATION

To help us celebrate, we want you to tell us how wearing the Harlequin wedding gown will make your wedding day special. As the grand prize, Harlequin will offer one lucky bride the chance to "Walk Down the Aisle" in the Harlequin wedding gown!

There's more...

For her honeymoon, she and her groom will spend five nights at the **Hyatt Regency Maui.** As part of this five-night honeymoon at the hotel renowned for its romantic attractions, the couple will enjoy a candlelit dinner for two in Swan Court, a sunset sail on the hotel's catamaran, and duet spa treatments.

Maui • Molokai • Lanai

To enter, please write, in, 250 words or less, how wearing the Harlequin wedding gown will make your wedding day special. The entry will be judged based on its emotionally compelling nature, its originality and creativity, and its sincerity. This contest is open to Canadian and U.S. residents only and to those who are 18 years of age and older. There is no purchase necessary to enter. Void where prohibited. See further contest rules attached. Please send your entry to:

Walk Down the Aisle Contest

In Canada	In U.S.A.
P.O. Box 637	P.O. Box 9076
Fort Erie, Ontario	3010 Walden Ave.
L2A 5X3	Buffalo, NY 14269-9076

You can also enter by visiting www.eHarlequin.com
Win the Harlequin wedding gown and the vacation of a lifetime!
The deadline for entries is October 1, 2001.

HARLEQUIN®
Makes any time special ®

PHWDACONT1

1. To enter, follow directions published in the offer to which you are responding. Contest begins April 2, 2001, and ends on October 1, 2001. Method of entry may vary. Mailed entries must be postmarked by October 1, 2001, and received by October 8, 2001.

2. Contest entry may be, at times, presented via the Internet, but will be restricted solely to residents of certain georgraphic areas that are disclosed on the Web site. To enter via the Internet, if permissible, access the Harlequin Web site (www.eHarlequin.com) and follow the directions displayed online. Online entries must be received by 11:59 p.m. E.S.T. on October 1, 2001.

   In lieu of submitting an entry online, enter by mail by hand-printing (or typing) on an 8½" x 11" plain piece of paper, your name, address (including zip code), Contest number/name and in 250 words or fewer, why winning a Harlequin wedding dress would make your wedding day special. Mail via first-class mail to: Harlequin Walk Down the Aisle Contest 1197, (in the U.S.) P.O. Box 9076, 3010 Walden Avenue, Buffalo, NY 14269-9076, (in Canada) P.O. Box 637, Fort Erie, Ontario L2A 5X3, Canada.

   Limit one entry per person, household address and e-mail address. Online and/or mailed entries received from persons residing in geographic areas in which Internet entry is not permissible will be disqualified.

3. Contests will be judged by a panel of members of the Harlequin editorial, marketing and public relations staff based on the following criteria:

   - Originality and Creativity—50%
   - Emotionally Compelling—25%
   - Sincerity—25%

   In the event of a tie, duplicate prizes will be awarded. Decisions of the judges are final.

4. All entries become the property of Torstar Corp. and will not be returned. No responsibility is assumed for lost, late, illegible, incomplete, inaccurate, nondelivered or misdirected mail or misdirected e-mail, for technical, hardware or software failures of any kind, lost or unavailable network connections, or failed, incomplete, garbled or delayed computer transmission or any human error which may occur in the receipt or processing of the entries in this Contest.

5. Contest open only to residents of the U.S. (except Puerto Rico) and Canada, who are 18 years of age or older, and is void wherever prohibited by law; all applicable laws and regulations apply. Any litigation within the Province of Quebec respecting the conduct or organization of a publicity contest may be submitted to the Régie des alcools, des courses et des jeux for a ruling. Any litigation respecting the awarding of a prize may be submitted to the Régie des alcools, des courses et des jeux only for the purpose of helping the parties reach a settlement. Employees and immediate family members of Torstar Corp. and D. L. Blair, Inc., their affiliates, subsidiaries and all other agencies, entities and persons connected with the use, marketing or conduct of this Contest are not eligible to enter. Taxes on prizes are the sole responsibility of winners. Acceptance of any prize offered constitutes permission to use winner's name, photograph or other likeness for the purposes of advertising, trade and promotion on behalf of Torstar Corp., its affiliates and subsidiaries without further compensation to the winner, unless prohibited by law.

6. Winners will be determined no later than November 15, 2001, and will be notified by mail. Winners will be required to sign and return an Affidavit of Eligibility form within 15 days after winner notification. Noncompliance within that time period may result in disqualification and an alternative winner may be selected. Winners of trip must execute a Release of Liability prior to ticketing and must possess required travel documents (e.g. passport, photo ID) where applicable. Trip must be completed by November 2002. No substitution of prize permitted by winner. Torstar Corp. and D. L. Blair, Inc., their parents, affiliates, and subsidiaries are not responsible for errors in printing or electronic presentation of Contest, entries and/or game pieces. In the event of printing or other errors which may result in unintended prize values or duplication of prizes, all affected game pieces or entries shall be null and void. If for any reason the Internet portion of the Contest is not capable of running as planned, including infection by computer virus, bugs, tampering, unauthorized intervention, fraud, technical failures, or any other causes beyond the control of Torstar Corp. which corrupt or affect the administration, secrecy, fairness, integrity or proper conduct of the Contest, Torstar Corp. reserves the right, at its sole discretion, to disqualify any individual who tampers with the entry process and to cancel, terminate, modify or suspend the Contest or the Internet portion thereof. In the event of a dispute regarding an online entry, the entry will be deemed submitted by the authorized holder of the e-mail account submitted at the time of entry. Authorized account holder is defined as the natural person who is assigned to an e-mail address by an Internet access provider, online service provider or other organization that is responsible for arranging e-mail address for the domain associated with the submitted e-mail address. **Purchase or acceptance of a product offer does not improve your chances of winning.**

7. Prizes: (1) Grand Prize—A Harlequin wedding dress (approximate retail value: $3,500) and a 5-night/6-day honeymoon trip to Maui, HI, including round-trip air transportation provided by Maui Visitors Bureau from Los Angeles International Airport (winner is responsible for transportation to and from Los Angeles International Airport) and a Harlequin Romance Package, including hotel accomodations (double occupancy) at the Hyatt Regency Maui Resort and Spa, dinner for (2) two at Swan Court, a sunset sail on Kiele V and a spa treatment for the winner (approximate retail value: $4,000); (5) Five runner-up prizes of a $1000 gift certificate to selected retail outlets to be determined by Sponsor (retail value $1000 ea.). Prizes consist of only those items listed as part of the prize. Limit one prize per person. All prizes are valued in U.S. currency.

8. For a list of winners (available after December 17, 2001) send a self-addressed, stamped envelope to: Harlequin Walk Down the Aisle Contest 1197 Winners, P.O. Box 4200 Blair, NE 68009-4200 or you may access the www.eHarlequin.com Web site through January 15, 2002.

Contest sponsored by Torstar Corp., P.O. Box 9042, Buffalo, NY 14269-9042, U.S.A.

Double your pleasure—
with this collection containing two full-length

Harlequin Romance®

novels

New York Times bestselling author

DEBBIE MACOMBER

delivers

RAINY DAY KISSES

While Susannah Simmons struggles up the corporate
ladder, her neighbor Nate Townsend stays home baking
cookies and flying kites. She resents the way he questions
her values—and the way he messes up her five-year plan
when she falls in love with him!

PLUS

THE BRIDE PRICE

a brand-new novel by reader favorite

DAY LECLAIRE

On sale July 2001

HARLEQUIN®
Makes any time special ®